T0274590

It's Only a Game

It's Only a Game

KELSEA YU

BLOOMSBURY

NEW YORK LONDON OXFORD NEW DELHI SYDNEY

Content Warning: This book contains depictions of violence

BLOOMSBURY YA
Bloomsbury Publishing Inc., part of Bloomsbury Publishing Plc
1385 Broadway, New York, NY 10018

BLOOMSBURY and the Diana logo are trademarks of Bloomsbury Publishing Plc

First published in the United States of America in July 2024 by Bloomsbury YA

Bloomsbury books may be purchased for business or promotional use.
For information on bulk purchases please contact Macmillan Corporate and
Premium Sales Department at specialmarkets@macmillan.com

Library of Congress Cataloging-in-Publication Data
Names: Yu, Kelsea, author.
Title: It's only a game / Kelsea Yu.
Other titles: It is only a game
Description: New York : Bloomsbury, 2024. | Audience: Ages 12+ | Audience: Grades 10–12 | Summary:
Marina Chan, living under a fake identity to escape her past, risks exposure when her online gaming
team accepts a tour of their favorite game company, only to find themselves entangled in a deadly game.
Identifiers: LCCN 2024006452 (print) | LCCN 2024006453 (ebook) |
ISBN 978-1-5476-1335-9 (hardcover) | ISBN 978-1-5476-1336-6 (epub)
Subjects: CYAC: Video games—Fiction. | Identity—Fiction. |
Murder—Fiction. | LCGFT: Thrillers (Fiction) | Novels.
Classification: LCC PZ7.1.Y896 It 2024 (print) |
LCC PZ7.1.Y896 (ebook) | DDC [Fic]—dc23
LC record available at https://lccn.loc.gov/2024006452
LC ebook record available at https://lccn.loc.gov/2024006453

Book design by Jeanette Levy
Typeset by Westchester Publishing Services
Printed and bound in the U.S.A.
2 4 6 8 10 9 7 5 3 1

To find out more about our authors and books visit
www.bloomsbury.com and sign up for our newsletters.

For my brothers, Corbin and Collin—
my first gamer friends

It's
Only a
Game

PROLOGUE

The world was out of focus, like water spilled over an ink portrait. Heads turned to look as I raced down the boardwalk, faster than I'd ever run. Fast enough to blur all the strangers around me.

I needed to get away. Before it was too late.

I stumbled over a nail sticking out from the wooden boards beneath me. Pain shot through my knees as I hit the ground hard. I reached out to break my fall, but my hand slid forward, overwhelmed by momentum. The splintered wood slashed the tender skin of my inner forearm.

I swallowed a scream as the cuts on my arm tore back open. They'd been so close to healing.

"Oh my God!" An unfamiliar woman ran over and knelt beside me, hand clapped over her mouth. "Are you okay?"

More people stopped to glance our way, their eyes keen and watchful. Others shifted on their feet, looking around uneasily like they were waiting for someone to tell them if they should offer help.

They shouldn't. They couldn't. No one could help. My throat went tight, clogged with fear. I couldn't afford to draw any more attention.

I had to get away.

I pushed to my feet, wincing as pain seared through my knees.

"You're bleeding." The woman reached out a hand. "Is there anyone with you? Should I call—"

A shiver raced down my spine. I shoved her hand away and took off. The faces around me blurred once more, obscured by tears and my desperate pace. I forced myself to ignore the burning in my lungs and the blisters forming on my heels.

I would not look back. I would not let myself get caught. Pain was a small price to pay when I had a shot at freedom.

ONE
YEAR
LATER

CHAPTER 1

I'm far from squeamish, but this volume of blood would appall anyone who isn't a vampire. Luckily for me, the blood's not real.

"Night? Is everything all right?" Rock's British accent sounds
through my headset. My teammates would have seen the urgent
flash of red on their screens as my health bar dwindled.

"I'm fine," I reply. My character, NightMar3, is fine. The
Wraithwolf Ancient that attacked me a minute ago is not. It lies on
the ground, head separated from its body, in a pool of crimson.

In-game, I sheathe my steel scimitar just as footsteps sound
from behind. I whip around to look, adjusting my night vision
goggles.

"Damn, Night!" Dread whistles as he drops down beside me.
"You just hate being rescued, don't you?"

"I prefer 'kill with finesse' over 'damsel in distress.'"

Dread snorts. I can practically feel his eye roll through the
screen as his character, Dreadnaughty, runs down the corridor
ahead of me. He wields a giant, wicked blade that's even more dramatic than mine.

I don't stop to heal up—we're on a timed mission and every
second counts. We learned that the hard way by failing the mission

twice already. The first two times, all four of us stopped to kill every enemy mob. This time, the plan is for Syl and Rock to keep the mobs distracted while Dread and I sneak past undetected, steal the quest item, and escape out a nearby window.

"Are y'all almost there yet?" Syl's voice betrays a hint of impatience. She draws out each syllable in an irresistible drawl that makes my breath hitch. Syl's family moved from Atlanta to Seattle three years ago to be nearer to Dread's family. Dread and Syl are cousins. Rock, meanwhile, has known Dread since junior high, when Rock's family moved from London. The three of them have been playing *Darkitect* together for years. I'm the only one who's never met the team in real life.

But tomorrow night, that's going to change.

My stomach clenches with nerves at the thought of finally meeting my teammates, but I force my mind back to the game as Dread and I turn a corner. "One more hall . . ." His words trail off as we both stop short. "Oh, hell."

"What is it?" Syl asks.

"I *think* we found the rest of the Wraithwolf pack."

"Cíxǐ keeps things interesting." Unlike the others, I pronounce the reclusive game designer's name with the proper Mandarin inflections.

The others murmur agreement. We're all a little starstruck. This is the first time Cíxǐ has invited us to beta test one of her missions—an honor bestowed upon us because we've worked our way up in the rankings to become one of the top *Darkitect* teams. Cíxǐ combines *Darkitect*'s in-game tools with expert programming knowledge. She builds challenging puzzle levels that require clever strategizing to beat and always look stunning. Cíxǐ's only been around for half a year, but she's already wildly popular. There's a whole forum dedicated to speculating on her real identity, but no one's figured it out.

On my screen, a sea of wolfish yellow eyes glow in the darkness. In unison, they turn toward us.

"Flash 'nade?" Dread is already heading back up the way we came.

"On it!" I toggle the tinted lenses on my night vision goggles and my screen darkens. As the Wraithwolves run toward me, growling, I set off the flash-bang grenade. They whimper and cry out. I toggle the tinted lenses off and run through the pack, toward the window. In the chaos of wild slashes and snapping jaws, my health bar drops.

"I'm back!" Dread clutches the severed head of the Wraithwolf Ancient I killed earlier. Enraged by the death of one of their elders, the group howls an eerie pack call, snarling as they chase Dread back up the corridor, away from me.

"What's the plan, cuz?" Syl asks.

"You know me," Dread says.

"You have no plan," Rock says.

Syl's already thinking ahead. "Can you kite them to that room with the lanterns and oil jugs? I'll ping it. We'll trap them inside. Rock can heal me while I AoE them to bits."

"'Kay."

Syl always has the best plans. Rock's healing will keep her in a protective bubble while she sets the ground aflame, igniting the jugs of oil and burning the Wraithwolves alive.

I'm all the way down the corridor now. My heart races as I reach the door bearing the glowing red Chinese characters our mission instructions said to look out for: 公道. Gōngdào. Justice.

I draw in a sharp breath as a memory hits, reminding me of the life I left behind. Sitting at my desk, filling page after page with hànzì until my wrists ached. It's been a year since my last lesson.

"I'm in the final room." As the door swings open, I spy several large, shadowy creatures and instinctively swing at them with my sword. My blade makes a metallic sound as it slices through one, but no blood appears. Instead, it breaks into dark chunks that crumble to the floor.

It's a statue. Blinking, I flip on my flashlight. The room is huge, and it's filled with modern-looking tables and chairs. The walls are covered in posters of creatures from *Darkitect*.

"It looks different from the rest of the palace," I say. "The decor here doesn't even look remotely Chinese."

I check the countdown timer. Less than ten minutes left to steal the artifact and escape. I scour the room, interacting with statues, inspecting images, and looking under all the furniture. The "Stolen Artifact" we need to complete the mission is nowhere to be found, but it has to be in here.

There's a noise from somewhere behind me.

I jump out of my desk chair, pulling my headset off as I swivel around, searching the dark room. There's no one there.

I squeeze my eyes shut and take a deep breath. The sound came from the game.

It's been ten months since I started living in the back office of this restaurant. Though I have the owners' blessing, I can't be caught here, or their restaurant will be shut down. I don't want to be responsible for that, but I have nowhere else to go.

And there are other reasons I'm always listening for someone trying to sneak up on me. I still can't shake the fear that I'll be found.

My dog, Slate, gets up from his bed and leans against me, soft and warm. His reassuring nuzzle pulls me back to the present. He always knows when I need him most. I give him a quick pat on the head before putting my headset back on and continuing my search for the artifact. Thankfully, no one seems to have noticed my jumpiness.

I'm passing one of the desks when I nearly step on a man lying on the floor. He has short brown hair and wears jeans and a hoodie. He doesn't fit into the level's aesthetics at all.

It's a game, so I do what you're supposed to do with a corpse—I loot him. His body contains four sealed envelopes. Strange.

I'm about to move on and search a nearby desk when I see something glowing underneath the dead man. I pull it out from under him.

"Found it!" I click on the carved ivory vase to pick it up. "The dead guy was hugging it."

"Cixi is weird," Dread says.

"I want to meet her." Syl sighs.

"Excellent work," Rock says. "Now kindly get the hell out of there, Night."

"Aye aye, Captain."

I head for the window we scouted out earlier. Then I down a potion to slow my falling speed and jump out the window to victory.

It takes me two minutes to reach Cíxǐ. Not Cíxǐ, the reclusive creator of this level, but her in-game avatar who looks just like the stern-faced Qing dynasty empress dowager she was named for. Cíxǐ wears her signature yellow silk robes, with precious gems and gold hairpins woven into her elaborate hairstyle. Every detail is right, down to the clawlike, six-inch golden nail protectors the real empress dowager wore on her ring and pinky fingers.

I turn in the Stolen Artifact, and Cíxĭ offers me a shrewd, satisfied half smile before handing me the reward to share with my team.

"Hell yes!" Syl shouts. "Did we get it?"

I open the quest reward. "We got it!" Sure enough, it's the legendary helmet Syl's been wanting for ages—the reason we ran this mission in the first place. Well, that and the simple fact that when the most renowned private *Darkitect* level designer invites you to a new mission, you *always* accept.

"Ahhh! I love you!" Syl squeals. My heart nearly jumps out of my chest. If only she really meant it.

"That level was awesome!" Dread says.

"It was absolutely brilliant," Rock agrees.

"Yeah! Almost as cool as tomorrow's going to be," Syl says.

My stomach flutters with anticipation at the reminder. Dread landed a summer internship at Apocalypta Games, the company that makes *Darkitect*, and he set up a tour for the four of us.

I'm excited to see the studio, but I'm most excited—and nervous—about meeting my friends for the first time IRL. For the past nine months, we've been talking and gaming together almost every day. I'm desperate to meet them.

But what if they don't like me? What if they decide I'm not interesting and kick me off the team?

Or, worse, what if they realize what I'm hiding?

"Hey, there's something else in the reward box." I click the extra item. "Four tickets inviting us to the Haunted Royal Opera Theater tomorrow at eight p.m."

Syl gasps. "Does that mean what I think it means?"

I grin wide. "I think so."

Dread taps out a drumroll. Rock cheers. "We have a new mission, people!"

We've been invited to Cíxǐ's next level.

CHAPTER 2

Ten Years Earlier

"Mama, who is my daddy?"

Mama coughed, spitting out her tea. "Why would you ask that?"

"Jenny at school wanted to know." For as long as I could remember, it had just been Mama and me in our tiny apartment.

"Jenny should mind her own business."

"But, Mama . . ."

Her hand shook as she set her teacup down. "He's dead."

I felt like someone had pushed me on the playground. "Dead?"

"Oh, bǎobèi." Mama came over to hug me. "I didn't want to tell you until you were older, but I should have known other kids would ask."

"What happened to him?"

"Your dad was involved in some . . . things. Bad things." She looked like she was going to say more, but then she hesitated. "Lia, it hurts to talk about him. You don't want to hurt me, do you?"

Guilt stabbed my stomach. "Of course not. I'm so sorry, Mama."

CHAPTER 3

Friday, 5:10 p.m.

After last night's mission, we went over the plan for today's meetup. We'll all check in for the studio tour at 5:30 p.m. Then we'll grab dinner at my favorite place in the world, Bette's Battles and Bao, before playing Cíxǐ's next level together.

I've barely been able to sit still all day. I'm so nervous, I swear my heart will burst out of my chest at any minute.

I'm about to meet my teammates in person for the first time ever.

I tug on the hem of my shirt and smooth down my black leggings, reminding myself that I talk to them every night in *Darkitect*. I know them. It'll be fine. Plus, I'm twenty minutes early, so I should be the first one here.

Before entering the building, I take a moment to stare up at the sleek, modern tower. It's five stories tall, nestled in among other office buildings in downtown Seattle. A metal plate engraved with "Apocalypta Games" says I'm at the right place. Inside, summer sunlight filters in through the glass ceiling. A giant spiral staircase in the center swirls around a glass elevator, and sky bridges shoot out in every direction from the stairs, connecting to various floors.

Straight ahead, a burly man with brown skin and a stubbly

beard sits at the front desk, looking down at a computer screen. Behind the guard, two larger-than-life statues of rival overlords from *Darkitect* lore stare each other down.

My heart flutters with both apprehension and excitement when I spy a slender Indian guy dressed in slick jeans and a polo leaning over the counter. He says something to the guard at the front desk, who looks up and laughs. I walk up to them, trying to act casual. My right hand itches to trace the familiar scars on my left wrist.

The boy turns as I reach the counter, and his mouth transforms into a wide grin.

"Night? Is that you?"

"Hi, Rock!" I hope my voice doesn't betray my anxiety. "You're early!"

His familiar laugh eases my tension. "So are you."

"Guilty." I pull my left sleeve down to cover most of my hand. I can't help it; it's a nervous habit, even though I know my wrist is already covered.

I always keep it covered.

The security guard looks up from his screen, drawing my eye. I note the name on his badge: Carlos.

"Are you Marina Chan?" Carlos asks.

"That's me."

"Let's see. It says here that you're fifteen, so you'll be bringing in a permission form instead of an ID."

"Fifteen!" Rock says. "Sometimes I forget you're such a baby."

I roll my eyes at him. "Right. And at seventeen, you're *so* worldly. Besides, I'm almost sixteen."

Three more days until my birthday. A memory pops into my mind. One lone candle flame in the endless darkness. I try to hide my shiver.

"All right, all right." Rock nudges my shoulder playfully. "I'll let you finish checking in." He heads toward a set of black velvet wingback chairs, pulls out his phone, and sits.

I'm relieved he won't hear the lies I'm about to tell.

Once Rock is seated, I turn back to Carlos. "I did bring my permission form. My mom signed it last night."

I wipe my sweaty palms on my leggings before opening my shark backpack and rummaging inside. After pulling out a piece of paper, I glance at it one more time, even though I've already looked it over so many times I almost missed the bus here. The "parent or guardian signature" line is full of Joan Chan's loopy signature, crisply forged this morning. I hold my breath as Carlos accepts the paper. No turning back now. Silently, I will him not to look up Joan Chan.

If he does, he'll discover she doesn't exist.

Carlos glances at the form, types something on his keyboard, and files the paper away behind his desk.

"Read and click accept when you're ready, then we'll do the photo."

I frown. "You're taking a picture of me?"

"Company policy for all visitors. Fine print's on the screen. Take your time."

He flips a mounted tablet to face me. I scroll through, skimming the tiny text. Was it a mistake coming here today?

I remind myself that nearly a year has passed with no one coming after me. I've been careful. Nothing from my past has followed me here.

Still, I don't like having my photo in their system.

Carlos eyes me and I realize I've spaced out. Quickly, I click accept.

"Most people don't read the whole agreement." His scowl softens. "But I always teach my kids that they should. You don't know if you're signing away your soul unless you check the fine print."

The fondness in his voice makes my heart ache, and I have to clench my fist to keep my expression clear. I mumble something but don't look up, afraid of what he might see on my face.

"Ready?"

"Yeah." I look at the camera. *Click.*

An image appears on the tablet screen. I can't remember the last time anyone took my photo. Thanks to Bette I'm no longer gaunt, but I'm still worryingly thin. I'm looking straight at the camera with eyes that some call almond-shaped, while Chinese people love to remark that they're huge. My heart-shaped face looks the same as it always has except for one change: the dark circles under my eyes. I don't think almost-sixteen-year-olds are supposed to have big eye bags, but I haven't slept well in a year. I've been too afraid of who might find me.

"Welcome to Apocalypta Games." Carlos hands me a visitor's badge. "Someone will be down to meet you all shortly."

I walk over to sit in a chair across from Rock.

"This place is so dramatic." He eyes one of the statues. "I absolutely love it."

"Yeah, it'll be cool seeing the inside."

It's hard to believe I'm in the actual place where my favorite game was created. When Dread first landed his internship here, he described Apocalypta HQ to us, but hearing about it is one thing. Seeing it is entirely different.

Rock and I talk about tonight's mission as we wait for the others. I fight the instinct to check the door every few minutes.

My hands take on a life of their own—pinching the velvet on my armchair, picking fuzz off my shirt, and playing with my hair. I finally have to sit on them to stop from fidgeting.

At 5:40 p.m., the door bursts open. Rock and I stand as a guy and a girl dash in, heading for the front desk. The confident clack of high heels makes my heart leap. I'm just as nervous now as when I handed my permission form to Carlos, but for entirely different reasons.

They're here.

She's here.

In her heels, Syl looks around my height, which means she's probably 5'2" without them. The way she walks makes her look taller than she is: broad shoulders back, head held high, with a confident stride. Long microbraids run down to the small of her back. She's wearing a knee-length green dress and gold pumps that perfectly highlight her dark skin and brown eyes.

Syl lifts her hand to wave, and her nails sparkle gold; they match her shoes. Suddenly, I'm embarrassed of my two-for-twelve-dollar leggings and black thrift store hoodie, even though I'm usually proud of the way I altered it. A few months ago, I cut out panels and hand-sewed in pieces of a red thrifted shirt to re-create the *Darkitect* icon on the front—four slash marks, as if torn out by a creature's claws.

"Rock! Night! Want some?" Dread holds a supersized bag of Funions. Rock and I shake our heads and Dread shrugs, biting into an onion ring.

Though Syl and Dread are cousins, they're polar opposites. Dread is lanky and freckled, with pale skin and barely styled brown hair. He has a hint of beard stubble and towers over all three of us.

He just came from work, but no one outside the Seattle area would guess that based on the way he's dressed: sarcastic nerdy T-shirt, basketball shorts, and flip-flops. Seeing his outfit, I relax a bit.

"Hey, man." Dread and Carlos do some kind of secret handshake. Syl checks in, which is how I learn her real full name: Tamyra Johnson. Wordlessly, I roll the name around on my tongue until I notice Rock looking at me with a confused expression. I stop, cheeks red.

Since Dread works here, he already has a badge with his photo and "Andrew Hunt, Intern" printed across the top.

"How did you manage to be late for a meeting right after work, *at* your workplace?" Rock asks.

Syl gives Dread a friendly glare. None of us are surprised, though. Dread is always late for missions.

"We had a company-wide offsite today, so I actually *wasn't* here, thank you very much. Then I had to pick up her sorry ass." Dread points a thumb at Syl, who rolls her eyes. "Besides, I knew it would be fine. Ethan's always late."

Syl and I turn to stare at Dread.

"Did you say . . . Ethan?" I ask.

"Ethan *Wainwright*?" Syl adds.

Dread stops chewing for a minute and gives us a sheepish, caught-out look.

"Um, pretty sure giving your favorite cousin a *heads-up* when the CEO and founder of their favorite video game company is planning to be their *private tour guide* is part of our cousin code or something!" Syl punches him lightly. "If I'd known, I would've dressed up."

If this isn't what Syl considers dressing up, I'm afraid to know what is.

"I think it was supposed to be a surprise? I overheard HR talking about it. My bad," Dread says. "Besides, Rock knew."

Syl turns to Rock, about to say something when an unfamiliar voice cuts in.

"You've ruined the surprise already? Guess you might as well all go home."

The four of us turn to look at the man who has somehow managed to sneak up on us. He's a tall white guy who's maybe in his late thirties, with a big, mischievous grin on his face. A face I've seen before on countless magazine covers.

"Andrew, right?" he says to Dread. "You're one of the summer interns?"

"Yeah! I'm on Michael's team."

"Oh yes, mission design! Your team does excellent work." Ethan turns to Rock. "Hi, Raj! How's your dad doing?"

"He's been busy since giving his speech at Black Hat. Apparently, it was very popular."

Syl and I glance at each other. Her eyes widen and I know we're thinking the same thing. Rock knows *Ethan Wainwright*? He's told us his parents' company runs security for Apocalypta Games, and Dread mentioned that they put in a good word for him when he applied for his internship, but Rock never mentioned knowing the CEO personally.

Ethan laughs. "Good. The praise is well deserved. Sanjay practiced that speech on me last month."

I'm still reeling when Syl introduces herself to Ethan, shaking his hand firmly.

When Ethan finally turns toward me, the weight of his attention is palpable. There's an intensity to his gaze that's tempered by his kind smile. "You must be the last member of the team."

"Yep, I'm Marina."

He nods, possibly waiting for me to say something else, but nothing else comes out. I wish he'd turn his attention back to the group. Instead, he compliments my shark backpack, and I blush, nodding my thanks. The colors are fading, and the fin is fraying, but this bag has been through a lot with me.

Finally, he addresses the group. "As some of you know, I'm Ethan. On behalf of Apocalypta Games, I'm pleased to welcome you to our headquarters! I apologize for the chilly air. Our air conditioner seems to be on overdrive today, but we have someone working on it right now. Shall we get this tour started?"

"Yeah!" Our collective exclamation is followed by a loud crunch. Everyone turns to see Dread shamelessly laying waste to his bag of Funions.

Ethan starts talking as we wait for the elevator. "Apocalypta Games was founded six years ago. Our goal has always been to create games that invite players into the game design process. Why limit level design to our employees? There are numerous talented designers in every population of gamers, as evidenced by the sophisticated mods released by third parties for practically every application."

The glass elevator arrives, and we all file in.

"Does this mean you plan to release more games with built-in design tools like *Darkitect*, or will you be focusing on other aspects of game design with your next project, Mr. Wainwright?" Syl asks.

"I'd really prefer if you all called me Ethan. We're not the stuffy formal type around here." Ethan's statement is supported by his rich nerd attire: a company hoodie, 7 For All Mankind jeans, and black Ecco sneakers.

"Sure, Ethan." Syl's unfazed.

He smiles. "And to answer your question, yes. I can't offer specifics until we've announced our next project, but we have exciting new things in the works."

The elevator stops and the doors open.

I gape at the scene in front of me. The entire office is filled, floor to ceiling, with *Darkitect*. I'm staring at everything like a total fangirl as we trail Ethan, but I'm too excited to be self-conscious about it. Next to me, Syl and Rock are doing the same, while Dread wears an I-told-you-so grin.

The walls are alive with scenes from the game in the form of concept sketches, posters, and murals. There's even a giant monitor showing real-time stats like how many players are currently signed into *Darkitect*. There are no cubicle walls to block the view, so we can see every desk. They're organized in pods as if they belong to cliques of conspiring workers.

"Our game teams work collaboratively, and team compositions change as needed, so we're constantly reconfiguring," Ethan says. "While there are areas where you'll see clusters of, say, environment artists or quality assurance testers, it's not uncommon to see a pod where everyone is in a different discipline. They'll work closely together on a specific project, then split up and join another pod for the next venture."

"Where is everyone?" Rock asks.

"It's after hours. Plus, the offsite," Syl says.

"Yeah, but no one came in to catch up on work?" Rock sounds skeptical.

"We believe in team building. With the exception of the security guard, our offsites are mandatory. And we encourage everyone to go home and enjoy their weekend afterward."

Now that Rock's pointed it out, the silence surrounding us is a bit eerie.

As we walk, I narrowly dodge a statue of a Wraithwolf pack. They're mid-leap, jaws open in a snarl. A Dragonfae woman suspended from the ceiling breathes fire at her lupine adversary. I reach out and run my hand along the metal flame. It's cool to the touch.

"How does anyone concentrate around here?" I lean down to inspect the Wraithwolf's jagged, sharp teeth.

"They don't, mostly."

At my wide-eyed look, Ethan smirks. "Okay, they all work really hard, so we try to make it a fun place to be. I think we achieve that, don't we, Andrew?"

Dread nods enthusiastically. "We're about to reach my favorite room."

We turn a corner and follow Dread into a side room. Rows and rows of snack dispensers line the walls, filled with treats of every imaginable kind.

"Of *course*, the snack room would be your favorite," Rock says. But he fills up a cup with a mix of cereal and candy just like the rest of us.

Snacks in hand, we continue down the hallway. I have a brief sense of déjà vu even though I've never been here before. Then I remember last night's level.

"This looks just like the room from last night's game," I blurt out, looking around. Everyone turns toward me, and I bite my lip, wishing I hadn't said it aloud.

"What do you mean?" Syl asks.

"This." I gesture to everything around us. "You were all busy burning up Wraithwolves so none of you saw, but the room where I retrieved the Stolen Artifact had statues and posters just like these."

I realize I'm tracing my scars through my sleeve again and stop, letting my hands drop to my sides.

"Whoa, really?" Dread asks.

Ethan looks curious, so Rock fills him in. "We tried a new level by Cixi last night."

"Oh!" Ethan's eyes light up. "She's such a talented level designer."

"Do you know her real identity?" Syl asks.

Ethan shakes his head. "Wish I could hire her. She seemed to come out of nowhere, showing up suddenly with these amazing, detailed levels. Her ideas are out of this world."

"If the level looked like your headquarters, maybe she already works for you," Syl says.

Ethan's brows lift. "You may be onto something."

After touring the fifth floor, we stop by two more floors, including the merchandise department, where Ethan insists that we each choose an Apocalypta sweater. Syl puts hers on immediately, and I realize she must have been freezing with the AC on overdrive. I hadn't noticed because of my always-wear-long-sleeves policy.

Ethan hands us each a goody bag full of *Darkitect* swag. I peek inside to see a Demonrapter plushie, and I feel like the excitement is going to burst out of me at any moment in a big, embarrassing squeal. I'm here with my best friends, whom I've just met *in person*, Ethan Wainwright is giving us a personal tour, and I just got exclusive swag from my favorite game. I stuff the goodies in my backpack. Who could have imagined a year ago that my life would turn out to be this awesome?

Too soon, the tour is over, and we're back on the first floor. The security guard is gone. He must have left for the day.

I'm preparing to thank Ethan, figuring he'll go back to

whatever multimillionaire techies do. But instead of waving us off, Ethan turns to me. "Marina, may I speak with you briefly?"

The question catches me completely off guard, and I stutter out a reply.

"Mind waiting here for a few minutes?" he asks my friends, and they all agree.

Ethan and I walk back into the elevator, alone this time, and I wonder what he could possibly want.

I'm seated across from Ethan in his office, which is not at all what I expected based on the rest of the building's design. It's almost dizzying, going from the explosion of *Darkitect* creatures and colorful artwork to this. The walls are plain white, filled with things like industry leader awards, Ethan's framed computer science degree from the University of Washington, articles about Apocalypta and *Darkitect*, and more. The large wooden desk in the center of the room looks sturdily built. Behind it, floor-to-ceiling windows offer a grand view of the waterfront.

"This must seem completely out of the blue." Ethan sounds apologetic. "As you may know, Raj's father is one of my close friends, and his family is kind enough to invite me to dinner once a month or so. At a recent meal, Raj mentioned that his teammate, Marina, is a talented fan artist. He gave me your Instagram account name. NightMar3 is a great handle, by the way. Clever play on your name."

I feel my cheeks warm. I'm both embarrassed and delighted that Rock thought my drawings worth mentioning.

"Thank you. It didn't work, though. I thought by calling

myself NightMar3, my nickname would end up being Mare, short for Marina."

"Let me guess. Instead, they call you Night."

I nod and relax a bit. He speaks like a gamer, like he knows we usually shorten player names to the first pronounceable syllable, unless it's something super awkward. It makes me think he must play video games. Then I feel silly. Of course he plays. He founded a video game company. Still, Ethan seems like someone I could talk to, maybe even game with. Not some all-important, unknowable CEO.

"Well, Marina, after seeing your art, I thought you might be interested in working on a piece for either our website or the quarterly magazine."

"Really?"

"Yes! You could submit a piece for the October contributor comic—that's a fun one since we usually do something Halloween-themed. Or you could do a guest post on the official blog. We'd credit your page, of course, and we always compensate our contributors."

I don't think my eyes can get any wider. "Oh . . . wow!"

Ethan smiles. "We also have a booth at PAX West this year! You and your team could come in as our guests of honor. We have a few extra exhibitor badges that haven't been claimed yet."

I was wrong—my eyes *can* get wider. His casual mention of giving all four of us behind-the-scenes access to one of the world's biggest video game conventions boggles my mind. This year, four-day PAX badges sold out within twenty-five minutes. Plus, Apocalypta Games legit wants to pay me for my art? I could finally get a new headset, and maybe a new toy for Slate. "That sounds amazing!"

"Great! Consider it done. I'm curious, Marina, is art something you'd consider for your career?"

"Maybe? It would be cool, but . . . I haven't decided yet."

That's the best answer I can give. With no official ID, I'm not registered for school. Most of the time, I try not to think about the future. Right now, all I can handle is surviving.

Ethan's about to say something else when a beep startles us both. He looks down at his smartwatch. He sighs. "I'll be right back."

I immediately text the team.

He likes my artwork AND he invited me to do the October contributor comic or a guest post on the Apocalypta blog! But here's the best part . . .

I hit send, feeling a rising thrill. Then I start typing again. *Okay, I'm drawing out this announcement dramatically, but PAX BADGES!*

None of them are typing back. Maybe they all got distracted?

A little red-circled exclamation mark pops up, and I frown. The message didn't go through.

I realize my phone has no reception, so I try the Wi-Fi next, but the network is down. Ironic that a tech company doesn't have a working internet connection. Guess my news will have to wait. Sighing, I look around the office instead, wondering how long it'll take for Ethan to return.

That's when I hear the gunshot.

CHAPTER 4

Ten Years Earlier

"Lia!" Mama's voice was sharp. I spun around in my chair in the after-school program's computer lab, startled. Normally, Mama worked late and didn't come to pick me up until almost all the other kids were gone. "What are you doing?"

I avoided her eyes. "Playing *Minecraft*."

Mama grabbed my hand and tugged me sharply out of my seat. She didn't let go until we were on the sidewalk outside. "You know you're not supposed to play computer games," she hissed. "They rot your brain."

"But other kids get to play them," I whined.

Mama crouched down in front of me and took my hands. Her eyes darted back and forth, checking to see if anyone was near. She didn't look mad anymore. She looked . . . scared.

"Lia, people can track you through computers. And if anyone wanted to hurt you . . . Computers make it easier for them to find you."

My heart pounded. "Why would anyone want to hurt me?"

Mama squeezed my hands, a little too hard. "Just . . . stay away from them, okay?"

I swallowed. I didn't understand, but I didn't want to make Mama upset. "Okay," I agreed.

CHAPTER 5

My body reacts before my brain catches up. I'm out of my chair in an instant, head turned toward the source of the gunshot.

Someone collapses in the hallway.

This can't be happening.

I don't see the shooter. Only a flicker of movement, like the shadow of someone's arm lowering a gun.

I dive behind Ethan's giant desk.

My heart pounds as I crouch there, making myself small. Small and quiet. My throat is tight. It's hard to breathe, like something clogs my airway.

Fear. You remember how it tastes.

I squeeze my eyes shut. Try to go blank.

No. That's a bad idea. I need to stay alert. Quiet but alert.

I force myself to open my eyes. To shift ever so slightly. To peer out through the narrow gap below his desk.

The doorway is open, and the lights in this room are on.

Oh my God, oh my God . . .

The need to trace the scars on my wrist is so overwhelming that I nearly give in to temptation. Just once. I'll trace them each once, and . . .

No.

I need to stay focused. Take stock of the situation. Figure out what to do. For a moment, I pretend I'm NightMar3, on a mission.

The thought, ridiculous as it is, calms me a little. Some of the fear recedes.

And then I see a pair of heavy black boots coming my way.

I'm going to die.

And it turns out, I'm not like NightMar3 at all. I'm not brave. I'm a scared little mouse, squeezing her eyes shut until the bad things are over. Again.

The footsteps grow louder as they approach. I keep my eyes closed, but my mind builds the scene for me anyway. Boots casting shadows on the carpet as they step through the doorway. Cold eyes staring out from under a ski mask, scanning the room. My shark backpack on the floor, catching their attention. Them lifting the gun. Walking around to search his desk and . . .

The footsteps recede.

My head feels light from choking back all the terror that's desperate to come bursting out.

In the distance, I hear the turn of a doorknob, then the swing of a door before it slams shut. And then I'm shaking uncontrollably, and it's all I can do not to vomit.

When the worst of it subsides, I do my best to steady myself and listen.

Nothing.

Nothing but a horrible, endless silence.

I'm alone on this big, empty floor again.

Except I'm not alone. I saw someone fall, right after the gunshot.

And Syl, Dread, and Rock are downstairs. Oh God, what if the shooter finds them?

I picture all sorts of horrible scenarios as I push to my feet, the movement dizzying. I keep going anyway, grabbing my backpack and half stumbling, half running down the hall toward the person crumpled on the floor. I have to check on them. They could be bleeding to death.

It has to be Ethan. It doesn't make sense for it to be anyone else. But part of me can't believe it. He's too important to fall victim to something like this. He's supposed to be untouchable.

But it's him. He lies face down on the ground in a pool of blood, so still.

"Ethan?" I whisper.

Silence.

My knee brushes against the dark carpet as I press my fingers to his wrist, looking for a pulse. When I don't feel any movement, I shift my fingers and try again.

Still nothing.

Pushing with all my strength, I flip Ethan onto his back. He lands with a thump, and something rolls out from underneath him. I stare at the off-white vase, carved with a scene depicting an ancient Chinese village.

Suddenly, the neckline of my hoodie feels too tight. I tug on it, trying to get more air.

The vase looks just like the icon of the Stolen Artifact from last night's game level.

I think back to that level. To the strangeness of the modern office setting, of the dead man I found there.

The dead man who looked a lot like Ethan Wainwright.

But . . . that's impossible.

Video games don't come to life.

So, what the hell is happening?

Footsteps pull me back to the present. Instinctively, I duck behind a nearby desk. Is the shooter back for a second round?

Someone lets out a strangled cry, and then the footsteps grow louder and faster. From my vantage point, I see someone running toward Ethan. It takes me several heartbeats to register that it's Rock. In seconds, he's kneeling on the floor, muttering to himself, "No, no, no . . ."

Syl and Dread follow closely behind.

"Oh my God." Syl covers her mouth.

Dread stands there, looking dazed.

It's just my friends. Not the killer.

I stand slowly, trying not to startle them.

"Marina?" The relief in Syl's voice combined with my real name on her tongue makes me want to run into her arms and cry. All the tension I've been keeping in suddenly floods out, overwhelming me.

I should have realized Ethan was the dead man from last night's level. If I'd understood, I could have warned him.

I could have prevented his death.

My heart drops, and I slide to the floor, wrapping my arms around myself. It's all too much.

"What happened? Are you okay?" Suddenly, Syl is beside me, her arms around my shoulders, enveloping me in a warm hug. I shake my head, and Syl hugs me tighter.

I open my mouth to tell her everything, but nothing comes out. At the sound of a sniffle, I look over to where Rock still kneels on the floor, face in his hands. Dread has a hand on Rock's shoulder.

Rock knew Ethan personally.

I give myself one more moment, then take a deep breath and shakily extricate myself from Syl's hug. I mouth *thank you*. She nods and stands up, walking over to put her hand on Rock's other shoulder.

"Rock, are you all right?" she asks. He doesn't respond.

I feel lost. I talk to Rock every night, but I don't know how to comfort him or show him support in real life. He might not want me here, seeing his vulnerability. I stand, hands in my pockets, and wait.

After a minute or two, I break the silence with a whisper. "What do we do now?"

Dread looks up at me as if he's just remembered I exist. He rubs Rock's shoulder and then stands. "We heard something . . . the gunshot, I guess . . . it was hard to tell, and came up to make sure you're okay."

"We checked our phones on the way up. None of us have reception," Syl says. "You?"

I shake my head.

"One of us should leave and find help, then," Dread says.

"No way," Syl says. "We're safer sticking . . ."

Her words trail off as the giant monitor on the wall behind Ethan's body flickers on. Words form on the screen, one letter at a time, as if someone is typing.

I wouldn't go for help if I were you.

Syl gasps. We all gape at the screen as words continue to appear.

THE RULES OF THE GAME
1. Tell no outsiders. This will be our little secret.
2. An exclusive level will open each night at 8:00 p.m.

3. To prevent a randomly selected misfortune, successfully clear each level before the next level opens.
4. Everything you need to know is in *Darkitect*.
5. Follow the rules and play through all four levels and you have nothing to fear.
6. Break the rules, and you'll be charged with his murder. You were the last ones to see him alive, after all — suspicious, no?
7. Still not convinced? Check the envelopes. ☺

And don't forget! GLHF.

—Cixi

"Good luck, have fun? What the *hell*?" Rock gets to his feet, furious. Before any of us can stop him, Rock reaches for one of the cords and yanks on it.

"Wait!" Syl says, but it's too late. The screen goes dead.

He turns to face her, eyes full of fire.

"You actually want to participate in this bullshit?"

"Of course not!" Syl sounds frustrated. "But we need to figure out what's going on, and that screen was a clue."

"We know what's going on. Someone shot Ethan, and they're acting like it's a game!"

"Yeah, it's messed up. That's exactly why we need all the information we can get about the killer."

"This was in *Darkitect* last night." My voice comes out strangled. Everyone turns to stare at me. My gaze slides downward toward Ethan's body. I want to squeeze my eyes shut, to blink and skip over the dead man in front of me, but I force myself to look.

To confirm. The blood and the hole in his chest. His hair. His outfit. It matches.

"*What* was in *Darkitect*?" Syl asks. "These so-called *rules*?"

"No." I draw a deep breath. It fails to calm my breathing—or my heart, which beats so loudly I can barely think. "Him. This. Ethan was the body in the last room." In the room labeled "justice" in Chinese.

Dread shakes his head. "That can't be."

"He had a bullet hole in his heart. And the Stolen Artifact— the quest item—looked just like that vase." *And it wasn't the only loot on his body.*

My eyes land on something peeking out from Ethan's hoodie pocket. I reach for it and pull out four envelopes. They're just like the ones I found on the body last night in *Darkitect*.

"The last *rule* said something about envelopes," Syl says.

I flip them and see writing on the back.

The Misfortune of Andrew Hunt
The Misfortune of Rajesh Mukherjee
The Misfortune of Marina Chan
The Misfortune of Tamyra Johnson

I hand them out. Dread tears the seal on his immediately, while Syl opens hers carefully. Rock's hands shake, grip tight enough to curl the envelope.

I open mine, unsure what to expect. But whatever I might have guessed, what's inside is worse. Judging by the faces everyone makes, theirs are just as bad.

"What do yours say?" Rock's voice sounds hollow.

"It's a threat against my mom," Dread says. "Framing her for fraud at her company. I don't understand how . . ." He shakes his head.

"My parents' security business would be completely destroyed by the threat in my envelope," Rock says.

"This implies she'll burn down my . . . workplace." I almost say *home*, but change my mind at the last minute.

"My *misfortune*"—Syl spits out each syllable like a curse—"is that Cixi will kill my brother."

Misfortune.

To prevent a randomly selected misfortune, successfully clear each level before the next level opens.

These must be the "misfortunes" we can prevent . . . by following these horrible rules. If any of us falls out of line, Cíxǐ will follow through on these threats.

And frame us for Ethan's murder.

"Are we really supposed to believe Cixi is behind this?" Dread sounds incredulous. "As in renowned *Darkitect* player Cixi?"

"We all saw the sign-off after the rules," Syl says. "And Night saw this scene in yesterday's level, which Cixi designed."

"This makes no sense," Rock says. "What, so we have to try her new video game levels or she'll ruin our lives?"

We're all quiet for a moment.

"There has to be more to it," I say, because he's right. The rules make it sound so simple. Too simple. Play the game and no one—no one *else*—gets hurt.

I look around, suddenly chilled. There was a killer in here just a few minutes ago, and they've already shown us that this murder was very, very premeditated.

I want to trace the scars on my wrist over and over until my fingers are numb. I want to wrap a blanket around myself and shrink away from this whole mess. I want to throw away the envelope in my hand, run home, bury my face in Slate's soft gray-and-white fur, and pretend this day never happened.

I thought I'd left trouble behind. I thought I'd created a new life where things would be okay. Where I'd be safe. But trouble keeps finding me.

I must be cursed.

"There has to be something we can do," Dread says. "Maybe if we try to prevent the threats from happening, we can keep everyone safe, and *then* we can tell someone?" As soon as he says the last words, his mouth snaps shut. I see the others tense with the same realization. Last time he suggested telling someone, the rules popped up on the screen right afterward.

Cíxǐ is listening.

"We're not telling anyone." Rock wrings his hands, the movement at odds with the calm in his voice. I can't tell if he means what he's saying or if it's for Cíxǐ's benefit. "We have to play along."

CHAPTER 6

Nine Years Earlier

Grace Zhou wanted me to come over and play.

We passed notes back and forth all through Saturday afternoon Chinese school while Lǎoshī taught us about Empress Dowager Cíxǐ, who ruled China for nearly five decades. As soon as class finished, we ran outside to beg my mom to let me go over for a playdate.

But Mama said no.

"Why can't I go?" I asked after Grace left with her mom. I stamped my foot on the sidewalk. "It's not fair!"

"Why do you want to leave me, bǎobèi?" Mama bent down to look at me, her eyes swimming with hurt. "Am I not enough for you? Am I so bad that you have to get away from me?"

Instantly, guilt filled my stomach. "Of course not, Mama. But why can't I go over and play?"

"Because I love you too much." Mama reached out to smooth my hair. "Do you know what kinds of horrible people are out there in the world? You don't know what Grace's parents are like. You don't know what kinds of bad things they might do."

I stared. Could Grace's parents really be bad people?

"I used to trust people, but I was wrong. Terrible things happened to me. I won't let those things happen to you." Mama sucked in a sharp breath and pulled me into a hug. She was squeezing so hard it hurt, but I didn't complain.

What kind of terrible things had happened to Mama?

THE MISFORTUNE OF MARINA CHAN

CONTENTS OF ENVELOPE:

- Four articles with the following headlines:
    - » "Mexican Restaurant Destroyed in Ballard Fire"
    - » "Fire Destroys Popular Seattle Bakery"
    - » "Firefighter Injured in Restaurant Blaze"
    - » "Tacoma Trattoria Severely Damaged in Fire"
- Photograph of a restaurant with the sign displayed clearly: Bette's Battles and Bao.
- Note, which reads as follows: Kitchen fires happen far too frequently. It would be a shame for a beloved gem like Bette's to go the same way as all these other restaurants.

CHAPTER 7

Friday, 7:20 p.m.

After leaving Apocalypta HQ, we decide to follow our original plan. Dread drives us all to the restaurant. Cíxǐ's new level opens soon, and we only have until 8:00 p.m. tomorrow to beat it.

The bell jingles as I pull open the red door.

"Hey!" The hostess on duty, Christina, waves as I step inside. "Welcome to Bette's Battles and Bao," she says to my friends as they file in after me. "Marina, your favorite table is free."

"Thanks!" The restaurant is loud enough to mask the shake in my voice. I grab menus and head toward the fox booth with my friends trailing behind. I sit first, holding my breath to see where Syl will choose.

"Scoot over." Syl slides in beside me. Despite everything that's happened tonight, I feel my heart flutter. She inspects a framed kitsune sketch that hangs on the wall above Rock's head. "That looks like your art."

I blush. "It is." Bette insisted on putting it up. Each table boasts a different theme and they're all decorated with knickknacks she's collected over the years. This whole restaurant is her love letter to the world.

"How long have you been working here?" Dread asks.

"Ten months." Thinking about the first time I set foot in the restaurant, last October, I feel a surge of gratefulness for Bette and Jimmy. They're the reason I'm not living on the streets—or dead in a ditch somewhere. I owe them everything.

"This place is really cool." Syl looks around. "It's like an internet café and a cozy Chinese restaurant had a baby."

"It used to just be a Chinese restaurant," I say. "Then the owners, Bette and Jimmy, realized their best bet for staying in business was to cater to the techie lunch crowd. A lot of the regulars work for local startups or tech, and they play games on their lunch break." I gesture at the corner full of floor cushions, a television, and several game consoles. "They also host events. Last week, Spiked Lizard Games rented out the whole place for a game jam."

"Brilliant business strategy," Syl says.

"They're smart people." I hand out menus, wishing I could tell my friends that I live here too. But Bette and Jimmy put their livelihood on the line every day by letting me and Slate live here in violation of Seattle's strict zoning laws and restaurant codes. The least I can do is keep my mouth shut.

Syl glances over the menu. "What do you recommend?"

"The guàbāo is their bestseller. It's popular in Taiwan, where Bette and Jimmy are from. It's traditionally made with braised pork belly, but my fave is their crispy oyster mushroom guàbāo. I order it in the combo platter with sesame noodles, garlic cauliflower, and veggie wonton soup. Plus lychee bubble tea. Oh, and we *have* to get the cōngyóubǐng to share. It's this delicious, flaky, fried scallion pancake, and it will change your life."

"That sounds amazing. I want what you're having," Syl says.

While Rock and Dread peruse the menu, I crane my neck, looking for my favorite being in the whole world. As if he can hear my silent summons, the door to the restaurant's back office opens and a big, fluffy husky saunters out, heading for our booth.

"Slate!" I call out.

"He's gorgeous." Syl sets down the menu. "How old is he? Can I pet him?"

"He's nine. And yep, he's friendly."

Syl reaches for Slate. I go completely still as her thigh leans against mine. My giant fur baby wags his tail and sneaks under the table. He pops back up, wriggling until his head is wedged in between us. He sniffs Syl, who smiles. It's the first time any of us has smiled since finding Ethan dead.

"Does the dog *live* here?" Rock sounds skeptical.

"Only during the day, of course, and he's never allowed in the kitchen, just the office and eating area." I tell Rock the same thing we tell every new customer that asks. Most of it's true. "I should take him for a walk."

"Méi guān xi." Bette swoops in, carrying a plate of appetizers, which she sets on our table. "Wǒ yǐjīng liúgǒu le."

I shouldn't be surprised that Bette already walked Slate. She's the best. Slate *loves* her—and not only because she sneaks him scraps of chicken. "Thanks, Bette. These are my friends." I don't miss the way her eyes light up when I say "friends." "Everyone, this is Bette."

"Marina! Your friends are so lovely! What are your names?"

They introduce themselves, and Bette repeats their names, taking the time to say something complimentary about each of them. As always, I'm in awe of how naturally kindness comes to her. From someone else, this level of effusiveness might feel showy, but Bette's delight is warm and genuine. And I know better than anyone how deep her selflessness runs.

"Jimmy!" Bette yells. "Marina's friends are here!"

I blush at how big of a deal she's making, but it's nice too. Jimmy hurries out of the kitchen, and Bette beckons him over. "This is Tamyra, Raj, and Andrew."

Jimmy grunts and nods at them. He's a man of few expressions and even fewer words. But I can tell he's pleased I brought my friends.

Rock asks for a recommendation, which Bette's happy to give. Dread gets the beef noodle soup, a Taiwanese classic, and Syl says she'll have whatever I'm having, plus a milk tea. Bette flashes me a grin before she and Jimmy leave to place our orders, and I can tell she's already planning to bring us extra food. For the space of a few minutes, the shock of the last few hours' events lifts for all of us.

And then they're gone, and the tension settles back in, even as we start in on the appetizer platter of salted peanuts, chili garlic cucumber, and pickled mustard greens. Beneath the table, Slate is curled up by my leg, back paws on Syl's feet. The booths here are roomy, tables designed to fit laptops and plates of food, so Slate has plenty of space. He's just sitting on her feet because he likes her.

You and me both, pup.

"So, Night." Syl turns to me. "What happened when you were up there with Ethan? Did you see anything?"

My mind flashes back to the gunshot, and I tense as memories flood in.

Crouching behind the desk, listening to the sound of footsteps getting closer, closer...

I realize I've unconsciously started tracing the scars on my left wrist. It's become a habit in the past year, a way to calm myself down.

Afraid to draw attention, I force myself to stop and look up. Everyone's staring worriedly at me. I take a deep breath. Then another. Syl rests a hand on my shoulder. I focus on her touch until I can breathe again.

"He said Apocalypta wanted to commission an art piece from me. He said . . ." I trail off. The PAX badges won't happen anymore. Apocalypta won't be paying me for my artwork. I hate myself for being disappointed. "It doesn't matter. He got a message on his smartwatch and left the room. While he was gone, I heard the gunshot and hid behind his desk. It was . . . loud."

"Did you see the shooter?" Syl asks.

"Just that they wore black boots. After shooting Ethan, they left through the stairwell."

I leave out the part where the killer walked into the office and stood there breathing the same air as me. The thought of having to recount it makes me feel like hyperventilating.

"What about all of you?"

"Nothing really." Syl shrugs. "Before . . . *it* happened, we almost went to find you."

"Why?"

"You know. Adult man asks to talk to a teenage girl he doesn't know alone in his office? You just never know. Then we heard the gunshot."

"We weren't sure if it was real," Dread adds. "It was far away and seemed unlikely."

"We argued about leaving to find help, in case it was real, or coming up to investigate," Syl continues. "We decided we couldn't leave you there, so we came up to check."

Oh. I bite my lip. They came back up for *me*.

"None of this tells us much." Rock sounds frustrated.

Syl chews her lower lip. "Y'all . . . even if we play this *game*, someone's going to find Ethan before the levels are up. One level per day, four days . . . I assume Monday is a regular workday?"

Dread nods. "And, sometimes, people work weekends."

Syl covers her mouth. "Someone could find him tomorrow."

My palms start to sweat. Apocalypta has my photo in their system. Once Ethan's body is discovered, the police will check the security logs and see that we signed in for our tour. They'll realize I forged the signature, and they'll look for me, and—

Slate sits up and licks my hand, snapping me back to the present. I lean down to pet him, reminding myself that I can't afford to lose it now. We need to figure out who Cíxǐ is, fast.

I've missed whatever my friends have been talking about.

". . . Eight o'clock," Rock says. "The new level should be open."

An exclusive level will open each night at 8:00 p.m.

I force my thoughts away from imagining police officers questioning me. I'll figure out how to deal with that if it happens. We don't have time to panic. Cíxǐ made sure of it.

"This is so messed up," Dread says.

Everyone starts setting up their laptops. At the sight of Dread's sleek silver MSI, the armored ridges of Syl's Alienware, and the triple snake logo of Rock's black Razer, I hesitate. Usually, I'm proud of the way I worked double shifts and saved up tips to pay Bette back for my refurbished old laptop. It's big, clunky, and an ugly shade of gray, but it's mine. I earned it.

But their slick, flashy machines and equally cool matching mice make my setup look even shabbier than usual. I'm glad for the restaurant's dim lighting.

Reluctantly, I set up my laptop. Mercifully, no one comments.

As my ancient computer boots up, I feel the familiar anticipation of a new level call to me, followed closely by guilt. Cíxǐ murdered a man in front of my eyes. She's a monster. But the gamer part of me, the part that was excited when we were invited to try one of her levels last night, desperately wants to see what kind of content Cíxǐ has created for us.

I wonder if that makes me a terrible person.

As if he can sense my guilt, Slate nuzzles my leg. I reach down to scruff his ears, and he leans against me for a moment before wiggling out from between me and Syl and taking off, probably going to see if any of his favorite regulars will sneak him food.

We all put our headsets on. It feels weird now that we're all at the same table, but it's the only way we'll be able to hear the game sounds. When *Darkitect* finally loads, I'm in one of the shared areas where players go to trade items, run errands, and show off awesome gear.

"Porting over." I click on the pocket portal that'll send me back to our team base.

Darkitect is a mix between a massively multiplayer online role-playing game and a level builder. There are shared zones with quests to complete, monsters to kill, treasure to find, and places to explore. Most players also enjoy running instances—separate levels that a team can enter via portal and work together to beat. There are plenty of official ones designed by Apocalypta Games, but I think players who stick purely to shared zones and official instances are missing out.

Unlike most MMORPGs, Apocalypta put a lot of work into their level-building tools and builder interface for *Darkitect*. Then they made those tools accessible to the public. Which means that in addition to the official levels, there are numerous player-designed levels. Most players don't have the expertise to design anything really complicated, but people with programming skills can tweak the existing tools and create truly phenomenal levels.

Cíxǐ's levels are among the most spectacular, which is why she became so well known in such a short time.

At our team base, I switch out a few items, bringing a mix of things that could be useful for different scenarios. We have no idea what we're getting into.

Rock does a ready check, then we all click on the tickets we received last night.

Haunted Royal Opera Theater.

The words flash across all our screens as our characters drop into a courtyard paved with stones. It's nighttime here, but lanterns illuminate a massive three-story building with pillars holding up each floor.

"It looks like a Chinese temple," Dread says.

I squint at the screen. The building looks familiar . . . oh. That's the Grand Theater in the Beijing Summer Palace. I remember learning that Empress Dowager Cíxǐ—the real one—had it built during her reign. Cute reference.

The theater's exterior is exquisitely detailed, with curved roof tiles and intricate, lacquered red-and-yellow designs. Its walls are open, but it's too dark to see inside.

A countdown timer pops up in the top right corner of my screen. We have until 8:00 p.m. tomorrow to clear the level.

"Enjoy the show," a voice says behind us. We all spin around.

Cíxǐ wears the same embroidered yellow robes as she did in yesterday's level. Tonight, she sits on a huge, padded throne. Sitting next to her is a ghostly man. His features are elongated and grotesque, and he's wrapped tightly in translucent chains. He looks appropriately miserable.

"It's Ethan." Rock clenches his jaw.

"Discover his dirty little secrets and he'll go peacefully to the afterlife," Cíxi's avatar says.

Rock growls, and I see Dread's gaze flicker over to his best friend. "You okay, man?"

"Cixi murdered him and now she's put him in the game as a ghost? That's twisted."

Suddenly, our characters are hurtling through the air, across the stone courtyard into the huge, open three-story building I was gawking at earlier. As soon as I hit the ground, I jump to my feet and pull out my steel scimitar. Rock is already healing us while Dread runs forward to pick up aggro for any mobs that might attack us.

A host of figures leap from the darkness, clad in flowing red-and-gold robes. The label above their heads says "Jing." As they near, I glimpse their faces, painted white with patterned red and black swirls. They immediately begin attacking with swords and staves.

"Syl, CC far right, then focus on Dread's target." Rock marks two targets for her to crowd control before she starts casting spells to help Dread kill the enemies. "Night, keep adds off me and Syl."

We all jump to obey. Dread runs around hitting as many Jing as he can, trying to anger them so they'll target him and leave the rest of us alone. He's our tank, which means he has the most health and armor and can take the most hits. Rock, our healer, sits back, focusing his healing on Dread to keep him alive. He's also our shot-caller, paying attention to the larger picture and giving orders.

Syl casts spells to root one Jing in place and banish another to a different dimension. She'll have to cast spells periodically to keep them occupied, but it gives us two fewer enemies to fight until then.

While the three of them work together in symbiosis, my role is more independent. Like Dread, I'm hardier than the others, but not enough to tank six enemies like he's doing right now. I can deal damage like Syl, but I can't crowd control anyone. And I can heal myself some, but unlike Rock, I can't heal anyone else. I can also sneak around mobs without them noticing. In short, I take care of myself and do a little of everything, which makes me perfect for taking on the odd jobs.

A Jing leaps away from the group and heads for Syl. Dread's knife throw misses the Jing, so I dive in front of Syl, slashing at the enemy with my scimitar. Enraged, it turns and attacks me, managing to cut a third of my health.

I raise my weapon, then smash it down on the Jing, finishing it off. Its body glows, indicating loot. I heal up and help my teammates kill the rest of the Jing before looting its body. "Found a yearbook for Redmond Preparatory Academy."

"That has to be important," Syl says.

I think back to the previous night, how different the final room was from the rest of the level. This school yearbook seems equally out of place in a Chinese opera house. "Probably."

"This one dropped a megaphone," Syl says. "Looks like I can type in a short message and my character will shout whatever I typed."

"Weird," Dread says.

In-game, something screams, making me jump. All three of my friends look up at me.

"Um . . . that startled me." Crud. I'm not used to having them here in person. I need to be more careful.

Thankfully, everyone's too distracted by what's happening in-game to question my jumpiness. On-screen, darkness descends fast, until the outline of the theater disappears.

Our food arrives just as the scene comes into view again, dimly lit. Syl reaches up to pull out an earbud as Bette sets our food down, but Bette shakes her head. Everyone here is used to serving gamers and techies, some of whom eat lunch here while playing games or calling into work meetings. Normal meal etiquette rules don't apply at Bette's. I wave at Bette, who winks before running off.

I turn my attention back to the screen. This time, we face just one enemy—a huge wooden puppet that towers over us, standing nearly as tall as the ceiling. Like the Jing, his face is painted, but instead of rounded swirls, his makeup highlights gaunt cheeks and angry eyebrows. His school uniform is both creepy and too modern for the setting. As he glares down at us, I read the name above him.

"Do yours also say 'Name Redacted' with brackets around it?" I've never seen that before and I don't know if it's intentional or an error.

"Yes," Rock confirms as lanterns light up the stage one by one. "Are we in a classroom?"

"Looks like it." Syl squints at her screen as she adjusts the settings.

There's a blackboard on one wall with stick figure drawings hanging next to it. Around us, the stage floor is full of kid-sized chairs with attached tables.

As [Name Redacted] looks down at us, I notice the design on his shirt. "Hey, that lion was on the yearbook I looted."

"Oh!" Rock starts typing, and Dread peers at his screen. A few seconds later, both their eyes widen.

"What is it?" Syl asks.

"Redmond Prep is a primary school," Rock says.

"And Wikipedia says Ethan went there," Dread says.

"Uh, cuz, a little help?" Syl says.

Dread's eyes snap back to his screen. "Shit!" He dives forward as [Name Redacted] lunges for Syl.

Rock tabs back into the game and heals Dread just in time.

"This dude hits hard," Dread says.

Through my headset, I hear a new voice speak in-game.

"I trusted him, fool I was," [Name Redacted] laments. "Best friends. He said we were best friends." He stops hitting Dread. Instead, he lets out a wail that drops all our health bars down 20 percent and spawns little white creatures labeled "Anguish Ghosts."

"Night, grab the adds?" Rock says.

"Yeah." I chase the Anguish Ghosts around the classroom, slashing at them. They don't have much health, but they keep spawning, so I switch to bow and arrow and begin picking them off.

Suddenly, they stop spawning. [Name Redacted] stops attacking Dread, sits down, and begins to wail.

"He's immune to my spells," Syl says.

"Same with melee strikes," Dread says.

My attacks aren't hurting him either. [Name Redacted] is at 75 percent health and staying that way. He's temporarily invulnerable, so we stop wasting our moves.

"There must be something we have to solve," Syl says.

While Cíxǐ's settings are always splendid, that's not the only reason players love her. It's her clever puzzles. You can't just mash your damage buttons and make your way through. There are always challenges or riddles to solve in order to win.

"Ethan struck away my name," [Name Redacted] cries, flailing his arms and knocking over several desks. "He took my creation. Took my credit. Now no one knows it was mine. Mine. Mine. MINE!" With a scream, he starts attacking again. Dread tanks [Name Redacted] while Rock frantically heals Dread.

"Syl and Night, look for clues," Rock says.

We split up and look around the level.

"There's a worn American flag and chalkboard here," Syl says, "with multiplication problems written out in chalk."

"Calendar hanging off this side and a bunch of little kid drawings." I inspect them in case they contain any hints. "This one is an elephant, maybe? And . . . oh, the drawing is signed! Henry Greenwood."

"Shout that name into the megaphone!" Dread says.

"What?" Syl asks. I'm confused too.

"The one you looted earlier, cuz. You can type something in, right? [Name Redacted] is complaining no one knows his name, and we're in a classroom. I think he's one of the students. If we say his name, maybe he'll stop attacking."

"Shouldn't we confirm which classmate he is first?" Syl asks.

"I'll explain later. Just type in his name!"

A few seconds later, Syldara's voice booms throughout the stage. "Henry Greenwood!"

[Name Redacted] stops attacking Dreadnaughty and for a moment, I think we've solved the puzzle. Then a snarl takes over his face, and his eyes turn red.

"Wrong, wrong, WRONG!"

With an enraged scream, his hands reach up to grab the ceiling. He leaps up, and we try all our ranged attacks on him, but they're ineffective. Then he stomps back to the ground, landing hard enough to crack open the floor. He falls to his knees and begins pounding the floor with his fists, like a kid throwing a tantrum. The building crumbles.

All four of us run for the courtyard, but it's no use. The building collapses with us still inside.

CHAPTER 8

Nine Years Earlier

Mama and I stood in line to watch a rerun of *My Neighbor Totoro* at Gold Mountain Theater. I hummed the theme song, bouncing up and down.

"Growing up, we used to love watching animated films," Mama said.

"*We?*" I perked up. Mama never really talked about being a kid.

She blinked. "Me and Mama and Baba, of course."

The man behind us in line tapped Mama on the shoulder. "Hey, don't I know you?"

Mama's eyes grew wide, and she pressed her lips tight. "No, you're mistaken. We've never met."

"Weren't we in a class together? You sat in the row in front of me. I . . ." The man stopped suddenly, his face twisted as if he was trying to remember something. "Didn't you—"

Mama grabbed my hand. She pushed past the man, dragging me away.

"Hey!" the man shouted, sounding startled. "Wait!"

Mama's grip on my hand tightened and we started to run.

CHAPTER 9

Friday, 8:40 p.m.

We all look at Dread.

He shrugs. "I was about to die anyway. That boss hits too hard. I need to switch gear. Couldn't wait too long."

"Dude," Syl says.

Rock sighs. "We'll have to start the level over."

"We might as well eat now." Dread digs into his beef noodle soup.

"It was a good idea," I concede. "It can't be coincidence that there were names on those kid's drawings up on the wall. Drawing, uniform, yearbook, classroom . . . they're all clues." I take a bite of my crispy oyster mushroom bāo. To me, Bette's cooking will always taste like hope and kindness. Like the night my new life began.

Dread finishes chewing. "We know this is all related to Ethan somehow. [Name Redacted] must be one of his classmates or his teacher, right?"

"[Name Redacted] was talking about Ethan taking credit for something of his." Syl sips her pearl milk tea. "Any idea what that's about?"

"Hm," Dread says. "We can probably check online. There's

always some controversy and people throwing around accusations when it comes to taking credit for various innovations."

"He wouldn't steal credit." Rock blinks rapidly and wipes his eyes. He doesn't look directly at us. The mask of composure he wore while playing the level has slipped. This isn't just a puzzle to him. He's known Ethan for years.

"Hey, man, your food's getting cold," Dread says. "Let's eat."

Syl and I glance at each other.

"Just because someone makes an accusation doesn't mean it's true," Syl says. "And none of us trust Cixi. Dread's right. Eat up. The food is *really* good. We'll figure out the right name in a bit."

Rock nods and closes his screen, half-heartedly picking up his fork. We eat in silence for a few minutes. I'm about to take another bite when my furry best friend wriggles out of another booth and heads toward me. He starts pawing at me and pointing toward the door.

"Again? I thought Bette just took you out!" I wrap the rest of my bāo in a cloth napkin. "Sorry, I gotta walk him," I say. Syl scoots over to let me out of the booth.

I grab Slate's leash and take him through the little back office we call home, then out the door to the alleyway. As soon as we're alone outside, he leans against me affectionately. I kneel down to hug him. "Missed you too." He whines happily.

Twenty minutes, two squirrel chases, and the rest of my bāo later, our walk is done.

When I return to the table, Syl looks excited.

"We figured it out!" she exclaims before I can sit down.

"Syl figured it out," Rock corrects, and I'm relieved to hear a bit of his usual wryness.

"The guy's name is James Steinberg," Dread says. "Apparently, he was Ethan's best friend at Redmond Prep. They had a huge falling-out when Ethan started Apocalypta Games."

"Steinberg claims Ethan stole their shared game idea, but he was never able to prove it," Syl says.

I lift my eyebrows. "That does seem like something an enemy of Ethan's might consider a dirty little secret."

We restart the level. This time, we're dropped right into the theater, where the Jing attack us immediately. We fight them again, going through the same stages until [Name Redacted] starts screaming about credit being taken from him.

"James Steinberg!" Syl's character shouts through the megaphone.

[Name Redacted] stops wailing. He looks at us, then wipes his face. He smears off most of the face paint, leaving faint smudges behind.

"That's him," Syl says. "There was a picture of him in one of the articles."

The words "[Name Redacted]" above his head disappear, replaced by new ones. "James Steinberg."

"Hey, he's vulnerable again!" Dread says.

We all attack, dropping James Steinberg's health bar down. At 75 percent, he flashes us a toothy grin and reaches up, pushing open a door in the ceiling. Then he leaps up through the door.

"Do we follow him?" Syl asks.

Before anyone can answer, James's huge hand reaches down through the ceiling hole, scooping us up and tossing us into the second floor with him. He grins at us. Strangely, he's changed into khakis, a button-down, and a tie.

I'm back in a familiar setting for the third time in less than twenty-four hours, surrounded by statues and game art.

"This floor looks like Apocalypta," Dread says as we start attacking. Flames flicker in James's eyes, and tiny red monsters labeled "Rage Demons" pop out of the floor.

"On it." I go after the Rage Demons like I did the Anguish Ghosts. Dread and Syl attack James until he's down to 50 percent health.

"He's invulnerable again," Dread says.

James cocks his head, inspecting each of us in turn.

"Are you *his* creatures?" His eyes flash with rage. "Do you know how *he* betrayed me?"

"I *hate* this," Rock says. "I know it's only a game, but it feels like agreeing with this guy means I believe him. And I don't." His hand curls into a fist. "Anyway, we know the answer to this one from Syl's research earlier. Type this into the megaphone: 'he stole your game.'"

"What if the wording's wrong?" I ask. "How are we supposed to guess the exact phrase?"

"Someone like Cixi will know how to create a dialogue response box that pulls and accepts certain key words in various forms," Rock says. "It's what some of the original text-based computer games used."

"Nerd," Dread says, and Rock's lips turn up at the corners. We're all nerds and proud of it, but Rock is our resident tech geek.

Next to me, Syl types something and hits enter, crossing her fingers.

In-game, Syldara shouts, "He stole your game!"

James stops attacking and grins wider. The Rage Demons melt away, and he claps.

Once again, he jumps up through another hidden trapdoor in the ceiling, pulling us up to the third floor. This time, he's in a suit, carrying a briefcase. I glance around. The stage is styled like a courtroom.

"There were only three floors, right? This should be the last," I say.

"It'd better be," Dread says. "I think the restaurant's about to close."

I look around, realizing he's right. I was so absorbed in *Darkitect* that I didn't notice Bette's has emptied. We can't afford to mess up or my friends will have to leave, and we'll need to start the level over.

This time, little green Greed Goblins appear. We repeat the same tactic, me chasing and killing them while the other three focus on attacking James.

At 25 percent, James becomes invulnerable again. He makes a *tsk* sound. "He kept me quiet." His grin widens. "Do you know how much it cost him?" His eyes twinkle now, little money signs visible in his pupils.

"Don't let me die," Syl says. I look over to see her tab out and open a Google search.

"What are you doing?" Rock asks as he starts healing us again.

"Looking for . . . I don't know. Information about the lawsuit? Earlier, I saw that James filed a case against Apocalypta Games claiming they stole his idea."

"Do we know the outcome?" I ask.

"I believe they settled out of court."

"Oh, can we look up the settlement amount? Matter of public record or something like that?" Honestly, I have no idea what I'm talking about, but hopefully one of my teammates does.

"No," Syl says. "It won't be. And the settlement terms are almost certainly confidential. Only the parties involved would be privy to the amount. Damn it, this is so frustrating! This isn't like the other answers. How are we supposed to find out something like that?"

We're all quiet for a moment, thinking.

Dread draws in a sharp breath. "I think there's a way to find out. Through me."

Syl and I look at him in confusion.

He grimaces. "There would be copies at Apocalypta, in the legal department. They have their own private office area. And it's piled high with filing cabinets. The settlement amount has to be in one of those files. I can't officially get into Legal . . . but I can badge into the building."

"Won't you get in trouble?" I ask. Dread's been gushing about his internship the whole summer. Breaking in and stealing legal records could get him fired, maybe worse.

Dread shrugs, but his eyes flick to his backpack, where the corner of his envelope sticks out of the front pocket.

We all know what's at stake.

"I guess we could go early tomorrow morning?" Syl says.

Dread shakes his head. "The company is full of workaholics. Someone might come in super early to get stuff done."

"And if they find him there . . ."

"They'll lock everything down," I say.

Dread's grim expression tells us enough.

"This is a bad idea," Rock says.

I agree, but what else can we do? Tonight could be our only chance.

"I don't think we have a choice," Syl echoes my thoughts.

"So that means . . ." I trail off.

Dread grimaces. "We go tonight."

While my friends pay for their meals, pack up their computers, and call their parents with made-up excuses to go out tonight, I sneak away to find Bette. As I walk toward the kitchen, I peer into the little restaurant office Slate and I call home. Part of me wants to ditch the whole risky plan and stay here. I could sign into the game and run around the shared zones instead. *Darkitect* is my safe haven.

At least, it *was* my safe haven.

Terrence, one of the chefs, waves at me from the kitchen as I pass by. I wave back but don't add a greeting. I'm careful not to get too close to any of the staff in case they ask about my family or why I'm at the restaurant so often. Bette's ahead, wiping down the kitchen. When she sees me, a huge smile lights up her face. Her smiles are magic. Everything weighs a little less when she gifts me one.

"Bette, can we talk in private?"

She sets the rag down and hustles me over to a solitary corner. With our voices down, no one will be able to hear over the clatter of Xiùlán washing dishes or the whoosh of flames as Terrence quick-dries the woks so they don't rust.

"I'm sleeping over at a friend's house tonight. Can Slate stay with you until tomorrow morning?"

Bette raises an eyebrow. "Shéi jiā?"

I blush.

"Tamyra?" Bette grins wickedly. "Wǒ dǒng le. The way you look at her and she looks at you." She taps her temple.

I can feel color creep into my cheeks. "It's not like that." Even if I wish it was.

Bette's gaze turns stern again. "Marina, you will be careful, yes?"

"I'm not . . ."

"Hǎo, hǎo." She waves dismissively. "But someday you will want to . . . you know." She winks. "Yīnggāi xiǎoxīn. People worry about pregnancy. Maybe you think with a girl there should be no worry. But there are diseases . . ."

I wonder if one can die of mortification.

"Bette, I promise! I'll be careful." Anything to end this conversation.

"Hǎo." She holds my shoulders in her hands. "I will watch Slate. I'm so happy to see you making friends. You deserve to be happy." She smiles, and the pride in her eyes brings tears to mine.

"Xièxie." I could thank her every day for the rest of my life, and it would never be enough.

As I walk back through the kitchen to rejoin my friends, a flame from the stovetop flares up, causing Terrence to leap back.

"Phew!" He gives me an I'm-okay grin. "Almost took out one of my eyebrows there. Chad would be *so* disappointed. He thinks they're my best feature."

He pauses, giving me the chance to reply with a quip. That's pretty much what all our interactions are—occasional light quips with zero personal information shared. Just the way I like it.

But, as I stare at the flame, my throat constricts. I can't muster a response, even though he's given me the perfect opening. My mind fills with the threats Cíxǐ put in my envelope.

Kitchen fires happen far too frequently. It would be a shame for a beloved gem like Bette's to go the same way as all these other restaurants.

All I can see is the roar of the fire, right before Terrence leaped back. In my mind, it grows bigger and bigger, swallowing the restaurant whole. Burning down everything and everyone inside.

CHAPTER 10

Nine Years Earlier

When we got home after running from the man on the street, Mama sat down on the couch and turned to face me.

"Lia, I wanted to wait until you were older to talk about this, but that strange man at the theater made me realize I can't put it off any longer." She took a deep breath. "Something happened a long time ago, and now there are bad people out there who might be looking for us."

"Bad people?"

"Scary people." Mama chewed on her lip. "People who want to hurt us." She pulled me close and hugged me. "But don't worry. I'll keep you safe, okay? Those people will never, ever find us."

THE MISFORTUNE OF RAJESH MUKHERJEE

CONTENTS OF ENVELOPE:

- Three articles with the following titles:
  - » "Another Private Security Firm Goes Under After Client Data Leak"
  - » "Black Blade Electronics Poaches Top Executive from Zenith Corporation (Decades-Long Rivalry Grows More Embittered)"
  - » "Interview with Sanjay and Gita Mukherjee, the Power Duo Behind King Security" (Accompanied by a black-and-white photograph of two smiling people.)
- Copies of the following:
  - » Zenith Corporation's Q2 Profit and Loss Statement, DRAFT.
  - » Zenith Corporation's Q2 Balance Sheet, DRAFT.
  - » Zenith Corporation's Q2 Statement of Cash Flows, DRAFT.
  - » Contract renewal between Zenith Corporation and King Security.
- Note, which reads as follows: It's hard to protect data these days, as many companies have learned. Imagine how unfortunate it would be for King Security to have their client's unpublished financial statements leaked directly to that client's biggest rival.

CHAPTER 11

Friday, 10:30 p.m.

"Soooo . . . your parents run security for Apocalypta?" Dread asks Rock.

Dread's driving, Rock's in the passenger seat, and Syl and I are in the back. We're stopped at a red light. Syl changed out of her heels and into the emergency pair of ballet flats she keeps in her backpack, and we're all wearing the hoodies we got during the tour. We figured it would be best to have hoods to hide our faces from the cameras inside.

"Yes, and?" Rock's reply is curt.

"Is there anything you can tell us about their security at night?"

"They don't exactly share specifics about clients with me," Rock snaps. "Am I supposed to call them up to ask how to break into a building whose security they're responsible for?"

Dread parks and turns off the car before facing Rock. "Look, man. I'm sorry about Ethan. I know this can't be easy."

Rock is silent for a minute. "He is—*was*—a really good guy."

All of us get out of the car, pull our hoods up, and walk the quiet block to Apocalypta. Someone moves in the shadows, and my heart clenches before I realize it's just someone sleeping on the sidewalk. Wordlessly, my friends alter their course to give the person a wide berth.

I wonder how they'd look at me if they ever found out about my past. If they knew that I used to sleep on the streets.

I wish I could help the person, but I keep walking. We can't afford to draw attention tonight.

"I still don't think this is a good idea." Rock stares up at the building, arms folded.

"None of us wants to be here," Syl says. "But we don't have a choice."

"Can we talk about this inside?" Dread looks around unsubtly before pulling out his badge. The lock clicks open, and he walks through, followed by me and Syl. After a moment's hesitation, Rock steps inside too. The security desk is empty.

"We're not asking enough questions about all of this," Rock says once the door shuts. "Yes, this could be the way to get the settlement amount. But *why* does someone want to know? The school info was available online. But this? We don't know how they'll use it."

"Except Cixi must already know the answer, or how will she know if we're right or wrong?" Dread says.

"Cuz?" Syl's sharp tone cuts through his words. "Didn't you say no one would be here?"

We follow her gaze up to the fifth floor, eyes still adjusting to the dim lighting. The outline of a figure is visible through the darkened glass. Someone stands, watching us.

"Shit, I thought it would be empty."

"I told you! Maybe we should leave," Rock says.

"And then what?" Syl asks. "Risk a random *misfortune* befalling one of our families? Let her frame us for murder?"

The figure stands for a minute longer, and the hairs on the back of my neck prickle. I stare at them until my eyes burn. It feels like I'm making eye contact with them, even though it's too dark for that to be possible. Then the person walks away from the window and disappears.

"If we go up, we might run into whoever that is," I say.

"Legal's on the second floor. Hopefully by the time we're done there, they'll be gone," Dread says.

Ten minutes later, we're outside Legal, putting on food prep gloves I took from the restaurant's kitchen before we left. Just enough moonlight streams in through the windows for us to see most of what we're doing.

I look around the room furtively, face hidden deep in my hood, and point. Rock pulls out a roll of masking tape we borrowed from Bette, tears off a piece, and sticks it over the lens of the security camera. He and I look around for more cameras while Syl and Dread watch YouTube videos on how to pick a lock. Cíxǐ must have been scrambling the cell reception earlier. We have no trouble getting a signal now.

When the third video they've watched ends, Syl and Dread dig around people's desks until they find a paper clip. Dread uses his phone's flashlight to provide light while Syl copies the video, carefully bending the paper clip into shape and sticking it in the lock.

"And . . . we're in!"

"You're amazing," I say. Syl smiles at me, and I'm glad the dim lighting hides my reddening cheeks. She pushes open the door, and we walk in.

Dread wasn't kidding. There are giant filing cabinets *everywhere*. We split up and start scanning the labels on each drawer.

"Looks like they're sorted by year," Rock says. We researched the lawsuit on the drive over, so we search until we find the right date.

It's locked, so Syl tries her bent paper clip, but it's too big for this keyhole. She pulls her phone out, looking up YouTube tutorials specific to picking these locks. Rock starts rooting around the desk drawers.

"What are you looking for?" I ask.

"People are by far the weakest part of any security system. My parents often mention adding extra measures to account for what they deem 'the foolishness factor.' I'll bet the workers here feel like their information is safe because the entire legal department is locked. They won't be concerned about keeping the filing cabinet key secure."

"I'd make fun," Dread says, "but my VPN token is in my unlocked top desk drawer." When Rock gives him a look, he adds, "Don't worry, it's buried in my candy stash."

"Airtight security." Rock seems to be loosening up a bit. I guess there's something about breaking and entering that brings people closer together. "Aha!" He pulls out a key ring with a bunch of tiny keys on it, and Syl takes them.

Using her phone flashlight, she inspects the keys and cabinet. There are little numbers on both, scrawled in Sharpie. She looks for a match.

"Anyone have theories on Cixi's identity?" Rock asks.

"Maybe she's related to James Steinberg somehow," I say. "Cíxǐ seems really obsessed with what happened to him."

"I don't know," Dread says. "Wouldn't he be incriminating himself?"

"Maybe it's someone who was hurt by the settlement, somehow. Or someone who cares about Steinberg."

"Possibly," Rock says. "Or Steinberg may have been included in the level for an entirely different reason."

"You knew Ethan best," Dread says. "What do you think?"

Rock shrugs, looking down. "He is . . . was . . . well liked. If he had enemies, I didn't know about them." He won't make eye contact. Is it hard for him to talk about Ethan or is he hiding something? I shake my head, trying to clear the thought.

"Cixi could also be more than one person," Dread muses.

"And Cixi also isn't necessarily a woman, just because they're assuming a female avatar," Rock adds.

"True. But none of this helps narrow down our pool of suspects." Syl turns a key in the lock, sliding the drawer open to reveal a set of hanging folders. We start checking file labels.

"Do you think Cixi is someone one of us knows?" Dread asks.

Rock turns to him sharply. "Why do you say that?"

"Because. I don't know about everyone else's, but the misfortune in mine is something that had to be set up months ago."

I shiver at the thought of someone researching each of us and making plans to orchestrate all of this months in advance. "Cixi went through all the trouble of showing me what would happen to Ethan the night before. Our being there was definitely not a coincidence."

"Maybe it's someone you work with, Dread," Syl says. "She knew what the inside of the building looked like and she's proficient at building game levels. Plus, she knew today was an offsite and she was able to connect to one of the internal screens."

I shudder, remembering the words appearing on the wall. Is Cixi listening in right now?

"I can pull a company roster through our intranet, just in case," Dread says. "But plenty of people who don't work here have seen the inside of the building. We give tours pretty much every week to local schools, teens interested in the internship program, influencers and media, and top gamers."

"Great, so we're back to it being pretty much anyone," Syl says.

"Well, not *anyone*." Rock sounds thoughtful. "Cixi has some truly impressive programming skills." He turns to Dread. "Hey, do you have access to the code for player-created levels?"

Dread frowns. "I've never tried. Maybe?"

"What about the code for official games? The one Apocalypta's developers use?"

Dread shrugs.

"If you can access those, I could try checking Cixi's code against everyone else's and see if any of them have the same signature."

"There are signatures in code?" I ask.

"Well, not exactly. It's more like everyone has a certain style. Formulas they like to use, how efficient they are, that kind of thing. There's a chance I'll be able to tell if Cixi works for Apocalypta by comparing code."

"I'll see what I can do," Dread says, "but maybe you should come with me."

"It'll take time. Can you grab your work laptop for me to look over later?"

"Yeah, that works. My desk's on the fourth floor."

"You shouldn't go alone though, cuz," Syl says. "It's probably better if we stick in pairs. I'll be your lookout. C'mon." She hands me the file cabinet keys.

"Just . . . hide if you hear anything, okay?" Dread says. "We'll text you afterward, and we can meet on the fifth floor."

They head out, closing the door behind them.

With Syl and Dread gone, Rock takes over Syl's spot. We riffle through folders in silence for several minutes. It's only now that I realize Rock and I never really talk directly. One of the others is always around. I want to get to know him better, though, so I decide to break the awkward silence. "Who do *you* think killed him?"

Rock turns to face me, wearing an unreadable expression. "I'm afraid it was me."

CHAPTER 12

Eight Years Earlier

Mama drew four Chinese characters on a piece of paper. "Did you learn any of these?"

相依为命

I shook my head. Ever since that man had recognized her on the street, Mama had stopped sending me to Chinese class. She'd stopped letting me go anywhere at all except for school. She was too scared that the bad people might find us. At first, I'd listened, but lately, I'd started to complain. I missed going to the playground and seeing other kids.

Mama pointed to each word, one at a time. "'Xiāng' means 'each other or one another.' 'Yī' means 'to depend on, to rely upon.' 'Wéi' means 'for, because of, or to become.' And 'mìng' means 'life, fate, or destiny.' Together, they form a phrase that refers to an unbreakable bond. People who are wholly and mutually dependent on one another for life. Who rely upon each other for survival. Without the other person, they are nothing."

I wasn't sure if I understood, but I nodded anyway.

"Repeat after me, Lia. Xiāng yī wéi mìng."

"Xiāng yī wéi mìng."

"Very good." She frowned. "If you ever start to forget why we have to be careful, just remember xiāng yī wéi mìng. We only have each other. We can't trust anyone else."

"Xiāng yī wéi mìng," I repeated, knowing it would make Mama happy.

"That's right." She hugged me again. "It means you're the only person in the world that I love."

CHAPTER 13

Friday, 11:00 p.m.

I'm afraid it was me.

Did Rock just confess to killing Ethan?

I drop the folder I'm holding and step back. My heart pounds. We're alone. If he knocks me out, he'd be in charge of the narrative. He could tell the others that someone attacked us, and he tried to stop them.

Rock must see the terror on my face because he puts his hands up. "Oh no, Night, I didn't mean . . . I mean. Not like *that*." And then his face crumples, and I feel horrible. Of course he didn't do it. The only way he could've done it is if all three of them were in on it. I'm the only one who was alone when Ethan was shot. And I caught a glimpse of the killer's feet. Rock wasn't wearing black utility boots.

He massages his face with his hands, then sighs. "I meant it might be my fault. He had enemies because of me."

"What do you mean?" My mind is still reeling from the surge of fear and adrenaline.

Rock clears his throat, then clears it again. He scratches the back of his head, then glances over at me and self-consciously sets his hand down back in his lap. I wait.

"I'm . . . trans." Rock's eyes flicker up to me, to my look of surprise.

"Oh!" It takes my mind a moment to catch up. Then after a beat, I add, "Cool."

He raises his eyebrow at me. "Cool?"

"I don't know what to say."

Immediately, I want to take my words back. Rock's putting his trust in me. I should be supportive—tell him he's my friend no matter what. But it doesn't feel like my place. Cis people don't have to work up the nerve to tell everyone they're cis, then wait to be supported or judged. My response shouldn't be up for debate. It's a messed-up world we live in.

And I've taken way too long to respond.

Rock starts laughing suddenly. "You look like that meme of the person staring at a mess of equations in front of them, trying to solve them."

"I like girls," I blurt out, and Rock stops laughing. My eyes widen. I hadn't meant to say that. For a second, he looks at me, and I look at him.

Then a grin spreads across his face. "Cool."

We look at each other, and then we're both laughing. Suddenly, I can't stop. I laugh until tears stream out of my eyes. I don't know if it's the buildup of everything that's happened tonight, the release of saying the words I've never spoken aloud before, or giddiness that I even have a friend I trust enough to tell, but for just a moment, I feel light and free and empty. I lean backward until I'm lying on the floor, looking up at the ceiling.

Rock leans over until he's looking straight down at me. I expect him to ask if I'm all right. Instead, he says, "You know that hundreds—maybe thousands—of dirty shoes have probably stepped in that exact spot, right?"

I prop myself up on my elbows. "Thanks for that. Wait, we're getting off track. What does this have to do with . . . him?"

Rock sobers. "You know my family and I moved from the UK, right?" I nod, and he continues. "That was five years ago. It's because I realized that who people thought I was didn't match who I am."

I turn this over in my mind and draw a dark conclusion, eyes narrowing. "Wait, did your *parents* make you move?" *Because they were ashamed?* I don't ask the second question aloud, but he catches my drift.

Rock shakes his head. "They're pretty great, actually. They moved because I asked them to. I was the one who wanted to start over, without judgmental relatives or classmates to make things harder while I sorted everything out."

I feel a pang in my heart. It's not fair that he felt he had to leave so he could sort out who he was. But he also has parents who were willing to leave behind everything they knew and start over for him.

"Anyway, it's a long story, but they met Ethan pretty shortly after moving. He helped them grow their business a lot." Rock swallows hard. "And despite everything, some jerk in my new school found out and started hassling me. Ethan learned about it and got him expelled somehow."

"Wait, you think that kid might be behind this?"

"Nah. That bully wasn't smart enough to plan something this elaborate. But . . . after befriending my family, Ethan started advocating for trans rights publicly and got a lot of shit for it. Made some enemies. You know, people who think my existence is an affront to God or some other bullshit. I just . . . wonder if that's why Cixi went after him. Why she's so desperate to paint him in a negative light. It's too much of a coincidence that she drew me into it all too. Ethan barely knows Dread and never met you or Syl before today. If it's about one of us, it has to be me."

"You know that even if some bigot targeted him, that wouldn't be your fault, right?"

Rock's smile is sad. "If he'd died because he tried to help you, wouldn't you feel a little bit at fault?"

I shrug. *I don't know* is the only honest answer I can give.

Rock and I turn back toward our respective file cabinets. We search for a few minutes. He pulls out a file. "This is it!"

"Let me see!" I take the folder and open it. I'm a few pages in when both our phones buzz. I check the message from Syl. "They got the laptop and they're packing up. They'll meet us on the fifth floor."

Rock inhales sharply. I turn toward him, wondering what's wrong.

Oh, right. Rock needs time to prepare himself to see Ethan's body again. He looks so small right now, so unlike his usual, confident self. A part of me wants to reach over and hug him, but I don't know if he would want me to. I haven't had many friends before; I don't know how this works.

"If you want, you can wait here." I try to sound confident, even though I don't really want to go up alone.

"No, Syl's right. We should stick together. Besides, I should see if I can find anything on his computer."

An involuntary shudder runs through me at the thought of

stepping foot in Ethan's office again, but I tuck the folder into my backpack and stand. "Let's go."

We put up our hoods, carefully pull the tape off the security camera, and enter the nearest stairwell. As we walk up to the fifth floor, it occurs to me that this is probably the staircase Cíxǐ used to escape.

Rock pushes the door open, and we head for Ethan's office. Dread and Syl are already there. As far as we can tell, whoever was here earlier has left.

"Someone should be the lookout." Rock's gaze travels down the corridor to where the body is. It's too dark to see, but I can picture Ethan lying there, perfectly still.

"I'll stand watch," Syl says. "Rock and Dread, the two of you are our best bet for getting into Ethan's computer."

"I'll join you," I tell Syl. "No one stays alone, right?"

She smiles. "Yeah. We'll text if we see anything. Don't take too long, y'all." Then she closes the door to the office, and we're alone in the unlit hallway. Syl leans close to whisper. "Let's find a good spot." She starts walking, and I reach up to touch the place where her breath warmed my ear.

I walk as close to her as I dare, wondering what she would do if I reached out and took her hand. Wondering if she feels what I feel. She's mentioned an ex-girlfriend, so I know she's open to dating girls, but I have no idea if that could ever include me.

We stop at a spot with a good vantage point of the paths leading to Ethan's office. "Should we stand across the aisle from each other or something?" I ask.

"Nah. Maybe we stay below desk level, so our silhouettes aren't obvious, and each keep an eye on one of the stairwells."

Happiness flutters through me as I set my backpack down, and we sit back-to-back beneath a desk. I try to focus on being a good lookout, but the feel of her back against mine makes it hard to think about anything else. If I lean closer, will she *know*? If I lean away, will she think I'm avoiding her? I try not to move at all.

The scent of her perfume drifts toward my nose. I breathe in deep, and I have a sudden urge to turn around. To see if she'd turn too. To lean in and kiss her and see if she'd kiss me back.

At the thought of her lips pressed against mine, a little gasp escapes me.

I'm suddenly on alert. Why did I do that? God, I hope she didn't notice. I pinch my leg hard and remind myself that we're here on a mission.

Syl shifts slightly, leaning back against me just a little more than before.

Countless times, I've dreamed of meeting her in person, and wondered if I'd realize we weren't compatible at all. But having her here next to me, I like her even more than I did before. She's beautiful and put together in a way I'll never be. She's smart and resourceful and kind. She's open and honest and she has a bright future ahead of her. All I have is a lot of secrets and a dark past I've left behind.

And that, right there, is why I can't let us get too close.

Even if she miraculously likes me back, I can't date someone who doesn't even know my real name.

With a monumental effort, I force myself to scoot forward a fraction, putting distance between us. I hear her swallow, but she doesn't move closer or say anything.

We sit that way for what feels like forever; I barely dare to breathe. Then there's a sound, and I jump, but it's only Ethan's office door creaking open. Syl and I stand up as Rock and Dread walk out, closing the door behind them.

Syl waves, and they join us. "Got everything?"

"Yes," Rock says. "We'll share the details later. Let's leave."

Dread's already walking toward the stairwell.

"Wait, cuz," Syl says.

"What?"

"I was thinking . . . maybe we should go that way." Syl nods toward the main staircase. "By Ethan's body."

"Why?" Rock sounds unhappy.

"Because Night said Ethan left after he heard his watch beep," Syl says. "Maybe we can find his watch or phone or something and figure out something about Cixi."

It's too dark here to see Rock's expression clearly, but I'm starting to learn his mannerisms; to match them up with the guy coordinating our game missions through my headset. I imagine Rock frowning and chewing his bottom lip, mind warring between Syl's smart suggestions and his desire to leave Ethan's body alone.

"It's a good idea." I hope my words help make up for earlier, when I moved away from Syl.

"Rock and I can meet you two downstairs," Dread says. "We have to stop by HR to grab a file anyway. I'll explain later."

"No." Rock's decisive team leader voice returns. "Syl's right. We should all go check."

"We'll make it quick," Syl says.

As we walk down the dark corridor, a shiver runs through me. Yet another path the killer took after shooting Ethan. I wonder if they're watching us right now.

"Did we go the wrong way?" Syl sounds puzzled.

"No, it was definitely this way." Then my eyes adjust enough to see what she's talking about.

"What the hell?" Rock says as we all stare down.

At the empty, bloodless spot where Ethan's dead body used to be.

CHAPTER 14

Six Years Earlier

I ran through the house, opening doors and cabinets and kitchen drawers. I couldn't believe how much space we had. Mama and I had gone from sharing a one-bedroom apartment to having a whole two-story house to ourselves. All because of Mama's new job.

I opened the door to Mama's office and ran inside. She had a fancy desk and chair I'd never seen before, and a stack of boxes sat in one corner of the room. I opened the desk drawer.

"Lia." Mama's voice was sharp. "What are you doing?"

I whirled around. "I wanted to see your new office!"

"This room is off-limits."

"Why?"

"It's for my work." Mama gently steered me out of the room and closed the door behind her. She took out her keys and locked the room.

"Your work?" I hoped Mama would tell me something about what she did. She never liked to talk about it.

"Yes. Now promise me you will never, ever go in there again." She gave me a serious look. I swallowed nervously.

"I promise."

CHAPTER 15

After finding Ethan's body missing, none of us wants to stay long. We stop by HR on the first floor, and Syl picks the lock with her paper clip. Dread grabs a file, promising to explain later.

We walk down the dark, empty street toward Dread's car. Inside, Dread downs a Frappuccino he swiped from the snack room so he can stay alert enough to drive us all home. I look outside, distracting myself by studying the lines of each vehicle, drawing them in my mind. The curve of a tire; the narrow, angry eyes of the headlights. The person sitting at the wheel, hidden in shadows.

I jump.

"What is it?" Syl's on alert.

I look again, but this time, I don't see anyone. I rub my eyes. So much has happened in the past few hours; it's no wonder I'm seeing things. "Nothing."

Dread drops me off first. I direct him to an apartment complex near the restaurant, where I act like I'm walking toward one of the tucked-away back units. After he drives away, I wait a few minutes, then walk back to Bette's Battles and Bao.

It's been nearly eight months since I've spent a night without Slate. Before I got him, I used to lie awake for hours each night while the world around me went still and dark, too scared someone would find me to close my eyes. After adopting Slate, I started curling up in my sleeping bag and going right to sleep, the air full of light snoring and contented snorts from my furry best friend.

I want so badly to walk to Bette and Jimmy's apartment, tell them I left Syl's place early, and pick up Slate.

But I don't. It's the middle of the night, and Bette and Jimmy deserve their rest. Besides, it would raise too many suspicions. I need to be strong.

I whisper good night to Slate as if he were here, wishing he could hear me somehow. Guilt curdles in my stomach as I imagine him awake and confused, wondering where I am. I wish I could reassure him that we'll be reunited in the morning. That I intend to keep the promise I made when we first met—that I will never, ever abandon him.

I get ready for bed in the employee bathroom before locking myself in the back office. Then I remove my shoes and pull my sleeping bag and pillow from the closet. As I set up my makeshift bed the way I do every night, my mind wanders through everything that's happened today. It feels like a week has gone by in the past seven hours. I wiggle into my sleeping bag and close my eyes.

Ethan's lifeless eyes stare back at me.

I scream and sit up. Breathing hard, I pull out my laptop and scramble into my desk chair. The glow of the screen is both reassuring and eerie. Once the desktop populates, I open *Darkitect*.

When my game finally loads, an in-game message pops up.

Syldara: what took u so long???

Knowing Syl was at her computer waiting for me to sign on helps soothe my panic. Syl and I are both chronic night owls; we often talk and hang out online late into the night. Compared to us,

Rock and Dread are total morning people and we'll never, ever understand them.

NightMar3: got hungry. had a snack.

Syldara: omg u hang out with dread for ONE EVE and this happens

NightMar3: yeah, those funions were just too irresistible

Syldara: speaking of, he's passed out on my couch lmao, he was too sleepy to drive home & my parents made him stay

Syldara: I think they're bored of me and want to replace me with my white ass cousin

NightMar3: as if anyone could ever be bored of you.

Syldara: :)

Syl and I sign onto voice chat. We don't worry about Cíxi's level since we can't complete it without the whole team. Tonight is just for us.

When we're not running team missions, Syl is usually out farming mobs—killing a certain kind of creature repeatedly hoping they'll drop specific loot—in an attempt to collect a rare pet. Right now, she's looking for a golden dragonfly, so I head out to the Sorrowful Swamp to help her kill giant bugs. I pull on my headset and adjust my microphone.

Syl's honey-sweet drawl pours into my ears. "Do you ever think about how unspeakably cruel our game characters are? Killing hundreds of creatures hoping to steal a baby from one of them so we can raise it as a pet?"

I laugh. "It is pretty rude."

"They'll call this the Great Dragonfly Massacre and vow vengeance upon us."

"We'll never be safe as long as the dragonflies remember," I agree.

"So, we'll need to watch our backs for at least five minutes," she says, and I laugh, wondering how long dragonflies' memories are. If they have memories at all. If they're haunted by them.

I sigh. "I should probably be reading through this hefty legal file."

"Probably. But we've had the world's longest day. We can all figure it out together when we meet up tomorrow."

"Yeah." I'm relieved. Today's events have been exhausting, and I don't really feel like reading legal documents.

"I figured out what Rock and Dread found in Ethan's office, though. You know how Rock said people were the least secure part of any security system?"

"Yeah?"

"They found a written sheet of passwords in Ethan's messenger bag."

"For real?"

"Yeah. Old people are ridiculous. They were able to get into his computer and scan some recent emails, which was enlightening. First, he's been talking with HR about his assistant, Nina Cohen. They were figuring out the best way to fire her."

I perk up. "So that's the file they took. Did the emails say what she did?" On my screen, NightMar3 fends off a swarm of angry insects.

"Nope, but we're hoping her personnel file holds some clues."

"Has anyone read it yet?"

"Nah. Figured we'll look together tomorrow."

Together. The word rolls so beautifully off her tongue. She means the four of us. For a moment, I wish it was just the two of us meeting. And that our meeting involved waffles and chatting, not court papers and stolen personnel files.

"Definitely," I say. "What was the second thing?"

"Apparently, Ethan hired a private investigator."

"What! To investigate who?"

Syl sighs. "No idea. It was just some cryptic email about calling Ethan with important news. But the guys wrote down the name and agency, so we can look 'em up tomorrow."

"Damn. Maybe Ethan *was* into something shady."

"Maybe."

I'm beheading a giant, angry dragonfly when my screen suddenly goes black. I groan. This laptop is old, but I need it to last at least another year or two. I don't have the money to replace it. Besides, we have game levels to beat.

I'm about to restart the computer when something flickers on the screen. Green words appear in an old-school font.

It's the same message repeated over and over, scrolling down my screen.

I can feel the color drain from my face as I stare at the words.

Hold your secrets tight, Lia.

CHAPTER 16

Three Years Earlier

I was in the lesson room drawing a comic of my favorite original character, Marina Chan. I'd started drawing her when Mom took me out of school two years ago. Marina got to go on all the adventures I didn't.

Our house was nice, but sometimes I missed our lives from before we moved. Whenever I brought it up, Mom would say we had plenty of space and everything we ever needed at home. Why leave? But I missed having friends, having classmates. I missed going to school. I missed going anywhere.

I pushed those thoughts away—they felt like a betrayal of Mom—and whispered the phrase to myself. *Xiāng yī wéi mìng.* Mom was only doing what she had to do to keep us safe.

The door opened. I looked up to see Mom with a bare-faced woman in pinstripe slacks and a green blouse. When our eyes met, she smiled. "Hello, Lia. I'm Helen Huang, your new teacher. You may call me Huang Lǎoshī."

"Hi, Huang Lǎoshī."

"In the future, some of our lessons will be conducted in Mandarin since conversing regularly is the only way to maintain fluency. For today, however, we will speak English. Getting used to a new tutor takes extra mental effort, and I'd rather you were less distracted so we can focus on the subject at hand. Any questions?"

"No, Huang Lǎoshī." I was surprised she'd explained her reasoning to me; none of the other tutors had. I liked this woman immediately. Maybe we could even be friends.

"Then let's begin."

CHAPTER 17

Hold your secrets tight, Lia.

Every time I closed my eyes, the words appeared, printing themselves over and over on the back of my eyelids. I thought I'd never fall asleep. Eventually, exhaustion from the day's events pushed me into a restless slumber.

Rock is wrong. Cíxǐ isn't targeting him or Dread.

She's after me.

No one from my new life knows my real name. For the past year, I've never spoken it aloud or written it down. I've barely allowed myself to think it, lest I slip.

But somehow, Cíxǐ knows. I rub sleep from my eyes, hopping off the bus and heading out to meet Dread and Syl. Everyone's houses have been vetoed as a meeting spot. They're all too worried their parents will overhear something they shouldn't. And Rock missed curfew last night, so his parents grounded him.

We decided to meet here instead. I round a corner and the central branch of the Seattle Public Library comes into view. It's a sight to behold, all weird angles like someone took a strange origami invention and turned it into a giant building made entirely of glass.

Syl and Dread are waiting for me.

"You're on time!" I say.

Dread rolls his eyes. "A certain annoying cousin of mine decided to be a human snooze alarm, bothering me every eight minutes until we left the house."

"You're welcome," Syl says.

We walk in as the library's opening for the day. Morning light shines through the diamond-shaped windows, illuminating the atrium as Dread, Syl, and I walk toward the neon chartreuse escalator.

The third floor is full of tables, chairs, and reading nooks. We pass a shop and a café, then walk through a big open area with an indoor garden, heading for the teen center. There are eleven floors at this branch of the library. I try to imagine how many books are housed here, and my head spins.

Since the library just opened, we manage to snag a table. Syl yawns as she sets down her backpack. She pulls out her laptop and a notebook covered in stickers—a rainbow flag, the *Darkitect* symbol, *Black Panther* fan art, and . . . another piece I recognize instantly.

I gasp. It's the birthday present I gave her last month. I told her I'd draw her anything she wanted, so she chose Zotia and Gaellina, who happen to be my *Darkitect* OTP. I sent her the file and told her she could use it however she pleased, and . . .

"You got it printed!" I tap the sticker to indicate which piece I mean.

Syl looks suddenly shy. "It's really pretty."

Despite everything, I find myself smiling.

"Stop flirting and focus," Dread says cheerfully, and Syl kicks him under the table. Dread checks his phone. "Rock says he's waiting for his parents to leave so he can sign on."

"We can look for the settlement amount while we wait," Syl says. "Got the file?"

"Right here." As I hand Syl the folder, our fingertips touch, lingering just long enough that I wonder if she's noticed. She opens the file and starts rummaging through papers.

"Do you think Cíxǐ wants us to look into this because she thinks the case was settled unfairly?" I ask. "She implied Ethan might be shady in some way."

"Yeah, but Cixi was on site when she . . ." Dread looks around. There's no one near us, but he lowers his voice anyway. "You know. Yesterday." *When she shot Ethan.* "Couldn't Cixi have grabbed the file herself?"

"Maybe she didn't have time." Syl's only half paying attention, busy skimming the file. She hands me and Dread pieces of paper. "Read these and see if there's anything interesting in them."

It's too early to be reading legal contracts. Though to be fair, there's never a good time for it. I rub the sleep from my eyes and give it my best shot.

"Even so, if she's had months to set this all up, there has to be an easier way to get this information," Dread says. "And the part I still don't understand is *why us?* By having us get the information for her, she's bringing our whole team into whatever she's planning. That can't be coincidence. I mean, I work at Apocalypta. I might be the reason Cixi decided to target our group."

Or it might be me.

I consider telling them about the creepy messages from last night, but that would invite questions about my past. Questions I can't afford to answer.

Maybe I should just run away. Ghost all of them. They might be safer without me around.

But there's no guarantee she'd leave them alone. We're in too deep now to do anything but follow her rules.

"Last night, Rock said something similar," I say. "He thought he might be at fault somehow."

Syl cuts in. "What if it isn't about any of us, exactly? What if we're just convenient for her plan? Look at the positions we're in. Rock's parents are besties with Ethan. Dread works at the company and could claim some insider knowledge of Ethan's dealings. Night and I . . . well, maybe we just came with the package. What if all of this is about defaming Ethan, and the four of us are just her messengers?"

"You mean like . . . Cixi is trying to convince us Ethan is evil or something?" Dread says. "Or she wants us to find her proof of something she thinks he's done? And then maybe she'll use us or our parents to tell the world what we've found?"

"Yeah, something to that effect." Syl considers. "It would be the ultimate destruction. Destroy him in body, and his legacy lives on. But destroy his legacy . . ."

"And you ruin everything he's built," Dread says.

"That's hardcore," I say. "But this will all be over by Tuesday night. That's a pretty short time frame."

"What if the levels escalate?" Syl says. "Like, what if for now she's showing us things she already knows the answers to, but for the next level, we have to get private info from Rock's parents' company or Dread has to steal something from Apocalypta?"

I look at the open file folder, thinking about how easily I slipped it into my backpack yesterday.

"Or what if Cíxǐ *doesn't* know the answer?" I ask. "What if the text box answers in the game aren't built in? What if she's on the other side of the levels, manually approving when we're allowed through?"

"How would she know if we found the right answer versus just typing in a guess?" Dread asks.

"Maybe she's watching us. Or maybe she's going to take the info from us somehow. After we've done the dirty work for her." I glance around. I don't see anyone watching our table, but we are in a public space. There was that person looking down at us last night, at Apocalypta. And the person I thought was watching when we got into Dread's car. What if they were the same person? I shiver, despite the sunshine filtering in through the library's massive windows.

"Doesn't really change anything," Dread says.

He has a point. We're not doing this because it's right. We're doing this because we all have something to lose.

"We could test the theory," Syl says. "I don't see how the settlement amount would hurt anyone. But we can play the level through to that point and put in an incorrect amount that's close to the real amount. See if it gets accepted."

Dread shakes his head. "We might not have time to play it through twice before Rock has to sign off."

"Yeah." Syl sighs, flipping through more pages. "Found it!" She holds up a wire transfer from Apocalypta Games to James Steinberg.

"The number we need?" Dread asks.

"Yep, and this." Syl hands him a sheet from the middle of the contract. "It states that the agreed-upon amount for the settlement will be wired to the claimant in one lump sum on this date. That proves the wired amount is the whole thing, not just an installment."

"How do you *know* all of this?" I ask.

"I interned at a law firm last summer," Syl says.

"They hire high school–age interns?"

"They do if they're a local human rights law firm and you go every day *begging* them to take you on as a volunteer until they give in." Dread laughs, and Syl swats at him.

"That's called creating your own opportunities," she says, chin up.

I look at the two of them, feeling oddly jealous. Syl already knows she wants to go into law. And, in a few weeks, Dread will be starting freshman year at DigiPen, a local video game–focused tech university.

I'm not sure what I want to do. It doesn't really matter anyway. I love drawing, but it's not like I have the equipment, software, or expertise to properly digitize it, which is what most art careers require these days. Besides, I don't have an ID. Without any way to get a school degree, my options are really limited. I won't even have a high school diploma.

Dread looks up from his phone. "Rock says he'll be on in twenty, so I'm gonna grab a pastry from Ivy's Bakery. Either of you want anything?"

"Ooh, that's the place with the brioche buns, right?" Syl asks.

"Yep."

"I'll take one of those. Savory if they have it. Sweet is fine if not."

"And you?" Dread asks me.

"I'm good." A pastry sounds amazing, but I'm saving up for a better headset.

"See ya." Dread leaves his backpack and heads out, a light skip to his step.

"Morning people." I roll my eyes, and Syl laughs. I turn my chair to face her now that it's just the two of us. "What's the notebook for?"

"I thought we could start a list of suspects." She flips to a blank page and begins writing slowly in a beautiful, bold font. Her penmanship is pristine. For a few seconds, I stop to watch as she writes out each precise letter. *POSSIBLE SUSPECTS.* She's shaded in the first three letters when she looks up.

"What?" she asks.

"I . . . um . . . you have beautiful handwriting." *And beautiful hands.*

"I'd love to learn calligraphy someday, but for now I just practice pretty fonts." She sounds shy, but proud too.

"Will you teach me sometime?" I blurt out.

Syl's face crinkles into a smile. "Yeah, I'd love to! You know . . . when we don't have a killer on our trail." The joke sours a bit as the reality of our situation hits again. She looks back at the page and continues filling in letters.

"I guess our first suspect is Steinberg, or someone affected by his court case."

Syl nods. In a neat scrawl below the heading, she writes *James Steinberg? Or someone related.* She leaves a few lines blank, then writes *Nina Cohen.*

"You said Nina is Ethan's assistant, right? He was trying to get her fired?"

"Apparently." Syl reaches into Dread's backpack and pulls a file folder out, handing it to me before going back to writing in her notebook.

I open Nina Cohen's personnel file. The first page has a photo of a woman with stringy red hair, round cheeks, and a sharp nose.

I can't help thinking she looks tired. I spread out the papers on the table. "Looks like she's twenty-eight and lives in Seattle."

"Let me see." Syl looks up the address, and her eyes widen. "That's in Ballard!"

A year into living in Seattle, I'm still not familiar with all the different neighborhoods. But even I know Ballard is expensive.

Syl finds the most recent house listing on Redfin. "That's a high price tag for someone living on admin wages. Even if she's renting, the cost would be ridiculously high. Though she could have family money, or maybe she's living with someone who makes a ton."

"Maybe we can find out." I dig through the file more. "Nothing came up in her background check. She's been working for Apocalypta Games since it was founded, so she's been there six years. Oh, and she changed her name last year, from Nina Kerry to Nina Cohen."

"She got married?"

"She has a five-year-old with the last name Kerry, and she sent in a request to remove someone named Zach Kerry from her insurance policy around the same time, so I'm guessing divorce."

Syl looks over my shoulder again. Her breath stirs my hair, making my cheek tingle. She points to something, and I notice that her gold nail polish from yesterday now has a chip in it.

"There. She requested a change in marital status in her W-4 filing. Married to single."

"Okay, so she's a single mom."

Syl writes this all down. Then she looks at the house listing again. "Wait, this house was built last year! If she got divorced, makes sense that she moved around then. Is her old address in the file?"

I dig through more papers until I find an address change request. "Right here."

Syl frowns. "She and her kid moved from Renton to Ballard after she got divorced? That seems unlikely."

She looks up the address to confirm, and sure enough, the Renton house costs half as much as the Ballard house.

We look at each other.

"Something isn't right," Syl says.

"Did you end up finding anything out about the private investigator?" I ask.

"Yeah, I looked them up on my phone on the way over. Their name is Sloan Kim, and there's virtually no useful information about them. We could try making an appointment, but I'm pretty sure they won't tell us anything."

"Plus, they might try to contact Ethan if they found out we're digging around for information on him."

"Good point."

Dread returns, holding a white paper bag. He opens it, and the scent of spiced apples and sugar wafts out. I almost regret not asking for a pastry. Instead, I try to visualize the shiny new headset I'm saving up for.

Dread pulls three napkins out and sets them down in front of us. He places a giant scone in front of me.

"I, um . . . didn't order anything."

Dread rolls his eyes. "Yeah, yeah. But you can't be the only one not eating." He lowers his voice. "We're not in a meeting room or special event space and this isn't one of the designated areas, so technically, eating here is forbidden. You're not getting away with being the only one following the rules."

"Your bag crinkling isn't exactly keeping it subtle." Syl reaches across the table to slide her fingers into the bag and somehow pulls out her pastry without making a sound. "But you get ten cousin points for getting me a brioche bun. You've *almost* canceled out the time I lent you my favorite book and you dropped it in a pond."

"That was an accident! And I bought you a new copy!"

"It had *sentimental value.*"

"Uh-huh."

"Thanks, Dread," I say. "How much was the scone?"

Dread waves me off. "Don't worry about it. Just hurry and eat it before a librarian notices."

Even though he's being nice, I feel weird, like maybe I owe him now. I should be grateful, but a part of me wonders if he got me a scone because he noticed my shabby computer and thrift store clothes. Then I take a bite of warm cinnamon apple goodness and all thoughts leave my head. "Wow!"

Syl turns to me. "Have you never had anything from Ivy's before?"

I shake my head. Dread and Syl gasp.

"You have to try a bite of mine." Syl hands me her brioche bun.

I accept it and pass her my scone to try. She and I take a bite of each other's pastries at the same time. It feels strangely intimate. Then we pass them back and I devour the rest of my scone, trying not to think too much about how my lips touched the pastry after hers did.

Dread's done with his croissant first. He wipes his hands carefully on his napkin, then glances at his phone. "Rock's online!" He starts setting up his computer.

I should pull out my laptop too.

My skin crawls, thinking again of last night's message repeating itself until I finally pulled the plug. I was too scared to turn the computer back on. Instead, after recovering from the shock, I texted Syl that my internet stopped working.

What if the message is still there when I boot up?

I have no choice but to set up anyway. Thankfully, when I turn on my laptop, the weird message is gone. Breathing easier now, I sign onto *Darkitect*. It takes us about half an hour to get through the level and back to the point where we failed last time.

"He kept me quiet." James Steinberg grins his creepy, wide grin. "Do you know how much it cost him?"

Syl has the paper in front of her. Carefully, she types the exact amount into the text box, checking three times before hitting enter. Her character shouts through the megaphone.

I hold my breath, hoping we have the right answer. If it isn't, I don't know where we'll search next.

James Steinberg starts cackling. The low, unsettling sound pours from my headset, and I'm tempted to pull it off my head. This doesn't feel like a typical game sound. It feels like there's a ring of truth to it, like someone recorded it and uploaded the sound file to *Darkitect*.

"He's vulnerable again!" Dread says, and we start attacking. He was down to 25 percent before Syl typed in the settlement amount. Based on the trajectory of the level, this should be the last phase before we defeat him and find out exactly how beating the level will "prevent a misfortune."

Mini Death Cry skeletons pop out of the ground and begin attacking us. As with the other adds, I pick them off with my bow while Syl and Dread continue dealing damage to the big boss.

When James Steinberg is down to 2 percent health, Rock calls out. "Night, ignore adds. Focus DPS!" I switch back to targeting

James Steinberg, letting the Death Cry skeletons spawn and roam free. I hit every cooldown I have, and my teammates do the same.

Steinberg lets out a long, keening cry and keels over dead. His giant body crashes to the ground, shaking the structure. The Death Cry skeletons collapse into piles of dust. I wait for his body to glow so we can loot him, but nothing happens.

"Weird, thought he'd drop something," Dread says. It all seems anticlimactic for the end of a boss fight.

"Something's wrong," Rock says. "We don't have the quest item."

"Maybe there are more mobs?" Syl says.

"Or another boss," I say.

Dread and Syl grimace. We assumed defeating him was the entire level. What if there's more to it?

Something rises from James Steinberg's dead body. It looks like a translucent, slightly bluish version of him.

"Think you can kill me so easily?" Ghost James's red eyes flash. "He tried and failed." He sneers, practically growling with anger. "But I paid the price anyway!" He presses a button and the trapdoors on every floor open. Then he sweeps us into the hole. We fall, whooshing past each story and through one extra trapdoor.

We're beneath the first stage. Above, the trapdoor clangs shut, leaving us in darkness.

A second later, there's a low hum as a blue glow interrupts the darkness. I roll my eyes. Dread loves any excuse to equip his lightsaber, a prize he won in a May the Fourth *Darkitect* event. It's not a great weapon—or a particularly good lighting device—but it does give us a peek, however fuzzy, of our surroundings. We appear to be in a storage area piled high with props.

Dread runs around with the lightsaber, checking out the room.

"No doors or windows. But there's a lantern and matches in this corner."

I shiver, thinking about the "misfortune" in my envelope, though Cíxǐ probably wouldn't use a box of matches to set Bette's Battles and Bao on fire. She's more likely to start an electrical fire.

We use the match to light all the lanterns and look around. We're surrounded by piles of junk.

"What is all this crap?" I ask. "Another puzzle?"

As if in response, Ghost James's raspy voice fills the room. I look up to see a blur of wispy blue through the trapdoor. "He took what was mine and paid for his betrayal. We were square. But that wasn't good enough for him, was it? People like him always need the last word. He had to have his revenge."

He draws out *revenge*, sending a chill through me.

"I can't rest until someone knows. Learn what he did to me. Find his weapon of choice!" The trapdoor swings open and something falls through the hole before it slams shut.

Syl picks up the object. "It's a ribbon with a tag attached. The only thing I can do with it is tie it to an object. Any guesses what the tag says?"

"Weapon of choice," Rock and I both answer.

"Got it in one."

We start looking around the room.

"There's so much random junk here," Dread says. "I guess we're looking for something that could be a weapon?"

"Yeah, but almost anything could be a weapon." I inspect the objects near me. "Like these. The butcher's knife is the obvious choice, but you could brain someone with the toaster."

"Ethan wouldn't do that," Rock says. Before we can respond, he adds, "I know, I know. We just need to figure out what James

Steinberg would consider an attack. Or what Cixi thinks he would, anyway. Is Syl still connected?"

I look over at Syl. She's tabbed out of the game and opened a browser window. Even with yesterday's mission, it's still strange sitting next to her in real life, playing *Darkitect*.

"I'm here. Just seeing if I can find anything out."

"I'll do the same," I say. "Keep us safe."

"We will," Rock says.

Syl and I start looking up James Steinberg, James and Ethan, James and Apocalypta, and any other combination that might lead to a result. Through my headset, I hear Dread and Rock talk about how various items in the junk pile could be used as a weapon.

"Anything?" Rock asks after twenty minutes.

I let out a frustrated sigh. "Nothing. Looks like Steinberg's gone radio silent since the case settled." I turn to Syl, who looks pensive. I follow her gaze to a Facebook post.

Officially closed today on our dream home! #blessed #steinbergsbuyahome :)

A couple wearing identical wide grins pose near a "SOLD!" sign in front of a gorgeous home with a perfectly landscaped yard. There's a smiling kid on James's shoulders. This version of Steinberg looks happier and much less terrifying than the one we've been fighting in *Darkitect*.

"What are you looking at?" I ask.

"Hm . . ." Syl's only half listening. Suddenly, her face lights up with recognition. "I knew it! I've seen that house!"

"You have?"

"Yeah! I thought the neighborhood looked familiar from some of the other photos. My cousin is a Cub Scout and was assigned a few neighborhoods to go door-to-door asking for food drive donations. I went with him!"

"You said you wouldn't tell anyone!" Dread says.

Syl gives him a *look* before turning back toward me. "Our seven-year-old cousin, *Chris*. We have, like, forty first cousins, and somehow, I get stuck hanging out with the most annoying one."

"He's useful, though. He has a car," I say, and then immediately wonder if my quip went too far. What if Dread thinks I'm just friends with him because of his car?

To my relief, Syl busts out laughing, and this time, Dread's the one who gives me a *look*. It's a mix between exasperation and playful annoyance. I've never had anyone to joke around with in person this way, and it makes me unreasonably happy.

"Brutal, Night," Syl says, "but also true."

Dread rolls his eyes.

"Do any of you realize how obnoxious it is having all of you in the same room without me?" Rock asks through our headsets. "I have no idea what's happening! Did you find something, Syl?"

"Yeah! James Steinberg's Facebook is private, but his wife's isn't. I looked through and found a post from last fall. I recognize the house from last month, when I helped a cousin of mine who *isn't* Dread. I don't remember exactly which neighborhood it was, but I have the route we took saved somewhere in my email."

"And this helps us how, exactly?" Dread asks.

"None of us have found anything on the Steinbergs that'll help us answer the question in-game," she says. "Diana shared a vague-post in June mentioning a recent struggle and asking her friends to keep her family in their prayers, but nothing conclusive. I don't think we'll be able to get the answer we need to complete the level online."

"Syl, are you suggesting what I think you're suggesting?" Rock sounds alarmed.

"Probably. Dread, do you have any plans for this afternoon?"

Dread shakes his head.

"Good. Because we need you to drive us around some swanky neighborhoods. We're going to talk to the Steinbergs."

CHAPTER 18

One Year Earlier

Someone was watching the house.

I was drawing Marina Chan comics in the backyard when I noticed a stranger in a long, beige trench coat holding up a phone like they were taking a photo.

My heart pounded. Mom was away on a business trip; I was alone. What if this was one of the people she always said were looking for us? What should I do?

Marina would be brave.

I approached the person. "What are you doing?"

They turned to face me, and I memorized their details. They had a short pixie cut, a narrow build, and sharp features, and if I were to guess, they were probably East Asian. "Hello! I'm Morgan, a reporter for the *Chronicle*. We're doing a series on San Francisco's historic neighborhoods."

"So, you have permission to be here?"

"We haven't contacted any of the homeowners yet. We're currently determining which homes would best visually represent the neighborhood."

I couldn't tell if Morgan was lying.

"Hey, while I have you here, would you be open to a brief interview? It would help to get some background information."

"Um . . . I'm busy right now."

I still wasn't sure what to think. But if Morgan *was* a reporter, Mom wouldn't want me to say anything.

Morgan shrugged. "All right. Maybe I'll see you around, then. If we pick your neighborhood."

"Yeah. Maybe." I went back inside and waited for a minute, then peered through the blinds. Morgan was still there, taking pictures. Their story made sense, but I couldn't shake the feeling that they were lying about something.

CHAPTER 19

Saturday, 12:15 p.m.

Syl's knock is steady and self-assured. I stand straighter, nervous we're about to get the door to this mansion slammed in our faces. Now that we've seen this enormous house and the settlement amount, all of us are even more befuddled. It doesn't seem like Steinberg got screwed over by the settlement.

Dread shifts from foot to foot. "What if they're not home?"

"We could ask the neighbors what he's like?" Syl rings the doorbell again. This time, to our relief, we hear the shuffling of footsteps. The door opens, and the kid from Diana Steinberg's Facebook photo stares up at us.

"We don't know you," he says.

"Hi!" Syl kneels down to the kid's eye level. "I'm Chloe." She sticks out her hand. We're using fake names, just in case.

"I'm not supposed to let strangers touch me." The kid doesn't budge. "And you talk weird."

"That's 'cause I'm from another part of the country." Syl pulls her hand back. "You're a smart kid. And you're right—you shouldn't let strangers touch you. That was a test to see if you're as smart as you look. You passed!"

"Oh. I'm the second-smartest kid in my grade." He points at me and Dread. "Who are they?"

"They're my friends. The three of us are on a mission."

"Like . . . spies?"

"No, we aren't here to spy. We're here to talk to your dad!"

"Is your dad James Steinberg?" Dread asks.

The kid nods. "Daddy's napping. And he doesn't like visitors."

"Do you mind getting him for us anyway?" Dread asks, and Syl elbows him.

"Wait," she says. "Maybe if you answer some questions for us, we won't have to bug your dad."

"I don't know how I can help. I'm only six."

"I have a six-year-old nephew and he's one of the most helpful people I know," Syl says, and the kid nods solemnly, like that makes perfect sense. "Do you know if your daddy ever talked to someone named Ethan Wainwright?"

From the look on his face, it's obvious he recognizes the name. "That's the bad man that stole Daddy's game!" He furrows his brows. "But then he paid lots of money for it later, so Daddy's not mad at him anymore. He says it's okay because we have a nice house now and I get to go to a nice school. That was before—" The kid claps his hand over his mouth and whispers, "I'm not supposed to tell anyone." He's on the verge of tears.

"It's okay," Syl says. "We already knew all of that, so you didn't tell us anything you weren't supposed to."

"Oh." He looks disappointed.

"You're really helpful, though. And that's really cool your dad invented a game! He must be smart, just like you."

The kid is positively beaming now. "He is! He—"

From somewhere inside the house, a door opens. Someone shouts, "Sawyer?"

"Daddy?" Sawyer runs off.

Dread, Syl, and I exchange looks.

James Steinberg shows up in the doorway. Like Puppet James in *Darkitect*, he's a thin, balding man with stern eyebrows. Unlike the game, Real Life James is in a motorized wheelchair. He glowers at us, expression resembling the boss version of him from *Darkitect*. "Who are you kids and why are you harassing my son?"

Dread chimes in with the cover story we invented on the drive over. "We're UW students doing a research project on Apocalypta Games's history of litigation. It's for law class."

"We actually came to speak with you," Syl adds. "Your son answered the door."

James crosses his arms. "You look too young to be law students."

"We're doing a group project for Management 200, an undergraduate course covering the basics of business law," Syl says. "We read about your settlement with Apocalypta and have a few questions."

"I have nothing to say about that company. And you're crossing a boundary. Next time, use email instead of showing up at someone's house." He wheels backward and then reaches for the door.

"Wait!" I say. "We're really sorry we came here without checking first. But we were too scared to use phone or email to contact you."

James frowns, but at least he's listening.

I hurry to continue. "Like Chloe said, we are UW students. We're not business students, though, we're computer science majors. We've been working on software together. But weird things have been happening lately. One of our flash drives went missing and we think we're being followed and . . ." I look around furtively. "This is going to sound unbelievable. But . . . we think someone high up at Apocalypta might be behind this. They have a mentorship program, and each project is assigned a mentor. Ours was from Apocalypta. All of the weird stuff started happening after that."

James is clenching his jaw tight, hands balled up in fists. He opens his mouth as if to respond, then presses his lips tight.

"We're really scared," Syl adds softly, and Dread nods. He's tapping his foot, which makes him look nervous—probably because of my freshly concocted lie. Ironically, it has the effect of making my words seem more plausible.

"Please," I say.

James sighs deeply, closing his eyes for a moment. Finally, he nods, seeming to decide something. "I can't legally discuss the details of the settlement." He worries his lip. "All I'll say is—while I'm still pissed I had to sue in the first place, I was happy enough with how the case turned out. But . . ." He looks up at each of us pointedly, expression serious. "It was too good to be true. You need to take care of yourselves. I don't know what this project means to you, but if you can, let it go. Some battles aren't worth fighting."

"You mean we should just give up everything we worked so hard on? Why would we do that?" Syl asks indignantly. If I didn't know better, I'd think she really did have a project to protect.

"Because. There are things that matter more than credit or money. Like your lives."

———

"Hurry," Rock whispers through the speakerphone in Dread's car. "I'm not supposed to be using my phone while I'm grounded, so

I'm hiding in the bathroom. I only have ten minutes or so before they think I've died on the toilet or something and come check on me. I need an update!"

"We found out Syl's our best bet for luring a child if we ever need to kidnap one," Dread says.

"She can also believably impersonate someone applying to the UW business school," I add. I call it U-Dub, like the locals.

"Dude," Syl says, "I actually *talk* to kids. It's not hard! And my brother, Jamal, is a business student."

"Stop bickering and tell me what happened!" Rock says.

"All right," Dread says. "From what we can piece together, James Steinberg claimed he invented *Darkitect*. He got in a legal battle with Apocalypta over the company stealing his game. As if we'd do that."

"That would be a lot to pay for a settlement if the lawsuit had no merit." Syl frowns. "Though Apocalypta might have decided it would be cheaper to pay them off than continue a long, protracted battle. Or maybe Apocalypta wanted the Steinbergs to keep quiet about the details for some reason. Whatever happened, we don't really know who's right or wrong there, but the point is, Apocalypta paid up, and everyone seemed fine with it."

"That sounds surprisingly tame," Rock says. "I thought there would be more to it, what with the creepy level and everything."

"That's not all," Syl says.

"Ah."

"Last year, James Steinberg was hit by a car. Hit-and-run."

"Is he dead?" Rock sounds horrified.

"No, he's alive," Dread says. "But he was paralyzed from the waist down."

"They think Apocalypta was behind it," Syl adds.

"But if they thought so, why wouldn't the Steinbergs go after the company?" Rock sounds defensive. "With the settlement money, they could easily afford another lawsuit. They must not have proof."

"The details were vague," I say. "Mostly, they're convinced because it happened on the anniversary of the final settlement date, and because the car that hit James looks like Ethan's car."

"He wouldn't be sloppy enough to hit someone with his own car," Rock says. "And he wouldn't do that anyway."

"Well, James Steinberg is convinced," Dread says. "He warned us, saying Ethan's a vengeful man. He thinks Ethan acted like he was fine with the settlement at first, to clear suspicion. Then he bided his time."

"That's such a leap in logic!" Rock sounds exasperated. "Did he say anything else? If they're so sure, why didn't he go to the police?"

"Maybe he thought no one would believe him," Syl says. "Or that Ethan would come after him again if he spoke up."

"Anyway," I say, "James can't be the shooter."

"True," Syl says. "But his wife could've pulled the trigger while he did the computer work. From everything I've read, James and Ethan were best friends for decades, in large part due to a shared love of programming and gaming. He would have the expertise. And with his claims about inventing the game, designing messed-up *Darkitect* levels would fit well too."

"If the Steinbergs are Cixi, why would they want us to learn all of this?" Dread asks.

"Yeah, that part makes no sense," I agree.

"Mum found me. Gotta go." Rock hangs up.

Dread starts the car. We head back to the library, stopping for coffee on our way. After the three of us get set up, we wait for Rock. We need him online to finish up the level.

It's another half hour before he manages to sign on. "My mum only agreed to give me some game time after I promised I'd do yard work for a few hours this afternoon," he says. "Yard work!"

"Ew. Hopefully no giant spiders jump on you," Dread says.

"Don't even joke about that."

Dread smirks. "I need to leave soonish anyway. Gotta take my sister to her tennis match."

"We should be able to knock this out before then," Syl says.

Assuming there aren't any more hidden surprises left.

Since *Darkitect* doesn't allow players to save mid-instance, we start over again, going through all of James Steinberg's many faces. The level is a lot creepier now that we've seen him in real life. After fighting our way through the different stages, Ghost James tosses us down the trapdoor, screaming at us to find Ethan's weapon of choice.

"Clearly, there are no full-sized cars here," Rock says.

"We must be looking for something car related?" Syl suggests.

"Maybe a tire," I say. "Since he was run over."

"Or car keys," Dread says. "A license plate. Something more symbolic."

We start digging through all the props in the room. I toss aside a hunting knife, a scalpel, a barbell, and a length of rope before finding something that gives me pause. "Hey, there's a Matchbox car here."

Syl checks my screen. "Damn, I wish we knew his license plate, so we could be sure."

"Let me see," Rock says through my headset. My character

hands his character the car. "This is it. I don't know his license plate, but this is the kind of car he drives."

"Should we keep looking in case there's something that fits better, or just go with it?" Syl's understandably worried. If we're wrong, we don't have enough time to play the level through again before Dread has to leave.

"We should submit it," Rock says. "That way if there are any more nasty surprises, we'll have time left to handle them."

"Yeah, I need to leave soon anyway," Dread says. "My sister will *kill* me if we're late this time, and we might hit Saturday afternoon traffic."

"All right." Syl passes Rock the bow with the "weapon of choice" gift tag. He sticks it to the Matchbox car, and we hold our breath.

"What is this?" Ghost James opens the trapdoor and presses his face against it so one of his giant eyes is centered in the opening.

Syl shoots a spell at him, but he's still invulnerable.

Ghost James reaches down to pick up the car, holding it up to his eye.

Then he sets the car down and begins sobbing, his ghost form melting into the floor. As his giant tears begin to fill the chamber, the four of us swim to the top along with various flotsam from the room. He keeps crying and melting until all that's left is a puddle of ghost and us four, now out of the trapdoor and back on the first floor.

James Steinberg's ghost is gone, leaving behind just one item—a miniature puppet version of James.

I pick it up. It's marked as the quest item in the tooltip. "This is it!"

Rock sighs in relief. We've beaten the level.

I leave the stage, leaping down to the courtyard and back to where Cíxǐ sits on her throne, watching us. I hand her the puppet and watch her give me the same not-quite-smile as she did Thursday night. She lifts a hand to reveal the orb sitting in her palm. There's something written on it.

真相. Zhēnxiàng. Truth.

Cíxǐ presses the orb into one of the chains wrapped around Ethan's ghost. With a zap, the chain breaks, falling away from him. There are three chains left. One for each remaining level.

"You've done well," Cíxǐ says, and I want to slash the ugly, self-satisfied look off her face. But she's just pixels on a screen. We need to find out who the real Cíxǐ is. She hands me an envelope containing four invitations and a wooden box.

"Got the reward." Usually, we celebrate beating a level, but today all I feel is nervous relief. "Looks like invitations to the next level. A dinner party tonight at eight. There's also a box."

"What's inside?" Syl asks.

"Opening it now." I click on the box and suddenly my screen fills with static.

I panic, thinking what happened last night is about to happen again. Those words filling my screen. *Hold your secrets tight, Lia.*

"What just happened?" Rock sounds alarmed.

I look over and see that Syl's screen looks the same as mine. A video begins playing.

"This doesn't look like *Darkitect*. That's real," Syl says.

On-screen, a manila envelope sits on a shelf labeled "Outgoing Mail." The camera zooms in on the envelope's shipping label.

"Black Blade Electronics." Dread coats the name of the addressee.

Rock's intake of breath is so loud we can hear it through our headsets. "That's the mail room at my parents' company. My 'misfortune' envelope said Zenith Corp's financials would be sent to Black Blade, their biggest competitor. Zenith is my parents' client."

"So that envelope must contain Zenith's financial statements?" Syl asks.

"I guess so." Rock sounds panicked. "But it's still in the mail room. I figured Cixi's threat was leaking the statements via email or something. There's an actual physical object? Does this mean we're supposed to go get it before it's sent out?"

There's a loud boom. We all jump, and my hands fly up to my ears. I stare at the screen. Syl gasps.

Charred paper flies everywhere, and there's a huge hole in the wall where the outgoing mail used to be. We watch in shock as a shelf, with its supports damaged, begins to slide. There's a cracking sound, and then it falls forward, everything on it crashing to the ground.

CHAPTER 20

One Year Earlier

It was almost dinnertime. I opened my bedroom door, but the sound of voices downstairs stopped me in my tracks.

Who could Mom be talking to? No one but Helen ever came to our house.

Heart pounding, I grabbed an X-Acto knife from my desk and crept into the hallway, tucking myself into a shadow just out of sight of the foyer.

"Stay away from us." Mom sounded angry.

A silky, unfamiliar woman's voice responded. "Aiya, Mèimei. Is that any way to greet me after all these years? I came all the way from Seattle to see you!"

Mèimei. Little sister. My eyes bugged out, and my grip on the knife loosened.

"How did you find me?" Mom asked.

"I have my ways." A laugh. "I know everything. Including what you took from me."

"You're lying."

"We're back together again."

"Then you're a fool, Jiějie."

"And *you* are still as jealous as ever. Even after all this time. He never wanted you. Here we are, decades later, and still, you pine after him. Pathetic."

"If you think that's what this is about, you don't know me at all."

"Oh, of all the people in the world to say that." The voice turned low and angry. "I know you better than anyone ever has or ever will. How could you forget the most important thing I taught you? Xiāng yī wéi mìng. You and I are bound together after *what you did*."

My mind raced. This stranger—my *aunt*—knew the phrase. She'd claimed it was *theirs*—hers and Mom's. It felt like she was taking something away from me.

"Well, where is she?" the stranger demanded. "Aren't you going to invite me in? The girl should know her own . . ."

A slap.

Then a slam and the thump of a body against the wall. Mom cried out.

The stranger's voice was barely audible now. ". . . Don't think that I won't hurt you, just because you're my sister. Sister means so little to you, after all."

"You say that like you had no part in shaping me!" Mom's voice was strained, like someone was squeezing her windpipe. Her words came out in a rush. "Perfect Kǎiwén, needing everyone to love her. You made me what I am. I did it for you. I did everything for you. But you've always been too selfish to notice! I saved Lia from becoming another one of your pawns. She doesn't need you. *We* don't need you."

There was a sharp gasp and a wheeze, followed by a muffled cough.

"Oh, but you *do* need me," the stranger—*Aunt Kǎiwén*—said.

"Now, just like then, you need me to keep quiet. I know how you get your money, little sister."

Another bout of muffled coughing, then Mom's choked voice. "What . . . do you . . . want?"

There was a crinkle. Paper? I peeked out from the shadows just in time to see a hand with long, delicate fingers and pointed red nails pass something into Mom's palm.

Aunt Kǎiwén sounded steely and calm. "Tonight, you will carry out this task *exactly* as instructed. Or I *swear* I will ruin you."

THE MISFORTUNE OF TAMYRA JOHNSON

CONTENTS OF ENVELOPE:

- Four articles with the following headlines:
  - » "The Allures of the Deep Sea"
  - » "Why College Students Are Spending Summers Fishing in Alaska"
  - » "The Dangers of Deep-Sea Fishing"
  - » "Deaths on Fishing Boats"
- Printout of Jamal Johnson's Facebook profile, showing a smiling young man.
- One note, which reads as follows: It's so easy for accidents to happen. Especially when you're far from everyone you know and isolated in the middle of the rough sea.

CHAPTER 21

Saturday, 1:30 p.m.

It's just me and Syl.

After Dread left to take his sister to her tennis match, my stomach let out a loud, embarrassing growl, and she insisted we get lunch. I let her pick, which is how we ended up at a phở restaurant. I was relieved when I saw how inexpensive it was.

Now Syl sits across from me in the dark green booth. Our waiter sets two big, steaming bowls of phở on our table. It's weird eating at a restaurant that isn't Bette's, but I'm excited to try something different.

After watching the video of the package blowing up, none of us were sure what to do. We couldn't tell anyone without explaining how we knew. But Rock's parents' alarm systems alerted them, so they're going to go check on it. Rock managed to convince them to let him tag along. He'll look for clues.

With Rock and Dread busy, it's up to me and Syl to make some progress on Cíxǐ's identity.

Hold your secrets tight, Lia.

I should tell her about the messages.

But what would I say, exactly? *Syl, I've been lying to you right from the start. I'm living illegally in the back of a restaurant. Marina*

Chan isn't my real name. If you tell anyone, the kind couple who took me in could lose their restaurant license, and I'd be in serious danger. Oh, and Cíxǐ knows my real name, somehow.

I imagine Syl making an excuse. She forgot she has somewhere to be. She runs out the door and never looks back. Or, even worse, her voice goes strange, strained. She keeps up polite conversation and plays out the rest of the levels with me for the next few days. Then, once everyone is safe, she, Rock, and Dread never speak to me again.

I don't tell her.

Instead, I continue the conversation we started in the library. "Rock has a point. James's evidence that Ethan was behind the hit-and-run seems flimsy."

"Yeah. I wonder if there's more to the story than he shared. His disagreement with Ethan clearly had a personal element, given their history." When she's talking about the case, I'm reminded that she wants to be a lawyer. That she's going places.

Unlike me.

Syl uses her chopsticks to pick up half the bean sprouts from the little plate the waiter brought us earlier. She drops the sprouts into her soup, then adds a jalapeño slice. Finally, she picks up a lime wedge and squeezes it into the broth before stirring everything.

I stare. If a stranger were asked which of us understands how to eat phở properly, they would point to me. I'm Chinese, not Vietnamese, but most people would just look at me and see an Asian girl. I'm supposed to know how phở works, but I grew up sheltered. There's so much I missed out on because of my mom's fear.

Syl has only lived in the area for two years, but she's already so comfortable here. It makes me wonder what kinds of things we could do together. The places we could explore, the cuisines we could try.

"Do you think Cíxǐ is someone one of us knows?" I ask.

Syl shakes her head lightly. "No. Maybe. I don't know. I can't imagine anyone I know doing something like this."

I wonder, like I have for the past year, what drives a person to hurt others. Is Syl right? What would she think if I rolled up my sleeve to show her my scars?

"This whole *game* feels personal, though, doesn't it?"

Syl sips her phở. "The threats do make it feel that way. I'm worried about Jamal."

"He's your brother—the one Cíxǐ threatened—right?"

"Yeah. This summer, he's deep-sea fishing in Alaska. He doesn't want to graduate burdened by a load of debt, and one of his college friends told him about it. It pays well, but it's also really risky. Something could happen . . ." She sits up straighter. "It's not going to, though. He promised our parents he'd be careful. And whatever's going on here, we have it covered."

"Do you think it's wrong of us to help Cíxǐ?"

Syl frowns, inspecting her nails, and I wish I hadn't brought it up. "Probably. But I don't know what else to do. I can't lose my brother."

And I can't let Bette and Jimmy lose the restaurant.

We're quiet for a moment. I watch Syl take a bite of rice noodles, wishing things were different. Wanting to tell her everything. Wondering how the hell we're going to keep everyone safe.

CHAPTER 22

One Year Earlier

After Aunt Kǎiwén left, I went back to my room and read until dinner. As we ate mápó dòufu and rice, I watched Mom, but she didn't bring up her sister's visit. So I pretended I hadn't overheard, even though my mind was racing. Aunt Kǎiwén's words—and her very existence—changed everything.

I wondered if she was one of the dangerous people after Mom. She had seemed scary. But why would Mom's sister come after her? And why would Mom hide that she had a sister? I didn't know what to think. I needed more answers. Aunt Kǎiwén's words burned into my mind. *I know how you get your money, little sister.*

My thoughts slid toward the locked office downstairs. Mom was going out to meet Aunt Kǎiwén; maybe I could find something out.

That night, I pretended to sleep, waiting until the garage door clattered shut. I watched Mom's car disappear down the street, then I crept into her room.

I searched the entire bedroom—the nightstand, under the bed, above the doorframes, inside Mom's pillowcase—but there was no key. Next, I checked every drawer and cabinet in the primary bathroom. Nothing there either. My palms began to sweat. This was taking too long.

Mom's walk-in closet was meticulously organized. After checking every shelf and rummaging through all the drawers, I nearly gave up. Mom must have the key with her.

Then I noticed how thick the wall mirror was. I pulled at one edge, and it swung open to reveal rows of jewelry pieces.

The key hung on a gold chain in the center. I took it and left, closing everything on my way out.

When I reached Mom's office, my hands shook. The last time I'd broken one of her rules, she'd been so angry she hadn't talked to me for a whole week. I didn't know what she'd do if she caught me here.

But I needed to know what was going on.

I turned the key, and the door unlocked. Then I pushed it open and stepped inside.

CHAPTER 23

Saturday, 8:00 p.m.

I rush into the restaurant office, smelling of soy sauce and sesame oil. My shift technically ended at seven thirty, but the restaurant was especially busy tonight, and Bette asked for help, so I worked an extra half hour.

Slate pads in behind me and curls up on his gray cushion as I close the door. I'm late, but I stop to pet him for a few minutes anyway. He's clingier than usual, and I feel awful about not having spent as much time with him lately.

"Once this is all over, we'll go on a long hike, okay?" I scratch behind his ears and kiss the top of his head.

When I sign on, everyone else is already online. The dinner party ticket in my inventory flashes green, and I click to accept. I stuff my headset on and log onto voice chat.

"Night, finally!" Syl says. In the background, I hear some indiscernible rumbling and two sharp barks.

"Sorry! My restaurant shift just ended. Where the heck *are* you?"

"Oh, Dread and I are at a big ol' Saturday night feast at our grandparents' house."

Their family seems to hold regular gatherings. It's hard for me to wrap my mind around. What would it be like to be surrounded by so many relatives?

"After your hundredth gathering, it becomes achingly clear that no one in the family is quite as interesting as they believe themselves to be," Syl says.

"Yep, we snuck away," Dread adds. "The food at these parties is stellar, though."

"Yeah, it's like a big flex fest. All the people in the family who like to cook bring dishes to outdo one another. Ridiculous competition with delicious results."

"Mm-hmm," Dread murmurs. His mouth sounds full.

"Will anyone see your screen?" Rock asks.

I think of ghostly Ethan in chains, from yesterday's level.

"Nah," Dread says. "No one will even notice we're gone. There are objectively five thousand people downstairs, zero of whom are interested in video games."

"Plus four dogs and one very angry hamster," Syl says.

The level loads. Like last time, words appear across the top of the screen.

Celebration at the Grand Palace

We're in a small, colorful room styled similarly to Cíxǐ's previous two levels. The ceiling is composed of intricately patterned tiles in green, blue, and red. Surrounding us are huge, heavy-looking gold vases on low pedestals. There's a black lacquer screen on one side of the room, painted with Chinese fairy-tale scenes.

Four figures labeled "Servant" step out from behind the screen, faces downcast, each carrying a folded piece of cloth.

"Watch out!" I fling a knife at one.

Syl casts a spell while Dread jumps into action, ready to pull aggro. But the figures continue to approach, unperturbed. Each

Servant stops before one of us, unrolling their cloth to reveal an outfit. Mine is a beautiful silk qípáo. The Servant hands me the dress, and it appears in my inventory.

"I suppose we don these disguises now?" Rock says.

Dreadnaughty's already wearing his, which looks identical to the Servants' garb. RockSplice wears plain, practical robes and sports goggles that look more steampunk than Qing dynasty. Syldara's clothes look regal but don't quite match the style of ours, like she's a foreign dignitary. I look the most like I belong here, in my green cheongsam with my hair tied in two buns and decorated with flowers.

"Hey, how come I'm the only one who looks like the Servants?" Dread asks.

Syl snickers. One of the Servants proceeds to unlatch a door to outside, and they all exit.

"Guess we follow them?" I say.

"I don't see any other exits." Rock ducks behind the screen, checking for anything we missed, while the rest of us head for the door.

Outside the room, there's a palanquin. I wonder if the four Servants are hiding around a corner, waiting to carry us to wherever our destination is. But when we click on it, each of us kneels by one of the poles. When Rock walks outside and sees us, he chuckles darkly. "Wow."

"Where's Cíxǐ? We don't have a quest," I say. In the previous two levels, she was the first person we saw.

Rock clicks on the palanquin, and then I can no longer control my character. A figure clad in yellow robes walks toward us. Behind her, Ethan's grim ghost floats along, still wrapped in chains. She steps inside, and he follows her in.

Cíxǐ has arrived.

"Someone has a rather inflated opinion of herself," Rock says.

Together, our characters lift the palanquin and begin walking.

Cíxǐ speaks. "Tonight, the palace holds a feast to celebrate the death of a traitor. The invite list includes government officials currently in favor, foreign dignitaries, and other guests of import. Four of tonight's guests are spies—threats to the stability of our empire. They must be removed discreetly and permanently, all at once, lest one warn the others. Each of you is responsible for one target. Draw them to a secluded spot, kill them, and bring me a token as proof. Find me on the balcony overlooking the event when you've completed your tasks. Good luck and have fun."

Through the side window, I catch the glimpse of a fleeting smile on Cíxǐ's face as she says the last phrase.

And then we're here. Our characters stop in sight of a grand pavilion and set down the palanquin. Cíxǐ steps off and walks away, with Ethan's ghost floating behind her. They both disappear down the path toward the pavilion. Finally, we're able to move again.

Our pockets all begin flashing. I click on mine.

Fourth Traitor's Dossier has been added to inventory.

I open it, and there's a crinkling sound as the scroll unrolls. There's a portrait drawn on it. I stifle a gasp. The woman on it looks like an older version of me.

Not me, NightMar3.

Me, Marina Chan.

My hands leap from the keyboard to cover my mouth. Slate sits up at my sudden movement and his ears stand up, alert. He lets out a slow growl, looking for danger. I rest my hand on his head, trying to convey through soft, calm strokes that I'm okay. There's no danger here. Nothing physical, anyway. Breathing hard, I force myself to lean forward and really look at the drawing.

It's not me. Her hair is thicker, fuller. Jet black, not dark brown like mine. Her lips are thinner, corners quirked up into a confident smile I don't think I've ever worn. And she's wearing tons of makeup.

But we have the same eyes.

I begin tracing the scars on my wrist.

"Do we all have dossiers of our respective assassination targets?" Rock asks. He doesn't sound like he's just seen an older version of himself on the scroll.

. . . six strokes, seven strokes, eight strokes . . .

"Yeah," Syl says. "Mine is someone named Lifeng Wu."

. . . thirteen strokes, fourteen strokes, fifteen strokes . . .

"Mine says Professor Eric Park," Dread says.

"That seems out of place," Rock says. "Not very nineteenth-century China."

. . . twenty-four strokes, twenty-five strokes, twenty-six strokes . . .

When I finish tracing the twenty-ninth stroke, my heart rate feels closer to normal. "What's the name on yours, Rock?" I hope my voice doesn't sound strained.

"Mei Ling Kang."

My heart's still beating way too fast, but my voice comes out calm enough. "Dread's target has the only Korean name, and it sounds more Korean American than Korean. Cíxǐ mentioned foreign dignitaries, but a Korean professor with a Norse first name . . . that seems weird for a royal Qing dynasty party."

"What's weird is that you knew 'Eric' is a Norse name." Syl's words make me grin, and the panic recedes further.

"I'm full of surprises."

And Helen, my last tutor, taught me history and mythology beyond the limited scope taught in most American schools. At the thought of Helen, my smile fades, and my stomach twists.

"That's not the strangest thing about Eric Park," Dread says. "His dossier includes some things to know about him. One of them says he works for UW."

"What!" Syl and I say simultaneously.

"I'll look him up," she adds.

"Put your character on auto-follow," Rock says. "We'll scope out the party."

Syldara follows RockSplice in jerky, computer-generated motions as the rest of us head for the brightly lit pavilion. The hum of chatter mixed with Beijing opera music gets louder as we approach.

The decor inside is lavish. I look up and gasp. The tall ceiling lends the room grandeur, and the air is filled with floating Chinese lanterns, all luminous. It's absolutely stunning. I'm in awe, imagining how much time must have gone into programming each element. For a moment, I forget.

Then my eyes land on a massive throne on the second-floor balcony overlooking the party. Cíxǐ wears her usual yellow robes embroidered with dragons. She rests her hands on the railing in front of her, and her gleaming, wickedly long nail protectors curve over the banister like glittering claws.

She's looking straight at me.

Ethan's miserable ghost hovers in the air beside her, eyes unfocused.

"I wonder what those percentages are for," Rock says.

I draw my gaze back to the party around me and see what he's referring to. Everyone around us has two little percentage numbers above their head: one red, one green. I look at my teammates, but none of us have percentages.

"Only one way to find out." Dread approaches the closest NPC.

"Wait! I found Eric Park on UW's site. He's a computer science and engineering professor," Syl says.

"Any idea how he might know Ethan?" I ask.

"The tech world is surprisingly small," Dread says. "Everyone knows each other. Maybe Eric worked in tech at some point." His character leaps into the air and then lands lightly. He repeats the motion—his form of fidgeting.

"Didn't Ethan attend UW?" Rock says.

"Oh, duh." Dread laughs. "Occam's Razor."

"Found him," Syl says. "He's a CSE professor and he has tenure, so he may have been teaching around twenty or so years ago. Depending on when Ethan might have taken the class."

"Last night's level was all about Ethan's past too," I say. "Cíxǐ has to be someone who knew him a while ago."

"Good point," Rock says. "There could be history between Ethan and Cixi. Maybe this professor knows something Cixi wants us to find out."

"How are we supposed to do *that*?" Dread asks.

"Let's worry about it once we figure out how this level works," Rock says.

I see Syldara move away from RockSplice. She's back in the game, no longer auto-following his character around.

Dreadnaughty walks up to a random NPC and talks to her.

"Nǐ yào shénme?" She sounds annoyed.

"Uhhhh," Dread says.

"Do you have dialogue choices?" My heart beats faster. Did Cíxǐ put Mandarin in on purpose, knowing I would be the only one who could understand? Or is it just part of the way she styles her levels?

"Yeah," Dread says. "Three responses that um . . . are in English letters but have accents on them? And one choice that just says get out of the conversation."

So, they're in pinyin, not Chinese characters. That's a relief—maybe he can sound them out.

"Can you read them aloud?" I ask.

"Yeah, but there's a timer. I have to respond quickly." Dread reads the phrases, but between his poor pronunciation and the ticking clock, I have no clue what he's trying to say.

"Shit, I don't know."

"Just pick a random one," Syl says.

Dread clicks something, and his character says, "Cào nǐ zǔzōng shíbā dài."

I groan. "You just used *very strong* language to insult eighteen generations of their ancestors."

"What!"

The woman looks appropriately enraged. There's a ding sound, and then words appear at the top of the screen.

Target's suspicion level increased. Area suspicion and interest levels increased.

The red percentage above the NPC's head goes from 20 percent to 90 percent. Around them, other NPCs turn to look, their red and green percentages increasing too.

"Whoa, they're suspicion and interest levels," Syl says.

"Our mission is to lure our targets to a secluded spot, then kill them," Rock says. "Isolating them must have something to do with the percentages."

"That makes sense," Syl says. "We need to find one of the targets to test this on."

"Yes," Rock says. "We should split up to look for them. But it would be more efficient if we knew what all four targets looked like. Everyone, send a photo of your dossier to our group chat."

I gulp. I don't want anyone else to see my target; she resembles me too much for comfort. But it would be more suspicious for me to hide the sketch, and they'll see her face in *Darkitect* anyway.

Then I realize that's not necessarily true. The way the level is set up, each of us is supposed to kill our target in seclusion. Separately.

"My phone needs charging." The lie escapes my mouth before I can think more on it.

"You can email us a screenshot, then," Rock says.

That gives me the excuse I need to stop moving around in the game, but I'll need to be fast to pull this off. I turn down the resolution on my screen so it's blurrier and grab a screenshot of the dossier showing the sketched face. I import it into one of the free photo-editing programs I have downloaded. As fast as I can, I modify her face, drawing in the cheeks to make them look narrower. I sharpen her nose and tweak her eye shape to look less like mine.

I give her a five-second inspection to make sure I didn't accidentally warp something obvious in the sketch or leave a disconnected line.

Good enough.

I save the file and upload it to our shared drive. "I'm charging my phone, but also just uploaded the screenshot."

"I'm uploading everyone's now so you can see them too, Night," Syl says.

Her response to my lies is thoughtfulness. My stomach knots.

I watch as the files appear in our shared drive and open them, memorizing the targets' faces before switching back to *Darkitect*.

"Rock, I see your target!" Dread says. Rock hurries over to where he is.

"Yours is over here, cuz," Syl says.

No one spots mine, of course. I try jumping up on a table to look down at everyone. It's a bad idea. The characters around me all grow suspicious, their red percentages increasing by ten.

"This is a practice run anyway, right?" I ask.

"Based on the previous levels, probably," Rock says.

Since this round is for recon rather than beating the level, I stay on the table, scanning the room until my eyes land on a too-familiar face. She sits off to one corner, half-hidden in the shadows . . . where Syl's about to walk by. "I think I see yours, Syl!" I blurt out.

Syl stops and turns away from my target.

"Where?"

Quickly, I keep looking around the room, searching for the distinctive hairstyle her target is supposed to be wearing. It should be easy to find hers, given the unique look. Why isn't it?

"Ah, they ducked behind someone. Hang on." I keep looking. "There! In that alcove." I ping a location on the map and Syl heads for it. Relieved, I take off for the corner, where I come face-to-face with my target. "Now what?"

"Now we start the dialogue boxes," Rock says.

"Should we stagger them?"

"Doing so might trigger them warning each other. Let's just

each start the dialogue and take screenshots or record what they're saying along the way. We can analyze the conversation afterward."

"Sure thing, boss," I say.

"Three, two, one, now!" Rock says.

I click to speak with my target, taking note of the red percentage above her head: 70 percent. Great. She's already pretty suspicious.

"How may I help you?" my target says.

"She's speaking English." Dread sounds relieved. "Wonder why the other person spoke Mandarin."

"I guess that's how you know you have the right target?" Syl says.

A list of responses pops up. I scroll through them, heart sinking when I see the length of the list. In the corner, a timer begins counting down. I have five minutes to pick an answer before her suspicion goes up. Great.

"Do y'all have like ten possible answers?" Syl sounds dismayed.

"Yes," Rock says.

"Then there's no way we can guess randomly," Dread says.

"Of course not. Cixi would never make it that easy," Syl says.

"This is only the first round of responses too," I add. "If there are this many choices each time, it'll take us forever to get through one conversation by guessing."

"Everyone, please screenshot your possible responses," Rock says.

We all do.

"All right, then just pick a plausible-sounding one and see if it's right or wrong. Now!" Rock says.

I click on one at random and my target sneers at me, her suspicion level shooting up to 100 percent. She begins shouting at me, and soon the suspicion level of the other guests in the area starts rising. Elsewhere in the crowd, the same thing is happening to my friends. None of us got lucky with our guesses.

Guards leap from shadowy corners to descend upon me with giant, wicked blades. I slash at them, trying to jump out of the way while defending myself. Some of the guests scream and flee, while others pull knives from hidden sheaths and join in hunting me down. Blood splatters across my screen.

Syl casts an ice spell, causing several of her attackers to slip and fall in a puddle of ice, but it's her last stand. Rock and Dread work together and manage to last a little longer, but they're in the center of the fray, and they're soon overrun.

Then it's just me, with my last smidgen of health. My target, the woman with a face so like my own, deals the killing blow with a tiny knife. As I fall backward, I look up to see Cíxi's implacable stare, watching me die.

Everything goes dark.

CHAPTER 24

Mom's office looked like the rest of the house—neat and tidy and picturesque. There was a desktop computer hooked up to three monitors. I tried logging in, but after three failed attempts, the account locked up. I hoped Mom wouldn't try to use it anytime soon.

Next, I looked through the desk. Tucked away in the back of the bottom drawer, I found a notebook filled with Mom's neat handwriting.

There were names I didn't recognize at the top of each page. Below each name were checklists and notes. They were all dated, and some had giant red letters stamped across the top. *PAID.*

Paid for what?

I ran back out to grab my sketchbook and pencil, then returned. I didn't know how much time I had, so I started with the most recent few, copying what information I could.

Daisy Liang, 5/23. PAID.

Elias Sullivan, 7/2. PAID.

Lucas Arnold, 8/8.

The first two dates had passed, but August 8 was next Tuesday. Each of their respective pages had photos and other information in them. I recognized some location names, and numbers that looked like they might be schedules.

What was Mom doing with all of this?

I know how you get your money, little sister.

Scary as she might be, I wished I could speak with my aunt.

From the other side of the house, the garage door opened.

Heart racing, I stuffed Mom's notebook back in the drawer, turned off the light, and ran out of the office, locking the door behind me.

As the garage door creaked shut again, I rushed back to Mom's closet to return the key. I swung the mirror shut, then ran back to my room.

I stuffed my sketchbook under my pillow and tucked myself back in, heart pounding the entire time.

CHAPTER 25

After the team wiped, we didn't have time to play through the level again. I signed off to do one of my favorite things—take my fur baby for a walk.

Slate's been anxious all day, probably because I left him with Bette and Jimmy last night, so I hope this will help. The sun's setting fast, but I have my phone to light the way if it gets too dark.

It rained this afternoon, leaving little glimmering pools in the pavement where the surface is uneven. Slate licks rainwater from a pool, then sniffs the grass for a minute before returning to my side.

It's probably paranoia, but I still can't shake the sticky feeling of eyes on me. Of someone lurking in the shadows, ready to jump out and grab me.

I shiver and walk faster.

Slate and I head up the long concrete staircase to the top of the hill. Fremont Peak Park is tiny—just half an acre—but it has a beautiful view of the city. Slate tugs on the leash, eager, and I let him lead. My mind wanders back to *Darkitect*, to the face on my scroll.

She wasn't me.

But her features were too close to mine for comfort.

Is Cíxǐ someone from my past?

But how could anyone from my past have connected me to my game profile? I didn't put in any personal information. My new name, Marina Chan, isn't registered anywhere. I don't have credit cards, a bank account, or any paperwork. There's no trail at all.

Slate's tail wags. He's eager to sniff all the trees in the park, choosing the best spot to pee. He's picky about that sort of thing.

My phone chimes with messages from the team's group chat.

Dread: my fam is leaving the party

Dread: be home in 20

Syl: we're already back

Syl: meet online tonight?

Rock: I can sign on at 10:30, after my parents go to sleep.

Syl: works for me

Dread: ughhhh fine

I text everyone that I can make it too. Slate and I head toward a copse of trees, and I startle, realizing there's someone leaning against a tree trunk. Their face is shadowed by the black hood over their head; all I can see is that they're short and slender. They're staring at a phone screen. And maybe it's just coincidence, but the way they're angled, the camera is pointed directly at me.

I could've sworn they weren't there just a minute ago.

They're probably just playing a phone game or something. It's probably coincidence that it's pointed my way.

Probably.

But I have to know.

Without warning, I sprint toward them. Slate starts running too, excited that something is happening. If this is a stranger, I'm about to embarrass myself in a major way, but if not . . .

The person looks up, but their face is obscured by their hood. I expect them to shout or give me an odd look or something.

Instead, they take off running in the opposite direction.

Gotcha.

"Hey!" I call out. "Wait!"

Slate and I chase them.

"You okay?" someone asks. I ignore them and keep chasing the hooded figure down the stairs.

They're *fast*. And they have a head start. At the bottom of the stairs, they turn and vanish from sight. I curse. Slate barks, tail wagging. I wonder if the person we're running after looks like a giant squirrel to him.

We search for fifteen more minutes, but they're gone.

I pull out my phone and send a message to the team's group chat.

Me: Someone was following me. Just walked Slate and we saw them watching us at the park. We chased, but they escaped.

Syl: WHAT! OMG

The sun has almost set. Slate finally settles on a spot good enough to be his toilet for the night, and then we hurry back to the restaurant. I'm frustrated. This might've been our best chance to find out who Cíxǐ is, and I failed. But it does confirm that I was right about one thing.

Someone has been watching me.

───────────────────

Everyone else is gone for the night. Slate and I hide in the restaurant's back office, sitting in the dark as usual. After close, I always keep the lights off so that no one finds us here. Still, it's not a perfect system. If someone presses their face up to the window in the alleyway and peers in, they'd see the faint glow of my computer through the blinds.

I imagine the hooded figure from the park creeping up to my window. The thought makes me shudder.

On my screen, three faces pop up. We've all signed onto some secure video chat program our paranoid team leader made us install. Like me, Rock sits in the dark with his computer's glow casting shadows on his face. Dread's room is bright. His white walls are peppered with posters from classic horror films, and there's half a bookshelf in view, filled to the brim with collectible figurines. Syl's room is dimly lit, like she has a desk lamp on. It's harder to see how her room is decorated, but I can see her mint green walls and her bed behind her. Next to the bed I see . . .

"Does that poster behind you say 'Wakanda Forever'?" I ask.

Syl brightens. "Yeah! It's one of my favorite fan art pieces. My parents gave it to me for my birthday last year. Isn't the lettering gorgeous?"

"I love it."

Her room looks so friendly and inviting. I wonder what it would be like, sitting on that soft bed with her.

"Dread, you're on time." I act shocked.

"Yeah, yeah," he grumbles, yawning. "Let's get on with this." Wow. He is *really* not a night person.

"What did you find out, Syl?" Rock asks.

"Looks like Professor Eric Park has office hours tomorrow from eleven a.m. to one p.m."

"Who holds office hours on a Sunday?" Dread mutters.

Syl shrugs. "Professors are busy. From what I've heard, they hold office hours whenever they have time, so it can be pretty random."

"I guess." Dread looks half asleep already.

"I'm volunteering tomorrow until twelve thirty, so I can't make it this time." Syl looks genuinely regretful.

"You've done so much already," I say. "Don't feel bad! I can be there."

"Me too." Dread rests his head on his desk. "My sister lost the tournament today. She's a sore loser, so she's boycotting the rest of it."

"Callie is *vicious*," Syl says. "She was the first person to be banned from our family's online Settlers of Catan nights. At age *ten*."

"Well, I'll be stuck here again." Rock sighs. "Though I think I can sneak out tomorrow evening and meet up. I complained enough about my house arrest today that my parents are ready to ship me off anywhere. I'll ask my sister if I can stay over at her place. She'll cover for me."

Dread gives him a half-hearted thumbs-up.

"I spent some time researching this afternoon and found out more about Ethan," Syl says, and we all perk up.

"You are *magnificent*." Rock sounds so genuinely excited that a horrid, jealous thought crosses my mind. What if Rock and Syl started dating? I think I'd die.

"Well, that's true." Syl grins. "I read as many articles about Ethan as I could. He grew up in Redmond with two older sisters. His family runs a private investment firm, where he interned in high school. They wanted him to take over the family business, but he was determined to start his own game company. He majored in computer science at UW and ended up marrying the sister of a girl he met in one of his classes. He and his wife had a baby."

"What?" Rock says. "He had a wife? And a *kid*?"

"Yeah." The way Syl says it, there's a palpable weight.

"Something happened to them, didn't it?" I say.

Syl looks sad. "It's really tragic, actually."

Rock tenses, and Dread blinks. I sit up straighter, and Slate senses my tension. He lifts his head and comes over to curl up closer.

Syl draws in a breath. "His baby girl died. She was just eight months old."

My heart clenches. "What happened?"

"Ethan's sister-in-law took the baby out for a hike one winter morning and they both fell off Rattlesnake Ledge."

None of us speak for a minute, thinking about how horrible it must have been. Slate and I have hiked that trail. It's green and forested along the path. At the top, there's a stunning view of the valley. I can picture it now: sitting with Slate, watching light reflect off the surface of Rattlesnake Lake. It's beautiful.

It can also be slippery, especially after rain or snow.

"Shortly after that, Ethan and his wife separated. From all accounts, he went into near complete isolation, barely speaking with anyone for a year. When he came out of it, he announced that he'd been developing Seamless Server Technology."

"Isn't that kinda weird?" I ask. "He's grieving, so he works on his technology?"

Rock shrugs. "It sounds like him. When he's upset about something, he focuses his energy on one project."

"After selling SST, Ethan invested the money he made, and eventually had enough capital to start Apocalypta Games a few years ago."

"Hm," I say. "What about his ex-wife? Did he piss her off somehow? She could be our culprit."

"Maybe," Syl says. "But they were only married for two years, and they divorced over a decade ago. That's a really long time to hold a grudge."

"True. So, we still have the same two suspects. Nina Cohen and the Steinbergs."

"Could one of them be the person who followed you?" Rock asks.

"Maybe. I didn't see their face."

"Oh!" Syl looks excited. "Y'all, we've been approaching this wrong."

"We have?"

"Yeah! You just proved someone's following us, right? Forget trying to guess who has the biggest grudge against Ethan. All we have to do is catch our stalker. It *has* to be Cixi!"

"That's . . . brilliant, Syl," Rock says.

"How do we do that, though?" I ask.

"I have an idea. After you and Dread go to UW to interview the professor, I'll meet you in the U District." She grins. "We're going to set a Cixi-shaped trap."

CHAPTER 26

One Year Earlier

"Lia?"

I startled awake. "Sorry, Helen. I mean, Huang Lǎoshī."

"Are you okay?"

"I didn't sleep well." My eyes felt red and raw. After sneaking into Mom's office, I had been kept awake by adrenaline and my racing thoughts. I couldn't stop wondering about the names from Mom's notebook. Were they the people who were after us?

"Should I speak with your mother?" Helen asked. "Maybe you're getting sick."

Daisy Liang. Elias Sullivan. Lucas Arnold.

"No!" I hadn't meant to shout. I lowered my voice. "I don't want to bother her."

Helen looked concerned. "Are you sure? We can take a break."

"No need. I'm fine."

"I'll get you a glass of cold water. It'll help you feel more awake." Helen left the room.

Her laptop was still open.

Before I could think too hard, I grabbed the laptop and turned it toward me. Heart pounding, I looked up Daisy Liang, scanning the headlines that popped up.

Twenty-Two-Year-Old Woman Disappears

Two Weeks Later, Recent Stanford Graduate Daisy Liang is Still Missing

Vigil Held for Missing Bay Area Woman

My breath caught as I read the previews. Daisy Liang had gone missing on May 23. I grabbed my sketchbook from the shelf behind me. With shaky hands, I checked the notes I'd taken the night before.

The date matched.

I swallowed hard, then looked up Elias Sullivan.

San Francisco Man Dies in Boat Accident

Obituary: Elias Sullivan

Something had happened to him too, on July 2.

What did this have to do with Mom?

I looked up Lucas Arnold.

Congressman Lucas Arnold—Wikipedia

Top Stories: Lucas Arnold Announces Surprise Reelection Campaign

"Lia? What are you doing?" Helen stood in the doorway, holding a glass of water.

I clicked out and shut the laptop quickly before realizing that made me look far guiltier. "Sorry. I know I should have asked to use the computer first."

"What were you using it for?"

Tell Helen what you found. Helen had known me for two years now—far longer than any other tutor ever had. Maybe she'd help me make sense of what I'd learned.

But Mom was such a private person. She wouldn't want me talking about her business with anyone. I'd made the promise to her so many times. Xiāng yī wéi mìng.

"Nothing important," I said.

THE MISFORTUNE OF ANDREW HUNT

CONTENTS OF ENVELOPE:

- Vanessa Hunt's intranet work profile showing a photo of her smiling face. She is listed as an Accounts Payable Specialist for Ade Travel.
- Invoice from KT Marketing, charging Ade Travel $10,000 for services rendered. Stamped *PAID*.
- Proof of wire transfers for the following:
  - » $10,000 sent on June 13 from Ade Travel to KT Marketing.
  - » $10,000 sent on June 17 from KT Marketing to Celeste Incorporated.
  - » $10,000 sent on June 20 from Celeste Incorporated to Vanessa Hunt's personal bank account.
- Email from Vanessa Hunt to Tanya Hunt, with the following sentences highlighted: I'm so proud of Andrew! He applied to all these scholarships and ended up winning quite a few. The biggest one is giving us $10K a month for three months. How cool is that?
- One note, which reads as follows: Imagine your mom's surprise to discover the money for your "scholarship" came from her company. It'll be almost as great as the company's surprise. ☺

CHAPTER 27

Sunday, 10:00 a.m.

I wander the University of Washington campus, waiting for Dread to show up. If all goes according to plan, we'll catch Cíxǐ today. No more stressful levels, no more breaking into buildings, no more threats to us or our loved ones.

In a few hours, we could be free again.

I want to dance around and squeal at the thought. But since we're trying to lure Cíxǐ in, Dread and I have to act like all we care about is interviewing the professor. We can't change our behavior, or she might realize.

After twenty minutes, Dread finally shows up.

"What do you know about Ethan's assistant, Nina Cohen?" I ask as we start walking.

"I barely know her." Dread consults a campus map on his phone. "I know she's Ethan's assistant, but that's about it."

"Could she be Cíxǐ?"

He shrugs. "If she has that kind of computer expertise, she'd make a lot more working as a developer than an executive assistant."

"True. She could be working with Cíxǐ, though."

Dread nods. "She'd have known about the offsite, had access

to Ethan's schedule, and . . . oh! She might've helped book our studio tour."

"Huh. Also, any idea where we're going?"

"Nope." Dread stops to ask a random student for directions.

Soon, we're on our way to the Paul G. Allen Center for Computer Science and Engineering. As we walk, I study Dread. I've always liked how cheerful and easygoing he is. We occasionally chat one-on-one when we happen to be online at the same time, and he always makes me laugh.

But today, Dread looks unhappy. I hate seeing him down.

"You seem mopey."

Dread's shoulders slump. "I guess it's just hitting me that Ethan's really gone. I didn't know him as well as Rock did, but he was good to all of us employees. On the first day of the internship, he took time to welcome us to the company and gave a speech about why he had started the teen internship program."

"Why *did* he start it?" I feel guilty, realizing I haven't spent much time thinking about what Ethan's death really meant. He was a person, with people who looked up to him and people who cared about him.

"Ethan said that his parents never understood his desire to work in video games. They thought it was childish, and they pushed him to follow in their footsteps instead. He worked hard, going after his dreams and proving them wrong. Once he had his own company, he wanted to create a program where teens with an interest in the game industry could try it out and see if it was a career path they wanted to pursue."

We stop in front of a massive round fountain. It's nestled among evergreens and surrounded by majestic red brick buildings, but the most impressive thing about the view is snowcapped

Mount Rainier standing tall in the background. The urge to pull out my sketchbook and begin drawing is strong. Instead, I snap a reference photo with my phone.

Dread half sits, half leans against the lip of the fountain and I do the same. We're almost to the building where Professor Park holds office hours, but we're fifteen minutes early. Dread breaks the silence first.

"My family . . ." He pauses. "Syl is the only person in my family who understands my love for video games. My parents didn't want me to go to DigiPen."

"Really? I thought everyone here thought tech was a good career path."

Dread cocks his head at me. "Did you grow up around here?"

I freeze. I've never told my friends anything about my past. "I grew up in San Francisco." There are over eight hundred thousand people living in SF. Dread won't know anything about my past just because I told him I used to live there.

He nods. "Did you move up here recently?"

"About a year ago."

"Ah, so you're still somewhat of a newbie."

His words sting. I've come to think of this place as home. I don't need a reminder that I don't belong here. But Dread offers me a playful grin, and it's hard to do anything but grin back.

"The tech industry does rule much of the area," he says. "But video games are their own realm. It's a volatile industry, at the mercy of fickle player bases. That's what the VP of marketing says, anyway. In the game industry, you're either on top of the world or you're about to lose your job. My parents would prefer that I go for something a little more stable, like they did." He frowns. "Though my mom's job may be at risk now."

"The threat in your envelope from Cíxǐ?"

"Yeah. The whole thing is really strange. Did I tell you about the scholarship?"

"I don't think so. DigiPen gave you a scholarship?"

"No, we didn't end up getting much financial aid from them, and private colleges are expensive. I applied for a bunch of random scholarships. Figured if I won enough money, I could convince my parents to let me go to DigiPen instead of a state school."

"It must have worked." I think of the excitement in his voice whenever he talks about starting college this fall.

"Yeah, I won enough money that they didn't argue with my choice. One place called to congratulate me and told us they'd be sending the money directly to us. They even offered to send it early, to help cover textbooks and deposits. I was thrilled. My parents thought it was a little odd, but they weren't about to say no to free tuition money."

A knot forms in my stomach.

"We started getting wire payments a few months ago. And then . . ." Dread reaches into his pocket and pulls out an envelope, handing it to me.

THE MISFORTUNE OF ANDREW HUNT

I thumb through the contents. The first few sheets are records of wire transfers. I read the accompanying note.

"Cíxǐ is the one who sent you the money? And now it turns out she stole it from *your mom's company?*"

Dread nods grimly. He reaches over and points to the date on the first sheet. "The first one came through in June. If we fail, Cixi will make it look like my mom's been stealing from work for months."

I shake my head. "How are we supposed to beat someone this prepared?"

Dread, usually my cheerful, goofy, snack-loving friend, looks dejected. "I don't know if we can. But if it's possible, I guess it'll be the same way we beat out other top teams in *Darkitect*. By doing something unexpected."

Professor Park sits at a desk piled with paper, absorbed in his work. I knock on the partially open door, and he puts a hand up, wordlessly telling us to wait. He looks like an aged version of the professor from the photo Syl sent us. His black hair is peppered with gray, and he has a few more wrinkle lines.

Finally, he sets down his pen and looks up at us through round-rimmed glasses. "I don't recognize you. Are you students of mine?"

Dread clears his throat and steps inside, extending his hand. "Hi, I'm Ryan."

The professor shakes his hand, still looking confused.

"And I'm Anna," I say.

"We're business students," Dread says. "We don't want to take up too much of your time, but we're working on an assignment, and we'd really appreciate your help."

We both dressed to look older today. Dread ditched the shorts and flip-flops in favor of jeans and a collared T-shirt. I went with a nice purple top and black pants, one of the outfits Bette got me to wear for work.

"I see." Professor Park adjusts his glasses. "It's not quite dead week yet, and summer quarter is the slowest time of year for me, so I have time, as long as it's something relevant to my expertise. What exactly does this project entail?"

"We're giving a presentation about the uniqueness of the video game industry, using Apocalypta Games as our key example," Dread says. "We've done most of our research already, but one area where we're lacking is personal perspective about the founder. When we asked around, your name came up as someone who might be able to shed light on what Ethan Wainwright was like as a student."

Even though we practiced what we'd say, I'm impressed by how convincing Dread sounds. We decided he should take the lead—he's closer to college age, so our cover story will sound less flimsy coming from him. I'd rather not have anyone focus too closely on me anyway. My job is to secretly record our conversation so that Syl and Rock can analyze it later.

Professor Park looks excited. "That sounds like a brilliant presentation! I would love to talk to you about Ethan. He's one of my favorite success stories."

"Great, thank you!" Dread says. "We can ask questions if it's helpful, but if you're comfortable with it, we'd really just love to hear anything you have to say about Ethan."

"Sure, sure." Professor Park gestures at two chairs. We both sit. I pull out a notebook and pencil. "Here's the plain truth—I make no secret of it. I had Ethan in one of my intro courses, and he wasn't one of my top students. Truth be told, he was somewhat average."

I raise my eyebrows. Ethan, the programmer behind SST, *average*?

"That's surprising," Dread says, "given what he went on to accomplish."

"Yes, yes, exactly! He was an incredibly hard worker. He just didn't have a lot of experience. At the time, computer science had been around for a while, but in a very different form. When I studied it, I had to write out code on a piece of paper. Imagine that!" He chuckles to himself. "By the time Ethan took my class, it was a field on the rise. Some of my students were naturals—the type who grew up glued to their computers. But not Ethan."

"He came in not knowing anything about programming?" Dread asks.

"Well, I wouldn't say that. He had an interest in computers, which was less common at the time. But the main thing I remember is how hard he worked."

"Let me guess. By the end, he was one of your best students?"

"Not quite. He had a lot of catching up to do. But he definitely improved." The professor leans in conspiratorially, and we follow suit. "Everyone loves to complain that the introductory CSE courses are some of the toughest intro classes UW offers. And they're right. If he hadn't worked so hard, he would've been weeded out along with most of the class. But he was in here almost every office hour, learning and asking questions. I've had a lot of students, but I would've remembered him even if he hadn't gone on to such a celebrated career. He's one of the hardest workers I've ever met. He's living proof that hard work pays off."

I scribble some notes so Professor Park doesn't get suspicious.

"It helped that he often studied with his partner, Yumei, who was really talented. He actually ended up marrying her sister—who was also a student of mine a few years earlier."

"I think I read about that when we did background research on Ethan," Dread says. "I didn't know they met in your class, though!"

"They did. I know I sound like a stodgy old professor saying this, but that story is another favorite lesson of mine. I believe in finding positive influences, people you can learn from. Work hard and surround yourself with smart people, and you'll get places.

That's exactly what he did and look where he is now." His expression turns sad. "It's such a shame what happened to her, though."

"What do you mean?" Dread asks.

"Yumei, along with her niece—Ethan's daughter—both died in an accident. It happened a few years after she and Ethan graduated."

I remember the call from last night, when Syl told us about Ethan's baby. "We read about that. Rattlesnake Ledge, right?"

Professor Park nods. "I feel awful for that whole family, torn apart by tragedy. Yumei died so young. And Ethan lost his child."

Dread keeps the conversation going for a little while longer while I think about what the professor said. Ethan, struggling with school? It's hard to imagine.

Eventually, Dread elbows me, snapping me out of my thoughts. We both thank the professor for his time. He wishes us good luck on our presentation, and we leave, waiting until we're out of his line of sight to stop recording. Hopefully, we have the information we need to beat Cíxǐ's level.

An hour later, Syl texts that she's done volunteering, which is perfect timing. Dread and I are finishing up lunch. We're ready to set our trap for Cíxǐ.

"We have some time to kill before we have to go meet Syl. Want to walk around a bit?" Dread asks.

"Sure. I'm craving bubble tea."

Our conversation isn't exactly riveting, but it's all part of the plan.

We split the bill, which is thankfully small. Then we head to one of the numerous boba shops in the area while we wait for Syl to bus in from downtown.

I sip my watermelon smoothie, enjoying the satisfying pop each time I bite a bursting boba. We do our best to remain relaxed and casual, chatting about *Darkitect*. Hopefully, we look at ease, like we're not concerned about whoever might be following us.

After half an hour at the bubble tea shop, Syl texts that she's in place. Dread and I leave the café, strolling up the Ave. We stop several times during the walk, hoping it'll help Syl catch our tail.

First, we visit the University Bookstore on 43rd and browse their impressive sci-fi fantasy section. I read all the staff recommendation cards and end up buying a novel about queer space pirates. It sets me back on saving for a new headset, but it's signed, and it sounds really good. Dread gets a cookie and a monster board book for his baby niece.

Then we're off again. At the intersection of 45th, there's a girl sitting on the sidewalk holding a cardboard sign, with a one-eared dog lying on her lap. We stop to give her a few dollars, and Dread gives her his cookie. I silently promise myself that the next chance I get, I'll come back with dog food and whatever else I can scrounge up.

We keep walking up the Ave, past 47th. Dread "accidentally" steps on my shoelace and apologizes, giving us an excuse to step aside and kneel to tie my shoe. Even in the summer, with fewer students on campus, the Ave is busy. It would be easy for someone following us to blend into the crowd.

As I'm about to stand, a skateboarder flies down the sidewalk. There are curses as people jump out of his way, but I'm still crouched. He crashes straight into me.

"Hey!"

He shrugs and takes off again before I can say anything more. I glare at his retreating back.

"Night! Are you okay?" Dread bends down to help. He grabs my arm lightly, and I flinch. I've never gotten used to affection or anyone coming too close to me. Too late, I realize my sleeve is caught under my shoe. As I yank my arm back, the sleeve of my poor, well-worn shirt makes a terrible tearing sound.

For the first time since the day I ran away, the words scarred into my skin are exposed for all the world to see.

I stare at my wrist in shock.

A shock that's mirrored in Dread's face.

Quickly, I hug my arm to my chest.

Dread saw.

He *saw*.

He *knows*.

Suddenly, the busy street feels suffocating. I want to leap to my feet and start running. Ignore the shouts, never answer Dread's questions, just run home to Slate and . . .

. . . And what? Never talk to my friends again?

Instead, I stand, not quite looking Dread in the eye.

I have a story prepared for this. This isn't the end of the world.

But I thought if I ever had to use my story, it would be on a stranger. Not someone who knows me. Someone who might judge me. Someone who will see me differently and maybe tell other people we know.

I gulp and start walking again. Dread catches up quickly; damn his super long legs. I'm still hugging my wrist, keeping my secrets hidden, pressed against the fabric.

"Night . . . ," he whispers as we walk, "do you want to talk about it?"

I shake my head.

I feel lightheaded.

I feel like I'm trapped in a dark, musty room.

I feel like there's a blade pressing into my skin.

I need air.

"Did you know that in New Hampshire, it's illegal to collect seaweed at night?" Dread's voice cuts through my rising panic. The words sound alien, like I've never heard them before. Then the meaning starts to sink in.

"Huh?"

"In Ohio, every operator of an underground coal mine must legally provide an adequate supply of toilet paper with each toilet."

I blink at him.

"Really makes you wonder what's going on in Ohio, doesn't it?"

"What . . . ?"

"Oh, and in Illinois, it's illegal to possess a salamander whose value exceeds six hundred dollars." Dread shrugs and gives me a light smile. "When I'm stressed, I repeat funny state laws to myself. Come on, let's go."

My throat still feels tight, but my heart feels strangely lighter.

Dread starts walking, looking pointedly ahead. He's so careful not to glance at my wrist that I know he must be burning with curiosity.

By the time we reach 50th Street, I'm breathing easier again, and there are fewer people around. We turn right, and then right again, effectively doing a giant U-turn. We walk down Greek row, a beautiful street divided by a thin strip of green lawn. On each side, we're surrounded by giant houses labeled with huge Greek letters.

We're almost to 45th, which leads back into campus, when Dread's phone rings.

"Hey, what's up?"

I can't hear Syl's voice from where I'm standing. All I can do is listen to Dread's coded responses.

"Cool. We're headed to the car right now. I parked in the garage under Red Square. You know, entrance on 41st?" He pauses. "No, it's free on Sundays. Anyway, we're walking now. Should be there in ten, then we'll drive out to meet you. Send me the address." He hangs up.

I breathe a small sigh of relief, keeping my smile inside. We're not done yet, but Dread's call indicates that Syl's figured out who our tail is. Of course she did. Dread looks down at his phone. It's a blurry photo from Syl showing the back of someone. They're wearing a black T-shirt, jeans, and sneakers. They have short black hair and a dark gray messenger bag.

Dread switches to Find My Friends and a little blip pops up. It's Syl. That's how she's been tracking our location too, through Dread's phone. A text pops up at the top of the screen.

Syl: They're running! Headed south on 15th!

Dread and I don't hesitate. We turn and run south. He's holding out his phone, checking every so often to make sure we're going the right way. Syl's dot moves fast, and we run to keep pace. Dread starts pulling ahead of me. Unsurprising, since he was on the track team, but still, it rankles. I summon all the strength I can carry and dash forward, catching up to him.

Dread laughs. "You're so competitive. Can I remind you that we're *working together*, just like we are every time we're on a team mission and you *have* to beat me in kills?"

I don't respond because it's taking everything in me to maintain this pace. He flashes me a knowing grin, and I hate him a little bit for his easy pace. He looks so relaxed, he could be on a morning stroll. I run harder, getting ahead for a few glorious seconds. Then a stitch forms on my side, and I slow down.

Dread smirks, passing me. He doesn't say anything. Bastard.

His phone buzzes. He holds up his screen, reading me the text as he continues running. "At the car. HURRY!"

We look at the Syl dot. She's still a block away. I motion for him to run ahead, and he does. We can't leave Syl to handle this on her own.

I stop to catch my breath for a second before running after Dread.

This is it. Syl's plan *worked*! We're finally going to figure out who's been torturing us.

It's about to be over.

When they're finally in sight, I take in the scene. Dread and Syl stand facing me, leaning against a black car. They're blocking the driver's seat door. Syl has her arms folded, looking extremely unamused.

I recognize the black shirt and jeans from Syl's blurry photo. The person has their back to me, looking like they're in a heated discussion with Syl and Dread. They're throwing up their hands when I walk up and stand on the other side of Syl, the three of us forming a wall. They turn to look at me, about to say something.

I see their face.

And my mouth drops open.

CHAPTER 28

One Year Earlier

Mom and I sat at Lanhua Teahouse, a pot of dragon pearl oolong tea between us. She sipped from her teacup while I bit into my pastry. My teeth sank through the flaky outer crust, dough and red bean paste, and salted duck egg yolk. It was delicious.

Three nights had passed since my aunt's visit, and I hadn't slept well for any of them.

I tried to focus on the flavor. On the ambiance and decor. The beautiful carved wood screens and matcha green walls, the soft lanterns scattered throughout. I loved Lanhua Teahouse; it was the one place Mom and I continued to go. She'd worked here when she was a young single mom, and had fond memories of the place.

"How are your lessons going, Lia?"

"They're going well."

"Helen said you've been doing some interesting research."

My head jerked up. "She did?" Had Helen figured out what I'd looked up and told Mom?

Mom kept her gaze on me. "Yes. On the Cultural Revolution."

"Oh. Yeah." I tried to sound calmer than I felt. "Did you know that no one knows the exact death toll? It's possible *millions* of people died in it."

"I did know that. I learned about Wénhuà Dàgémìng as a child."

As a child. When Mom had grown up with her older sister, Kǎiwén.

Kǎiwén, whose existence Mom had hidden my whole life.

Kǎiwén, who showed up at our house, threatening Mom.

Kǎiwén, who knew Mom's and my phrase.

My head spun again.

I took a deep breath, releasing it slowly to build up courage. Mom seemed relaxed; it was a good time to fish for information. "Since my fifteenth birthday is coming up, I've been thinking about what to do when I grow up."

"No need to worry, Lia. Other parents see their children as burdens to unload once they reach adulthood. But I'll take care of you for life. That's why we're going to get matching 'xiāng yī wéi mìng' tattoos when you turn eighteen—so you never forget that I'll always be here for you."

I chewed my lip. "I know, but . . . I want to know more about what you do for a living."

Annoyance flickered across Mom's face. "I've told you before. I work for the government."

"But *what* do you do for the government?"

"I work as an analyst. It's not important, which is why I never bother you with details. You worry too much."

"I'm not worried. It's just . . . how will I know what to study so we can work together in the future?"

Mom sighed. "I can't tell you more. The information is

confidential. Anyway, all you need to do is be good and study hard."

The same answer she always gave.

Daisy Liang. Twenty-Two-Year-Old Woman Disappears.

I sipped my tea, wishing I could stop the names and headlines from repeating themselves in my mind.

CHAPTER 29

Sunday, 1:25 p.m.

I stare at the person who's been following us.

It's Morgan, the reporter who was taking photos of my house back in San Francisco. Their pixie cut has grown out some, and they're dressed more casually this time, in jeans and a fitted tee, but it's the same person.

My brain is frozen, and Syl has to elbow me before I remember to deliver my line. "You were following me last night." I sound more surprised than accusatory.

The not-stranger's eyes bore into me. If they were startled before, they're calmer now. They're not looking at Syl or Dread. They're looking at me.

I shift uncomfortably, wondering if they know that I haven't told Syl and Dread about my real identity. I have something on them . . . but they have something on me too.

"Why are you following us?" Syl demands.

Is Morgan about to spill my secrets?

Suddenly, this trap feels like it caught the wrong person.

"I'm not following *you*." They gesture to our group. "And if you don't move *right now*, I'm going to call the authorities."

"Really? Are you going to tell them about the *games* you play too?" Syl ignores the bystanders. Her normally sweet voice is more menacing than I've ever heard.

"What games?" They look completely puzzled.

"Don't pretend like you don't know, *Cixi*," Dread says.

"Cixi? Is that some kind of slang?" Their confusion seems genuine, and I have a horrible feeling that all of this is wrong.

We're starting to draw a crowd.

"I have your license plate down," Syl says. "I can report you for stalking underaged girls. Unless you come clean and have a damn good explanation." She's steely and strong, and I'm so in awe.

They shake their head. "Look, I don't know what you're all talking about, but I'm a private investigator. I'm here on confidential client business, and I haven't done anything illegal. Now if you'll excuse me, I'd like to get into my car now. You're causing a scene."

We look around and sure enough, people are standing on the sidewalks, muttering. It's only minutes now before some Good Samaritan steps in.

"Oh my God," Syl says, even as she moves aside to let them through. "You're Sloan." They look up at her sharply. One more piece clicks into place as Syl continues. "You were hired by Ethan Wainwright."

We're in Dread's car, driving back to the library. My mind hurts from desperately trying to piece together what I know.

We know that sometime before dying, Ethan Wainwright hired Sloan Kim, a local private investigator.

We know Sloan is following us around now.

I also know Sloan was following me over a year ago when I was Lia Tang. But I have no idea why.

I almost blurt out that I've met Sloan before. My friends deserve to have all the facts, don't they? I should tell them.

But then they'd ask me a lot of questions I can't answer. I can't risk it.

I hate having to hide so much from them.

"Sloan *could* be Cixi." Syl frowns. "But I got the feeling they had no idea what we were talking about. What do you two think?"

"I agree," Dread says.

"I don't think they're lying either," I say.

Syl sighs. It's a long, drawn-out sound that I feel in my bones. We're all disappointed. This was supposed to be our big moment. The end to the game. Instead, we're more confused than ever.

"Okay, let's run scenarios," Syl says, which makes me long to play a *Darkitect* level with the team instead of Cíxǐ's messed-up real-life missions. "Scenario one: Sloan isn't Cixi and has no clue about the game. What plausible reasons might they have for following us?"

"Maybe they found out something happened to Ethan," Dread says. "Maybe they're investigating us because of that."

"This is going to sound really coldhearted," Syl says, "but why would Sloan investigate if that's the case? Ethan hired them for something, which means he's their income source. If he dies, no one's paying them to investigate his death."

Dread whistles. "You *are* cold."

Syl holds her hands up. "Just being practical here."

"What if they *are* being paid to investigate his death?" I ask.

Syl leans forward. "You mean like . . . scenario two: Cixi hires

Sloan to investigate Ethan's death and hints we had something to do with it?"

"Yeah."

"That *could* be a way to cast suspicion on us, instead of her."

"Cixi's already threatened to pin it on us," Dread says. "Why bother with a PI?"

"It is convoluted," I say. "Besides, it feels like too much of a coincidence that Cíxǐ would've hired the same PI as Ethan."

Syl considers. "Maybe Sloan, Cixi, and Ethan all know each other through the same connection. Like they were all in a secret society together or something."

"My head hurts," Dread says.

"Scenario three: Sloan *is* Cixi, was hired by Cixi with full knowledge of the game, or they're part of a group that comprises Cixi. They're really good at acting, and they're in on the whole thing."

"How would they expect to follow all four of us, though? Shouldn't there be more PIs involved?" Dread asks.

"Maybe there are," Syl says. "And we've only caught one."

That's a chilling thought.

"Scenario four: just like in scenario one, Sloan was hired by Ethan and has no idea about the game at all. But in this case, they also don't know what happened to him and they weren't tipped off by Cixi. Instead, they're investigating us for some other reason."

As soon as she says it, I realize this must be it. I sit very still, apprehension bubbling up inside me. I think back to our conversation with Sloan.

Syl had asked, *Why are you following us?*

And Sloan had replied to her . . . *I'm not following* you.

They'd made a sweeping motion that presumably indicated the three of us. But they'd looked at me long and hard. What if they weren't gesturing at all three of us? What if they were only gesturing at Syl and Dread?

I close my eyes, replaying the scene. Sloan's words to Syl. The strange emphasis on *you*.

I'm not following *you*.

I'd thought their phrasing odd at the time, but now I understand.

They weren't following *Syl*.

They weren't following *us*.

They were following *me*.

They've been following me for over a year.

They probably have no idea their employer is dead.

Syl said it. Ethan hired Sloan for an unknown private investigation.

Except I now know what—or who—the subject of the investigation was.

Me.

By the time we pull up near the library again, Syl and Dread have given up on figuring out why Sloan is following us. To them, the scenarios all sound equally plausible and equally implausible.

I feel like screaming.

I'm the reason they're caught up in this game. I'm at the heart of this, somehow. Without me, my friends and their families would all be safe right now.

I'm a curse.

Dread drops me and Syl off while he looks for parking. Syl and

I walk side by side through the foyer. She turns to me. "Yesterday was your first time at this branch, right?"

"Yeah."

She smiles. "I want to show you something really quick."

I follow her into an elevator. My mind's still spinning, trying to understand everything, while guilt weighs heavy in my gut. Then the doors close, and I realize Syl and I are alone. We're standing so close that if either of us moves an inch, our hands will touch.

I don't think I breathe for the entire ride up.

When we reach the tenth floor, the door opens and Syl steps out. "This is the Reading Room."

"Doesn't that describe pretty much every room in the library?"

She giggles. "You'd think."

We walk past people busy reading or working on laptops. No one looks up; they're all absorbed in their own private worlds.

Finally, we reach a tiny balcony that juts out into the building's open middle. I read the sign hanging off the metal railing.

you are at the highest viewpoint

←—atrium outlook.

Syl steps forward without hesitation. The balcony is just wide enough for both of us to stand side by side. I join her.

"The view here is gorgeous, isn't it?" she says.

I look down. It is, indeed, stunning—like one of those cross-section diagrams, showing a peek of each carefully designed floor.

It's also dizzying. A wave of vertigo hits me, and I close my eyes, clutching the railing.

"Night? Oh my God. I should've made sure you were okay with heights."

I try to concentrate on Syl's words, but I feel like I'm floating in the air. My eyes are still closed. Maybe I should open them, but I'm afraid to do anything that might make it worse.

And then Syl's hand is on mine, her other arm around my shoulder. I cling to her steadying presence, letting her guide me away from the edge of the balcony. Gently, I turn until my back is to the railing, eyes still closed as I try to catch my breath.

"Night . . . Marina, I'm so sorry. I should've checked before bringing you up here."

I take a deep breath and open my eyes, feeling ridiculous.

But instead of annoyance, her gorgeous eyes are filled with concern. I'm suddenly conscious—of her hands, which have, somehow, landed on my waist. Of her perfume, light and floral. Of my racing heart, ready to burst out of my chest. Of how close her lips are to mine. All I'd need to do is inch forward and . . .

Syl's phone buzzes in her pocket.

I jump back, and Syl's hands fall to her side. I catch a look on her face—disappointment, maybe? And I suddenly want to take it back, to go back in time a few seconds, to ignore the buzzing phone. She didn't react. Why do I have to be so jumpy? I try to think of something to say to get the moment back, but then a stranger walks into view, clearly headed for the balcony we're still on.

"I think they're waiting." I don't look at Syl. I want to kick myself for my cowardice.

After a moment, Syl replies, "Yeah." She follows me off the balcony, and we wind our way toward the elevator. She checks her phone. "That was Dread. We should meet up with him. Are you feeling better?" Her voice sounds higher than usual.

"I think I'm okay now. Thanks for, um . . . thanks."

My heart is still beating fast. We walk the rest of the way to the elevator in silence, and I feel like I've ruined everything.

Dread meets us on the fifth floor, oblivious to the lingering weirdness between me and Syl. I try to act normal as we look around for a spot. We end up sitting at a counter, all facing the same direction.

As I set up in the middle, I sneak glances over at Syl. She's chatting with Dread, and she sounds like her usual self. I wonder if I imagined that moment between us. Maybe I read too much into it; she was probably just being a good friend.

Soon, we're all set up and signed on. Despite everything, sitting between Syl and Dread gives me a strange, warm sort of comfort. I'm literally surrounded by friends. While we wait for Rock, we look through the screenshots everyone took last night of their potential conversation choices. We play the recorded interview with Professor Park and use the new information to determine what the NPCs would want to hear. We settle on which responses make the most sense. It's time to test our guesses.

Rock finally signs on, and we all click on our dinner party invitations. A loading screen appears, and then we're outside the dining hall, standing next to the vacated palanquin. The four of us walk into the party, where we split up to search for our targets again. Luckily, it looks like they're traveling on a fixed loop, so we find them in similar places to last time.

I take a deep breath, staring at the woman in front of me. My face, but not my face. I'm waiting for Rock's signal to start the conversation.

"Shouldn't we look for secluded spots?" Syl asks. "We're supposed to lure the characters away and kill them somewhere private. How will we know where to take them?"

"Good point," Rock says. "We know generally where to find our targets now, so let's scout out places to lead them. Then we can find them again."

I pass by the woman with almost-my-face and look around the room's outer perimeter for doors or stairwells.

"Maybe I can draw my target back outside the way we came," Dread says.

"There were guards at the entrance, but there might be a private spot around a corner," Rock says.

I peer at Dread's screen. He's already halfway to the door, ready to scout the outside. It's still so odd to be gaming with Dread and Syl in person. To be able to look at their screens.

Which also means they can look at mine. They might see that my target doesn't look like the screenshot I sent them all last night. And I'm sitting right between them.

Crap.

I need to find a dark spot in the game so that if either of them looks over, it'll be harder to see my target's face. Or I need to kill my target first, while everyone else is still distracted, fighting their own.

"There's a staircase to the second floor here." Syl pings the location on our mini-maps. It's on the balcony opposite Cíxǐ's throne.

"You'll have to keep out of Cíxǐ's line of sight." I think of the previous round. Cíxǐ's fixed gaze as she watched me die.

"She gave us the mission. She has incentive not to raise the alarm."

"But she's also an asshole," Rock says.

"True."

My outer perimeter search leads me to a rectangular doorway. I open it to reveal a set of stairs leading downward. I shiver, trying to take my mind off the images that appear, unbidden, at the sight of the staircase.

I don't like basements.

I remind myself that it's only a game. This is what I need. A dark spot where I can commit murder without anyone seeing. No NPC party guests to witness the assassination, no friends to see my target's face.

"Found a basement to use." I click forward on my mouse, and NightMar3 walks down into the darkness. I stick a sound dampener to the wall and hot key items from my inventory that'll come in handy for a quiet assassination. Paralysis Poison to apply to my dagger. Stun Gun. Hypnosis Charm. Temporary Sound Booth, an artifact I acquired last month that lets me trap myself in a soundproof bubble with an enemy.

Once we're all set up, we head back to the party, moving toward our targets.

"I think my target's suspicion level increased from last time," Syl says.

I look at the little red percentage next to my target: 75 percent. Last time, she started at 70 percent. "You're right."

"We didn't do anything, though," Dread says.

"I noticed mine had increased by five percent when we first arrived," Rock says. "But I figured the base suspicion level was randomized within a range. Are you saying *all* our targets' suspicion levels increased?"

"Don't remember," Dread says.

"Mine went from sixty-five percent to seventy percent," Syl says.

"Five percent increase for me too," I say.

"Syl, your target began at sixty-five percent suspicion?" Rock sounds incredulous. "Mine was only at forty percent!"

"Yeah," Syl says. "Rock's target is now forty-five percent suspicious and mine is seventy percent. Dread? Night? What are yours?"

"Thirty percent," Dread says.

I bite my lip. "Seventy-five percent."

"Well, hell," Syl says.

Rock sounds tense. "Last time, when we gave the wrong answers, our targets shot up to a hundred percent suspicious, and that's when we were attacked. Which means that we only have five more tries to get this right. Otherwise, Night's target will attack her on sight."

"We might not have to be the first to speak with our own target," Dread says. "Maybe if I talked to Night's target, I'd be able to lower her suspicion."

"Or talking to someone else's target might raise it. And each round we fail, everything gets five percent harder," Syl says.

"I'd rather not test it either way," Rock says.

Each time we fail, there's a good chance we're closer to losing the level completely. *Darkitect* levels are meant to be challenging, but one aspect of the game we can usually count on is unlimited tries.

Five failed levels might be all that stand between Bette's Battles and Bao and a bucket of gasoline.

Rock counts down. I click on my target, and she turns toward me.

"How may I help you?" Again, her voice sounds familiar. I study her long, curled lashes, her flawlessly contoured cheeks, and her intricate hairdo, long locks swept up to resemble a Qing-style hairpiece. Her eyelids are a dark, smoky gray, and her bright red lips sit in a pout. She wears a cheongsam similar to mine, and her nails are crimson, like she dipped them into fresh blood.

Her nails, long and manicured.

Her voice, silky smooth and familiar.

Her face, an aged version of my own.

Could this be Kǎiwén? My aunt?

I stare until the response timer is under a minute. Then I click on my response.

A text bubble pops up above NightMar3. "I hear you deal in . . . *miracles*. There's a young, promising student. He works hard but lacks the skills to succeed in his field of study. Would you be able to help?"

The woman cocks her head to listen, and I can't stop staring. Wondering. I wish I'd been braver that day, a year ago. I wish I'd peeked out over the banister just for a moment. I wish I'd had the courage to look at Aunt Kǎiwén's face. Then I'd know if this is her.

"We may be able to come to an arrangement. For a price."

I watch as her red suspicion percentage drops down to 50 percent. I wonder how far I need to lower the percentage before she'll leave with me.

"How is everyone's conversation going?" Rock asks.

"First and second answers worked." Dread's talking to the professor about how Ethan's kid died. They're discussing grief and its effects on different people.

"My first answer worked, but I can't decide on the follow-up," Syl says. I lean over to look at her screen, scanning her list of choices until I settle on one that feels right.

Spread the rumors that "he" had help at the university. "He," presumably, refers to Ethan.

"That one." I point. "Spread the rumor."

"All right." Syl crosses her fingers, sighing in relief as her target's interest level increases to 40 percent, suspicion down to 55 percent.

"What about you, Rock?" I ask.

"The line about sensational new technology worked. He wasn't that suspicious to begin with, but his interest level was low. Now, both are at thirty percent."

We're not sure exactly what we need. Does the target's interest have to be above a fixed percent, suspicion below a fixed percent simultaneously? Does the interest percent just have to be higher than suspicion level? We assume there will be a dialogue option to lure them away once we've completed whatever secret requirements Cíxǐ built into the level.

I look back at my screen. The response timer is under two minutes now. Now or never. I select my next response.

"There's a girl under your tutelage," NightMar3 says. "I'm told she can help this promising young man."

The woman raises her eyebrows. "Indeed. Shall we retire to a quieter spot for further discussion?" Without waiting for an answer, she turns and slips out of the crowd.

That was easy.

"He's following me outside!" Dread says.

"My target lacks the requisite interest." Rock sounds grumpy.

"Still in conversation with mine," Syl says.

If this NPC woman is going to give me the perfect opportunity, I'll take it. I follow her—not to the basement where I had my sound bubble planted—but through a side door into a room full of servants. They drop in a deep bow as we enter. She ignores them, stepping on one servant's braid as she passes. I follow her, feeling more and more uneasy, but what choice do I have?

"I'm going to a quiet spot with my target," I say.

"I'm in the courtyard with mine now. Just gotta get them to follow me behind this giant tree," Dread says.

"Finally!" Syl says. "My person is coming with me."

Rock groans. "Mine is still not interested enough."

Tucked in the back of the room full of servants, there's a set of stairs leading to a small room. We enter, and she gestures toward one of two ornately carved chairs that face each other. I move toward the chair, surreptitiously drawing my dagger. When she goes to close the door, I quickly turn away and apply Paralysis Poison to the blade. But then, from behind me, my target speaks.

"I know how you get your money."

For a moment I'm in shock.

Her voice.

Her inflection.

Her words.

Those exact words.

"Now, just like then, you need me to keep quiet. I know how you get your money, little sister."

I gasp, and Syl turns toward me. She must notice my stricken look because she turns to look at my screen.

I don't remember turning NightMar3 to face my target, but I must have done so by reflex, because the face—not the face I altered and sent the group, but the target's real face—is turned toward me now, wearing a wicked grin.

She stabs me through the heart.

CHAPTER 30

One Year Earlier

It was August 8—the date next to Lucas Arnold's name. And Mom was away on business, leaving me alone for the first time since Aunt Kăiwén's visit. I snuck back into Mom's closet and opened her mirror.

The key was gone.

I broke out in a cold sweat. Did she know I'd taken it?

After leaving Mom's room, I paced back and forth in the hallway, trying to think about Mom. All of this had to have something to do with her work.

She hadn't been this secretive when we lived in our tiny, old apartment.

I might be sheltered, but even I knew there was something weird about how we'd suddenly been able to afford a house in the heart of San Francisco, a private tutor, and all the things Mom used to tell me were too expensive.

What kind of government analyst suddenly makes a lot of money at once?

I grabbed my sketchbook and sat on my bed, drawing.

Drawing made me feel calmer; it occupied the part of my brain that otherwise filled with worries. And Marina Chan's adventures let me escape my life for a time.

I drew Mom, frowning. Then I wrote notes around her in tiny text—things that might help me figure out what her job really was.

Scared of bad people who are after us.

Has an older sister, Kaiwen, who threatened to expose what Mom does for a living.

Started leaving on business trips seven years ago.

Moved us to a new house five years ago.

Has a mysterious notebook of names.

Two of the three names are people who died. One drowned, the other went missing.

I kept going, listing everything I could think of. On the opposite page, I drew Marina dressed as a detective, holding up a magnifying glass to Mom.

I drew little thought bubbles around Marina with possible theories.

Mom's a spy for the government.

It would explain the secrecy. At the teahouse, Mom said her work was confidential.

But the names and articles nagged at me. How did those fit?

Mom works for the government, helping people in witness protection.

I liked this theory best. It meant Mom hadn't lied to me. That she helped people. It explained the names, the articles. Maybe the government paid her per person helped.

But it didn't explain my aunt's threats to reveal what Mom did. If Aunt Kǎiwén had the names of protected witnesses, maybe. But then, wouldn't she have threatened to reveal that?

Mom doesn't work for the government. She helps people running from bad situations fake their deaths and start over.

It would hurt to know Mom had lied for years about working for the government. But it might be okay if she'd lied to protect the people she was helping.

Still . . . how was she making so much money? Did she charge people a fortune to help them start over? And why would a politician announce a reelection campaign right before he was trying to disappear and start over?

Mom is hired to look for missing people.

This theory might explain Daisy Liang. It could also explain our influx of cash, and why Mom was gone so often.

But Elias Sullivan and Lucas Arnold weren't missing.

I tore out the page, frustrated. None of the theories fit all the facts.

There was one more theory, but I didn't want to think about it.

Maybe I'd missed something.

Lucas Arnold, 8/8.

A little voice in my mind told me exactly what was happening today. What was probably happening right now.

I didn't want to think about it.

I buried it deep, forcing myself to go downstairs and make dinner.

Today was just an ordinary day.

CHAPTER 31

I watch as my target, the woman with a face like my own, calmly pulls the dagger out of my heart, wipes my blood on a handkerchief, and re-sheathes the blade. She must alert the palace guards shortly after that, because the dinner party turns into a bloodbath.

We only have four tries left before Cíxǐ's third level becomes impossible to beat.

"Five-minute break?" Rock suggests.

"Make it ten." Next to me, Dread removes his headset and disappears down a row of bookshelves.

Syl pulls off her headset and turns to face me. "What was *that*? She looked like you, but older. And her expression was so cold."

I say the first lie that comes to mind. "Her face changed at the last minute."

Syl's eyes narrow. My heart starts to race. She's going to call me out on my lie.

"Cixi is one messed-up person," she says, and I realize the narrowed eyes and the venom in her voice aren't meant for me.

I should feel relieved, but my secrets hang in the air between us, thick and cloying.

"Bio break." I practically scurry out of my chair, heading for the bathroom.

As I leave, I can feel her eyes on my back. Or maybe it's just my guilt, projecting itself.

I'm alone in the small bathroom. I stare into the mirror, looking at my face the way I might analyze an art subject. My mind starts to draw lines, to imagine strokes. The curve of my cheeks. The way my brown hair falls, wavy and finer than Mom's straight, jet-black hair. The way my eyelids have a small fold.

My brown eyes.

Just like the woman in *Darkitect*.

I look down at my wrists. Before I can overthink, I slide up my torn shirtsleeve, revealing the sharp words beneath.

Twenty-nine strokes.

They're faint white scars now. Bumps to remind me.

With my nail, I begin tracing the first character. I imagine my finger leaving a trail of blood, like my nails have been whittled into sharp points. Like my finger is a claw.

相

Xiāng.

As I trace, the anger begins to build.

I've spent so long trying not to think about what happened a year ago. The betrayal.

依

Yī.

By the time I'm tracing the second character, I'm breathing hard. My nails dig in deeper, leaving a chalky white trail of irritated skin and momentary pain. I feel the bumps and want to tear them out, pry them off.

为

Wéi.

When I begin tracing the third character, there's blood beneath my nail. I watch the trail of red seep out from the confines of my skin and a part of me is horrified, wants to stop, knows I'm in a public place, knows this is an awful idea. Knows I'm only hurting myself. But I can't stop.

The door bursts open and I jump, trance broken. Quickly, I yank down my sleeve to cover my wrist.

The woman who walks in has a librarian's name tag. She startles when she sees me. I feel frazzled and probably look like a mess, with my torn sleeve and bloody fingernails.

She steps toward me, reaching out a gentle hand. "Are you okay? Do you need help?"

I'm going to help you, Lia.

I'll make sure you get help.

"No!" I practically scream before I run past her, shoulder bumping her in my haste. She stumbles and reaches out a hand to catch herself, but I'm already out the door.

What's wrong with me?

I can't stop seeing echoes of my past.

A hand closes around my wrist. I yank it away. Is it the librarian? Did she come back out? I turn to yell at whoever has a grip on me.

"Hey, hey. Night! Are you okay?"

I recognize that voice.

"Dread?" I barely keep myself from sobbing.

He nods. "We need to talk." I've never heard him sound so solemn.

I follow him to a spot between two bookshelves. He looks around, but there's no one immediately within sight. I feel uneasy. Anyone could be listening in on the other side of the shelves.

Dread gulps, fidgeting absently. His shoe scrapes back and forth on the ground.

He's nervous. Why is he nervous? Did he see the face on my screen too?

I bite my lip, staying quiet. A minute passes. Two. Finally, he speaks.

"My sister almost died." He looks at the floor.

"Oh," I say, startled. "Is she all right?"

"She is now. But she wasn't. She thought she had everything under control. Thought the pain helped her keep it manageable. Just a little bit of release, letting out her sadness one slash at a time." He looks at me. "But it doesn't work that way. It's a destructive cycle. It gives you a temporary sense of control, but it's an illusion. You're left with less. And you risk destroying yourself. You risk death."

And that's when I realize what's going on.

He thinks I did this to myself.

I want to laugh almost as much as I want to cry.

I've always known someone might see my scars despite the precautions I take. I told myself I'd let people believe it was self-harm. It's the easiest explanation.

I need Dread to believe he's right. That way, he won't ask probing questions about my past.

So why does it hurt so much that he bought my unspoken cover story?

"It's not like that."

He gives me a sad look. I shrug, reminding myself I need him to believe.

"Don't take that risk. Every single time, you risk going too far. Leaving your friends and family behind," he says. "You don't deserve the hurt. And life, living, is worth it. There are people who love you."

A harsh laugh nearly escapes my mouth.

People who love me.

Who is that, exactly?

Instead, I nod. "Thanks. For telling me about your sister." Then I swallow and add, "You're not going to tell anyone about this, right?"

He gives me a long, searching look. "It shouldn't be shameful, you know. Depression lies. It's not your fault."

You've got that right.

"I know."

Dread sighs. "I won't say anything for now. But we should have another talk when this is all over, don't you think?"

I give him a wan smile. "Sure."

———————

It takes us two more tries to succeed in our mission. The first time, Rock gives his target the wrong answer, getting us all killed, and we pore over his dialogue choices as a group before we decide on one we think will work. Thankfully, the next time it does work, and everything goes smoothly.

I stab my target with the poisoned dagger and watch as she dies a slow, convulsive death. When she's still, I loot her, then grab a nearby cloth and cover her face.

We bring the looted items to Cíxi as a group, handing them in one by one, like we're supplicants making an offering. I'm the last to turn in my proof of kill, handing over a bejeweled dagger. It's the same one my target stabbed me with several rounds ago.

The same unpleasant, knowing smile lurks on Cíxǐ's face as she drops the four quest items into a vase, then pulls out another orb. Like the previous level, she uses it to break another one of the chains wrapped around Ethan's body. Two left to go. Then she gives us our rewards: a key to the underground complex beneath the palace, a schedule of the guards, and another wooden box.

Syl inspects the schedule and key. "Looks like the shift changes at eight p.m. A bribed guard will look the other way when we use our key."

"That must be our next level," Rock says.

I hold my breath as Syl clicks on the box. Like last time, the screen buzzes into static before a new video appears.

Instead of a mail room, this video shows a computer in a generic office cubicle.

"Anyone recognize the location?" Syl asks.

None of us do.

Dread taps his foot as we wait. The computer turns on as if by magic.

"Cixi must be using a remote desktop client." Rock sounds tense.

As we watch, an email program opens on the screen. I lean closer to see if I can read anything.

"Uh, cuz?" Syl says.

Dread's strangled sound tells me he recognizes the name.

Vanessa Hunt's Inbox

We watch as Cíxǐ remotely opens the draft folder, selecting an email that's scheduled to send automatically at 8:00 tonight. She deletes the email, then clears the trash.

Dread sighs in relief. "I guess we succeeded in stopping Cixi from framing my mom."

My jaw tightens. Next to me, I see Syl's shoulders stiffen. I want to be happy for Dread, but this means the remaining two threats are Syl's and mine.

"That was tame," Rock says.

I take a deep breath, reminding myself this is a good thing. We've solved both levels so far. We'll solve the next two also. I turn to look at Dread, reminding myself to focus on his relief instead of my own worries.

Through my headset, I hear a loud, frantic noise, like a fan speeding up. I turn to look, wondering if my laptop is glitching, but the sound isn't coming directly from my computer. Through the video, I watch in horror as application after application opens on Vanessa Hunt's computer. It grows louder and louder, like it's working impossibly hard.

"Shouldn't it shut down automatically or something?" Dread says.

"It should," Rock says. "Cixi must have found a way to override any fail-safes built in."

As we watch, the computer starts to short out. Then we hear the sharp sound of something sizzling and breaking inside the computer case. There's a static sound before the monitor goes blank.

"How much do you want to bet she'll need a new work computer?" Dread sounds glum.

"Cixi shouldn't have been able to do that," Rock says. "It's not just a matter of skill. Destroying a computer remotely like that isn't possible without direct tampering. Dread, that means she's visited your mom's workplace. *In person.*"

Dread's eyes widen.

"Hey, that means your mom might know something about

Cixi!" Syl says. "What's Aunt Vanessa doing right now, cuz? We should go talk to her."

"Meanwhile, I'll be off doing the last few things on my mum's chore list so I can earn some game time tonight," Rock grumbles. "Being grounded is the worst. See you all at eight." He signs off.

Dread turns toward me and Syl. "Mom's probably home."

"Night, want to come with us?" Syl asks. "Aunt Vanessa is cool. You can be our excuse to ask her about work. You could be interested in her field or something."

Three days ago, there's no way I would have turned down an offer to meet a member of Syl and Dread's family. But now that we've completed the level, my mind keeps going back to what I found out earlier.

Ethan hired Sloan to follow me.

We have a few hours before the next level starts, and I need to do some digging.

I deliberately glance at my phone before replying. "Sorry, can't. Emergency restaurant shift. My coworker is sick."

"Aw." Syl sounds disappointed.

My heart clenches. "Text the group if you find anything out?"

"We will." Syl and Dread head out while I take my time packing up.

When they're gone, I take my computer and backpack. Instead of heading down the escalator, I go up to the next floor and find a smaller table in a distant corner. Then I open my laptop back up, type *Ethan Wainwright* into the search bar, and press enter.

CHAPTER 32

One Year Earlier

I studied Helen as she explained a complex equation. For two years, we'd spent practically every weekday together. She was smart, organized, and well prepared for our lessons. If I didn't understand something, she'd explain in different ways until it clicked. She was endlessly patient, and she cared about me.

Helen Huang was the most consistent person in my life. I trusted her more than anyone.

Xiāng yī wéi mìng.

Guilt twisted my stomach. I wasn't supposed to trust anyone more than Mom.

But . . . shouldn't it go both ways? Mom didn't trust me with anything. I still didn't even know what she did for a living.

Don't you know, though?

I rubbed my eyes. Thoughts like these were why I'd been unable to sleep yet again.

It was August 9.

Helen set the dry-erase marker down. "Lia, is something going on? Your concentration seems broken lately."

Tell her.

No, you can't betray Mom.

"I didn't sleep well."

"Is something bothering you?" Her concerned eyes looked into mine.

I couldn't tell her. All I had were theories, assumptions.

How much proof do you need?

"Lia?"

"Have you heard of Lucas Arnold?" My question came out blunt, abrupt. I was so tired.

"Uh . . . yes. That name sounds familiar. A politician, I think?" She frowned. "Wasn't there something in the news about him?" She typed something on her laptop.

I watched her confusion transform into shock, and my stomach knotted with dread.

I knew what she was going to say.

"Awful news. He died yesterday."

He died *yesterday.*

Lucas Arnold, August 8.

I couldn't believe it. Wouldn't believe it. Mom would never . . .

I know how you get your money, little sister.

A choked sob escaped my throat. And then Helen's arms were around me, and I was breathing in the citrus scent of her shampoo, and I was crying; I couldn't stop crying. Helen had never hugged me before.

"It's okay, Lia. Whatever is going on, it's okay."

"It's not okay." The words came tumbling out. "I think Mom *murdered* him. She has a book of names in her office, and I looked them up and they're dead, they're *all dead*, and I have an aunt Mom never told me about who visited and threatened her and Mom says she works for the government but she won't tell me what she does or how we have money and . . ."

I was so tired of hiding away, so tired of keeping secrets, *so very tired.*

". . . I think she gets paid to kill people."

I felt dizzy with the release of everything I'd been keeping in, wild with guilt and worry and relief. Helen gave me one more reassuring squeeze before letting go.

The full horror hit me as I gazed into Helen's brown eyes.

I'd broken my promise to Mom.

I'd told someone something I should've kept secret.

And I couldn't tell if I regretted it.

"Mom is going to hurt more people," I whispered. "Or she's working with someone who will." Now that the words were out, what Mom had done felt even more monstrous. "You have to help me do something about it. Please."

Helen had never been this quiet before.

She looked at me for a long moment, her eyes full of sympathy.

Finally, she nodded. "I'm going to help you, Lia." She reached out both hands and rested them on my shoulder. "I'll make sure you get help."

CHAPTER 33

Sunday, 4:00 p.m.

I need to understand what connects me to Ethan. I'd never met him before Friday, and he pretended he'd only heard of me through Rock. But he hired a PI to follow me more than a year ago, and that PI is still following me now.

I pull out my sketchbook and begin doodling a timeline of Ethan's life using his Wikipedia entry as a guide. It's my first time reading about him directly rather than relying on my friends' second-hand info. Taking notes feels like taking control of the situation. If I write it all down and stare at the facts, they must form a shape, somehow.

He grew up in Seattle, the youngest of three children born to Edith and Richard Wainwright. He attended UW, where he majored in computer science. He met Yumei Li in class, and then started dating her sister, Kaiwen Li.

I stop short.

Kaiwen Li.

I've only ever heard of one other Kaiwen.

I stare at her name again. Her last name isn't the same as mine or Mom's, but her first name is unusual in the United States.

Ethan's ex-wife has the same, rare first name as my aunt.

Chills creep along my spine, and I keep reading.

Ethan and Kaiwen got married and had a baby, Brooke Madeline Wainwright. Brooke was eight months old when she and her aunt, Yumei, died from a fall off Rattlesnake Ledge.

Next to the entry for Yumei's and Brooke's death, I draw the view from the top of Rattlesnake Ledge. They died in January. Was it snowy or icy that year?

Ethan went into isolation for just over a year to mourn. Then he announced the project he'd been working on: Seamless Server Tech. Shortly after, he sold SST to Thinkly for a huge sum. He stopped programming and started investing in tech startups. He and Kaiwen got divorced. After eight years, Ethan sold most of his investments and founded Apocalypta Games. The company developed *Darkitect* for four years before releasing it publicly.

I end with things that aren't in the article. On Thursday, an NPC that looks like Ethan showed up dead in my *Darkitect* game. The next day, he was murdered IRL at Apocalypta HQ and everything went to hell.

I sit back, studying the timeline. I'm not sure what to make of it. The only new piece of information is Kaiwen's name. I don't have anyone to brainstorm with this time, but I can still run scenarios, like Syl did earlier.

Option one. It's coincidence. Kaiwen Li, Ethan's ex-wife, is not the same person as Kǎiwén, my aunt. In that case? Nothing changes. I still have no idea where to begin.

Option two. It's not a coincidence. Somehow, they are the same person. Where does that leave me?

My real name is Lia Tang and Mom's name is Jade Tang. My aunt's name is Kǎiwén. I had assumed Kǎiwén shared our last name, but I don't know for sure.

So . . . is it possible that she's Kaiwen Li?

There's a lot of reasons adult sisters might have different surnames. What if Kaiwen Li is the same person as my aunt Kǎiwén?

If so, she has two sisters: Jade and Yumei.

Which means I have a second aunt.

When Kǎiwén confronted Mom a year ago, she was angry about how they hadn't talked in years. What if Mom blamed Kǎiwén for Yumei's death? Had Kǎiwén been the one to suggest Yumei take baby Brooke on a hike that winter?

Ethan had divorced Kǎiwén after Brooke died too.

What if both Mom and Ethan had blamed Kǎiwén for the deaths?

There's only one person who might be able to tell me what happened back then. The person I came to Seattle to find, but never did.

It's time to start searching for Kǎiwén again. At least this time, I have the right last name.

CHAPTER 34

One Year Earlier

Helen put me to bed, promising that when Mom returned, she'd explain that I wasn't feeling well. I tried to sleep, but every time I closed my eyes, I imagined a twenty-two-year-old woman being kidnapped. A man pushed off a boat, drowning in the ocean.

Finally, I drifted off. When I woke, the delicious aroma of soy sauce and garlic filled the air. I followed my growling stomach downstairs.

The sun was beginning to set, and Mom held a big metal spatula. She stirred noodles, veggies, and tofu around in the wok. When she heard me step into the kitchen, she turned and smiled.

"Lia, you're awake. Just in time." Steam billowed up, leaving her face dewy.

I looked into the face I knew so well. She had wide cheeks that made her look sweet, almost cherubic. Her long hair was clipped up, held in place by a jade-green hair claw. There were faint freckles on her cheeks, the hint of lines on her neck. She had sharp, perceptive eyes and a small button nose, just like mine.

I tried to find signs that she was ruthless. That she hurt people. I knew I should be afraid, but she was just . . . Mom.

"I wasn't feeling well. Dinner smells good."

"It's almost ready." Mom's gaze lingered on my face just a moment too long. The flip of her spatula seemed almost . . . angry.

I was imagining things. I tried to relax as I set the table.

Mom and I sat opposite one another at the dinner table, eating noodles. We sometimes ate in silence, the way you do with people you see every day. Often, nothing has changed since you last saw them.

Sometimes, everything has changed.

I sipped my tea. It was burning hot. I blew, cooling it before the next sip.

"Did you sleep well?"

I nodded.

"Good, good." She watched me take another sip. The teacup was small. I drained it. She poured me more, smiling.

Something about her movements was strange, but my mind was too sluggish to pinpoint why.

I ate more noodles and washed them down with tea. "I might go to bed early."

"Good idea. I don't want you to feel unwell on your birthday tomorrow. I have something special planned for us."

She smiled.

A terrible part of me wondered if I could just forget about all of it. I could tell Helen it was a mistake. Now that I'd spoken the words aloud, I couldn't remember why they'd felt so urgent. What did I know, anyway? I hadn't even seen anything. Just a few names on a notebook and some articles.

The room felt wavy. My head felt like it could float away. Take off and balloon into the sky.

"It's all going to be okay," Mom said.

I looked at her, confused. What would be okay?

"Go to sleep, Lia."

I wasn't in bed, though.

Mom stood. My eyelids were too heavy. And suddenly, so was my head. No longer floaty and light. Mom cleared away my dishes. I lay my head down, cheek against the cold marble tabletop, smooth and polished and inviting.

Mom was behind me now, her hands on my shoulders, kneading. Rubbing my back.

My eyelids shut.

Mom loved me.

Everything was going to be okay.

CHAPTER 35

I run a photo search for Kaiwen Li and every form of her name I can imagine. Kai Wen Li. Li Kaiwen. A few intentional misspellings. The result is a plethora of photographs. Most show a shirtless male wrestler who must share her name, and the rest are various Chinese people of different genders.

I save all photos that could possibly be my aunt, but I really have no way to know which one she is, if any. None of them are listed as living in Seattle. None of them seem to have any connection to Ethan Wainwright, Yumei Li, or Jade Tang. None of them look like the woman in *Darkitect*.

I try a general web search next, and this time I find something promising. It's a simple website, listing a Kaiwen Li as a makeup artist at Emerald Artistry. When I see *Emerald*, hope rises in me. Emerald as in Seattle, the Emerald City? I click on their website.

Twenty minutes later, I'm on a bus to Capitol Hill.

My leg won't stop jiggling and the person sitting across the bus aisle glares, but I can't help it. If I'm right about Kaiwen, I'm about to meet the only other family I know about, other than Mom.

The salon is tucked between a bar with a huge rainbow flag out front and a used bookstore that looks like it's been around for a century. A cat stares at me through the window.

Emerald Artistry is loud and busy, filled with the buzz of blow dryers and chatter of conversation. The air is thick with scents that make me think *eucalyptus* or *fresh rain*. On one side of the open room, stylists apply dye, cut hair, and style updos with heat tools that look like torture devices. On the other, makeup artists with palettes apply various cosmetics to clients' faces. A few of the stylists glance over as I walk in, offering me half smiles before turning back to what they were doing.

I study their faces, but my heart sinks when I realize none of them look remotely East Asian. It's just my luck, coming all the way out here only to find that Kaiwen isn't in today.

A woman with exquisite makeup and long, wavy locks sticks her head out of a side door. "Be with you in a minute!" she hollers.

I scan the business card display, looking for Kaiwen's name.

"My apologies." The lady ties her apron as she comes out to greet me. "I'm Cathy. How may I help you?"

"I'd like to make an appointment with Kaiwen, one of your makeup artists."

Cathy's tone turns curt. "Unfortunately, Kaiwen no longer works here. Lars has several openings this month, though. Would you like to book an appointment with him instead?"

Disappointment claws my insides, but I've come too far to leave without finding out more. "I got a recommendation for Kaiwen from a friend. I really want her to do my makeup. It says on her website that she works at Emerald."

"Yes, we've contacted her to change it, but she still hasn't."

"Do you know where she's working now?"

"No idea." I can tell Cathy has dismissed me already. Without the promise of business, she wants to hurry me out the door.

"Please? I'd really appreciate it."

Cathy sighs. "I don't like to speak ill of anyone, but if you're looking to hire Kaiwen, I feel obliged to let you know we didn't part under the best terms."

"What do you mean?"

"I won't get into it all, but she was never all that reliable. She's a great makeup artist and she has this charming quality . . . well, people just loved her. But after the fourth time she was a no-show for an appointment, I was this close to firing her and then, surprise! She stops coming in altogether and never bothers to let me know. I'm sorry to say I have no idea where she works now, but I promise you we have a team of three reliable makeup artists here. I'd be happy to book you an appointment with any of them."

"I see. I'll have to think about it and let you know."

"Sure. Have a good day." Cathy goes back into the other room.

I turn to leave, frustrated by yet another dead end. I'm about to reach for the door when I notice one of the stylists looking at me. Her red hair is in an intricate fishtail braid and her waterfall earrings swish when she turns her head. Through her long lashes, she gives me a *look*. Why is she staring at me? Did she overhear? Does she know something about Kaiwen?

I sit back down, and she looks satisfied. She finishes up her client's hair and hugs them goodbye before coming over.

"I'll walk you to your car," she says.

"I took the bus."

"Then I'll walk you to your bus stop."

Once we're outside and around the corner, where we're no longer visible through the salon window, she turns to me and stops.

"You're not looking to book an appointment with Kaiwen."

I stiffen. "What do you mean?"

She rolls her eyes. "Come *on*. You're looking for her, aren't you?"

I inhale sharply. How does she know that? "Who are you?"

"I'm Emma. I was Kaiwen's best friend."

"Was?" I burst out. "Is she dead?"

"What? No! Who thinks that?" She gives me an odd look. "I mean, we were best friends when she worked here. I've talked to her a few times since she quit, but apparently the friendship meant more to me than it did to her. I was just a *work friend*." She puts air quotes around the phrase. "Anyway, I heard she lives in a big house on Queen Anne now, so I guess she doesn't need stylist friends anymore. No idea how she made that happen. I'm guessing . . . rich lover?"

"Why are you telling me this?" The question leaps from my mouth before I think better of it. I curse myself.

"Oh, come on." She smiles. I have the distinct feeling that I'm missing something major. "You're a stubborn one, but I know your secret."

My insides chill, and I'm tempted to ask, *Which one?* Instead, I shake my head.

"Girl, I don't know you, but I *know* you're related to her. You look just like her."

On the bus ride home, I stare at the newest entry in my phone. After nearly a year, I have it. Kaiwen's phone number, and a person who knew her saying I look like her. She really is my aunt.

It's a lot to wrap my mind around.

I tuck the phone away and get off the bus. When I step into

Bette's Battles and Bao, Slate greets me, and I lean down to pet him. He whines, ears back, probably nervous because I've been going out more than usual. I feel awful—with his history, he's likely afraid he'll be abandoned again. "Sorry, pup," I whisper, and he licks my face. I'm scratching behind his ears when I look up to see two familiar faces staring at me.

My heart sinks.

Dread has his arms folded, and Syl looks like she can't decide between anger and hurt.

I stand and try on a smile, but it probably comes out shaky. "What are you two doing here?"

"We got hungry and thought we'd stop by and surprise you, since you *said* you had to work," Syl says.

There isn't a single spark of laughter in either of my friends' eyes. They haven't accused me yet, but . . . this is where I'm supposed to fill in an explanation. Maybe an apology.

"I'm sorry." I mean it. I *am* sorry I lied. I'm also sorry I'm about to lie again. "This whole situation was just getting to be too much for me."

"You could have told us that." Syl's indecisive mood has slipped decidedly into hurt. I almost wish I could push it back the other way. Sometimes, it's easier to let people be angry with you than to let them down.

"I know. I just . . . felt like a jerk when you were both working so hard to solve the case. I felt guilty running off just because I need some alone time."

They still look unhappy.

"I shouldn't have done that. But I got some space and feel better now. Also, I have some information you'll both be interested in. Please don't hate me?"

Syl sighs and scoots over, patting the booth, and I slide in next to her. "Of course we don't hate you. We just want you to talk to us. You know you can tell us *anything*, right?"

Her eyes probe mine, and I look away first. Something about her gaze and the way she says *anything* makes me think of the secret scars on my wrist. Is she being nice, or does she know something? I glance at Dread, who shakes his head slightly. He didn't tell her.

"Yeah, I mean, I know you're newest to the group," Dread says. "But we care about you. I thought you knew that."

"I do. I'm sorry."

"We'll forgive you if you tell us what you found," Syl says.

"I talked to someone who knows Ethan's ex-wife."

"What?" Syl's eyes practically bug out.

"I thought you said you wanted to do something other than work on the case." Dread's tone turns hostile again.

"I did. But then I was browsing my phone on my way downtown. I ended up finding Kaiwen's website, which listed her workplace. A salon on Capitol Hill."

"Wait, did you *go* there?" Syl asks.

"Yeah, but she doesn't work there anymore."

Syl looks disappointed.

"One of the stylists knew her, though. She told me they've talked on the phone, but Kaiwen seems snooty now that she quit the salon and lives in a big mansion on Queen Anne."

"Hm," Syl says. "I wonder if Kaiwen owns the house. If so, the purchase would be public record. We could find her address and talk to her!"

I shift nervously in my seat, wishing now that I hadn't said anything. "We can't do anything to make her suspicious. What if she tries to contact Ethan?"

"We've talked to a few people without anyone getting suspicious. We'll be smart about it." She turns to Dread. "Do you think Uncle Zach would help us?" To me, she adds, "He's a Realtor."

They start talking family politics, completely losing me. As they talk, I imagine Aunt Kaiwen answering the door to her mansion in the posh Queen Anne neighborhood. She'd be charming, impossibly glamorous, perfectly made up, and delighted to see me. Maybe she'd tell me about her childhood. What it was like growing up with Mom and Yumei. She'd have an extra room I could stay in and a cool pet, like a snake or something.

I wonder again if I made a huge mistake running away. Aunt Kaiwen asked to see me. Would I have met her if I'd stayed?

But I *had* to leave.

I close my eyes again, shivering as the memories wash over me. Overhearing Mom and Aunt Kaiwen. Sneaking into Mom's office. Asking Helen for help.

Everything that came next.

CHAPTER 36

One Year Earlier

"Hello?" I called out. There was no response.

It's my birthday. Nothing bad can happen on my birthday.

The thought repeated itself, nonsensically, barely staving off the panic. It was dark, so dark. And I was tied up.

My breath came faster, and my heart felt ready to leap from my chest. Where was I? I squeezed my eyes shut, trying to drown out the darkness by imagining the day I'd been looking forward to. Long-life noodles, homemade birthday cake, and the trip to LA Mom had promised me. Mom telling me she loved me and wishing me a happy birthday.

The image faded, sharp discomfort winning as the ropes cut tight indents into my skin.

I opened my eyes.

"Hello?" I coughed. My throat was dry and irritated.

No response.

I tried to remember the last thing that happened.

I had dinner with Mom. And then . . .

Go to sleep, Lia.

No. Mom would never drug me or tie me up. She would never hurt me.

Just like she would never kill anyone.

"Mom?"

A flash of light hit my eyes. I blinked, adjusting. There was a tiny flame moving across a short wick. In the light of the flame, I could just barely make out a face. Two eyes, steady and familiar.

"*Mom?*"

The wick caught fire, and a scent filled the room.

Birthday cake.

In the light of the flickering candle flame, shadows danced across Mom's face. Had she been sitting in the dark this entire time?

"I heard you've been telling tales."

Fear pulsed through me. She *knew*.

Helen must have told Mom what I'd said.

"Do you remember our promise? For your eighteenth birthday?"

"Yes." My throat was tight. "Matching tattoos."

"It seems three years is too long to wait."

"Mom?"

"For your birthday this year, a reminder."

My voice shook. "I'm so, so sorry. I'll never do it again."

She held something up. Its sharp edge glinted in the light of the candle.

"Mom?"

Flames licked the knife.

What was she . . . ?

Mom grabbed my left arm, and I cried out, trying to wriggle out of her grasp.

"Stop," Mom commanded.

I stopped moving, afraid to defy her further, but I couldn't help my tremor.

The knife was still warm as the tip of the blade cut into my wrist.

I screamed as Mom dragged the blade carefully, deliberately across my wrist. One short, horizontal stroke.

Mom sounded calm. "Hold still, Lia. Twenty-nine strokes and all is forgiven."

"Why?" I whispered. I couldn't believe this was happening. "Why are you hurting me?"

A flash of rage crossed her face; an expression I'd never seen directed at me before, and I drew back. Her nostrils flared, and I let out an involuntary cry. I bit my lip, willing myself to stop shaking, to listen to Mom, even as tears leaked from my eyes.

An eternity passed before Mom's breathing evened again. "I taught you better, Lia. Betrayal is a wound that festers. It needs to be cauterized before it spreads. You need a reminder you'll never forget."

I closed my eyes, biting my cheek to keep from shaking, too scared to speak further. I tried not to think about the trickle of blood dripping down my arm.

The tip of the blade sliced into my skin a second time.

CHAPTER 37

"They finally left for dessert and drinks," Rock says through my headset, sounding the way he does when we wipe on a boss after getting their health bar down to 5 percent. "They're that gross couple who does *date nights*. It was a veritable comedy of errors watching them get in the car, then rush back in for an item one of them forgot. *Three times.*"

"Parents." Syl laughs.

Anytime my friends talk about their parents, it's hard not to think about Mom. But I don't want to think about her right now.

Instead, I think of Kǎiwén. Cathy's and Emma's descriptions have brought her to life in a way facts and speculation never could. Kǎiwén is fun-loving, maybe a little reckless. I can imagine her, straight black hair swinging side to side as she rushes back in to grab keys. Her wallet. A sweater for later.

"Did you find out anything from Vanessa?" Rock asks.

"Who's Vanessa?" I ask.

"Dread's mom," Rock says. I'm reminded again that the three of them have known each other for years, while I met them in person for the first time on Friday. When will we know each other well enough that I no longer feel left out of their conversations?

"Yeah, we talked to Aunt Vanessa," Syl says. "Sadly, she wasn't particularly helpful. We couldn't pry too much without letting on that we knew something. Now shush so I can call Dread."

The dungeon key in my inventory flashes green. It's 8:00 p.m., and Cíxǐ's new level has unlocked.

Dread signs on a few minutes late. "Sorry! Lost track of time. We all ready?"

Together, we click on our quest keys. Our base disappears, replaced by a loading screen. Cíxǐ's newest level begins in a dimly lit room that matches the rest of the palace complex.

The Royal Dungeon

This time, we don't have to seek her out. She stands on a dais, Ethan's ghost chained beside her.

"Let's play a game." Her smile is cruel. "These four prisoners will be executed tomorrow at nightfall. Each has pleaded innocence. Your task is to investigate them and report your findings. If I like your answers, you win. If not . . ." Her smile tells us all we need to know.

Cíxǐ presses a lever, and the floor drops out from under us.

NightMar3 makes an *oof* sound as we land on hard ground. It's pitch-black here. Rock flicks on a lantern at the same time that Dread equips his lightsaber.

In the distance, we hear an angry shout. I equip a sniper rifle and look through the scope, trying to make out any shapes in the darkness.

They're on us in an instant, leaping out from the shadows. At first, I think the creature attacking me is a leopard. Then I catch a glimpse of its almost-human face and ox ears, single eye glaring as it swipes at me. The name above its head reads "Zhujian."

I hit the creature with the butt of my stun gun, then quickly switch to my scimitar. It shouts and sinks its teeth into my leg.

"Hey! It stole my taunt," Dread says.

"Syl, can you CC?" Rock asks.

"Yeah." Syl's crowd-control spell misses. Instead of being lashed in place, it heads straight for her. She tries to dodge, but it's *fast*. Its paw catches her leg and drags her in.

Without his taunt, Dread is unable to pull aggro, and the Zhujian won't stay focused on him.

Before Rock can heal Syl, the mobs swarm her, and she dies quickly.

"Focus damage." Rock marks one with a skull symbol. Dread and I kill it.

"Watch out for the three-second cast where they glow slightly purple," Rock says. "That's when they steal abilities. And be careful. This mob took my main heal."

"Got my taunt back!" Dread says.

With his move back, he's able to pull aggro. The remaining mobs turn to focus on him.

"Wish I could AoE them down," Syl says.

There's a faded ghost icon of Syl's character hovering next to my health bar at the top of the screen. I smile. After twenty seconds as a ghost, players have the option of watching one of their teammates' screens, the way an esports spectator might watch their favorite team play. She chose to watch me.

I feel more aware of her eyes on my screen, but I try to play the way I normally would.

Finally, we defeat them. One drops a *Guide to Washington Trails*.

After Rock resurrects Syl, we all heal up and move farther into the complex. The next few trash mobs drop several quill and ink sets. Then we enter a narrow hallway, where cries and wails emanate from somewhere up ahead. Even though it's just a sound effect, the wails make the hairs on the back of my neck stand up. They're followed by a scream.

We all have our weapons ready as Dread opens the door at the end of the hall, revealing a cavernous square chamber. As we enter, red eyes turn toward us. Four demonic creatures bound out of the darkness, carrying what appear to be bloodied weapons of torture in their hands. Despite their sinister instruments of torture, they're not too hard to defeat, and soon we've killed all four. Each of them drops a blank scroll.

"I suppose we use the quill and ink sets on these blank scrolls," Rock says.

"Looks like it," Syl says. "When I apply it to the scroll, it gives me a text box I can type into. This must be how we complete the quest. I guess we're supposed to write up whether each prisoner is guilty or innocent and why."

"So . . . Cixi gave us homework. It's an essay question," Dread says.

"Which makes me wonder: How will she be grading it?" Syl asks.

"I think this would have to be checked manually," Rock says.

"Ooooh, can we figure out how Cixi is reading it?" Syl asks.

"Not unless I have access to Apocalypta's network traffic system," Rock says. "And someone who's been able to orchestrate this whole game likely knows how to mask their IP address."

"Oh." Syl sounds disappointed.

While they talk, I wander around the chamber, holding a lamp.

In one corner, there's someone shackled to the ceiling with a name painted on the wall above them. "Found one of the prisoners. Someone named Leo Anden."

"Huh," Syl says. "That sounds familiar."

"This corner has another prisoner," Dread says. "Yumei Li."

"What?" Syl and I say at the same time.

Yumei Li.

My dead aunt.

I abandon Leo Anden and run straight toward Dread. The hum of his lightsaber gets louder as I approach the figure shackled to the wall beside him. Her arms hang limp from the chains and her knees barely rest on the ground. The blue light of Dread's weapon colors her skin oddly.

But it's not her sallow skin, the blood dripping from her mouth, or the unnatural angle she's crumpled in that makes my breath catch.

It's when Yumei looks up, straight into my eyes, like she can see me through the screen.

I know those lines beneath her eyes, the unevenness of her eyelids, and her thin, sharp eyebrows. I recognize the beauty mark on her cheek.

For fifteen years, I spent every day looking at this face.

CHAPTER 38

One Year Earlier

I lay in bed. I was blank. I was nothing.

I turned to look out the window. To watch the gray clouds inch across the sky. To distract myself.

But my arm kept throbbing, demanding attention.

The door opened, and I sat up, wincing at the pain.

Mom gave me a sympathetic look that confused me. She set a tray on my nightstand and sat next to me on the bed. I tensed, pulling away.

Mom leaned to hug me, and I made myself small.

Helen had hugged me too.

Gentler than I'd ever known she could be, Mom laid my arm across her lap, turning it to expose my wrist. I knew I should be afraid. But this felt like *Mom* again. The mom I knew. Whoever she'd been in the basement was gone.

Mom took a washcloth from the tray and dipped it into a clear basin of water. She smiled at me, her voice soft and kind. "I loved you from the moment I laid eyes on you, Lia. I knew you'd be my good girl."

I shrank as she wiped away the blood around my cuts ever so carefully.

"One setback doesn't have to change things. I know children test their parents. You tested me, and children must be punished. That's how it was for me when I was growing up too."

Tears sprang to my eyes, and I wiped them away with my right arm. My good arm.

She was quiet as she carefully cleaned my cuts, dipping the cloth back in the basin several times. The water turned red.

"I don't enjoy punishing you. It hurt me as much as it hurt you."

I swallowed hard, trying to believe her. Wanting to believe her. Knowing I shouldn't believe anything she said. Hating her. Loving her.

Mom pulled up her sleeve and I drew in a breath at the sight.

Cut into her wrist were the same four characters as mine, her wounds just as raw.

相依为命.

We matched.

"When you hurt, I hurt, Lia. You did this to us when you told Helen those lies about me."

"I'm sorry, Mom." Confusion twisted me in knots as I stared at her wrist. I couldn't stop staring. She'd hurt me, but she'd hurt herself too. Did that mean she was right? Was it my fault? I had hurt us. I had broken my promise. "I'm sorry. I'm so sorry. I'll tell Helen I was wrong."

"There's no need. Helen will be *taken care of.*" Something in her expression scared me. I thought of the names in the notebook. "All is forgiven now, Lia. If you ever forget again, you have a reminder to look at." She clasped my hand in hers, connecting our newly marked arms. "Soon, you'll have a new tutor, and we'll never have to speak of this unpleasantness again."

January 23

RATTLESNAKE LEDGE CLAIMS TWO LIVES

By Chia Lovato
Seattle Times Staff Reporter

NORTH BEND—A Redmond woman and her eight-month-old niece died yesterday after falling several hundred feet off Rattlesnake Ledge in North Bend.

According to King County deputies, Yumei Li, 24, was hiking with her baby niece, Brooke Madeline Wainwright, early in the morning. Leo Anden, 25, witnessed the fall.

"I like to get in early before the hordes of hikers arrive. So, it was surprising that a woman was already there with her baby in one of those baby packs. I was inwardly wincing because they were pretty close to the edge and the baby was kicking its feet wildly and I just thought . . . what if they slipped? They were pretty far away, so I didn't say anything because I was afraid I'd startle her and then they'd fall. Then when it did happen, it was really surreal.

"I ran up, but of course it was too late already, and I didn't want to get too close to the edge—I mean, I just saw someone fall! When I finally picked my jaw up off the floor, I checked my cell phone, and there was no reception, so I ran down the mountain until I had reception. I didn't know if anyone could survive that fall, but I wasn't about to be the person who let someone die because they were too slow. The whole time I was running I just kept thinking about that baby, kicking its little feet."

Deputy Francesca De Rossi from the King County Sheriff's Department was the first responder to Anden's call. "I was in the area already, so I was first on scene. Unfortunately, the fall was lethal upon impact for both woman and child. This is not the first time Rattlesnake Ledge has led to fatalities. It's a beautiful spot, but it can also be incredibly dangerous."

Li and Wainwright's family are devastated. While Brooke's parents declined to comment, we spoke with Cynthia Wainwright, the baby's aunt. "It's still hard to believe my baby niece and Ethan's sister-in-law could be gone, just like that. We'll be looking into advocating for better signage on Rattlesnake Ledge and improved education on the dangers of local trails."

CHAPTER 39

That face.

It's Mom.

Yumei Li is *Mom*.

Either that . . . or Cíxǐ is messing with me.

Yumei *can't* be Mom. Mom's name is Jade Tang.

And Yumei Li is dead. She died on Rattlesnake Ledge forever ago along with her niece, Brooke Wainwright.

I stare at my screen.

Of course, if Yumei was Mom and Kǎiwén's sister, it would make sense that she and Mom look alike.

It's just . . . Yumei looks *exactly* like Mom. She even has the braid Mom often wore when I was young, before she cut her hair shorter. And that expression on her face.

"Who's Yumei?" Rock asks.

"She's Kaiwen's sister," Syl says.

"Wait, did you say Kaiwen?" Rock says.

"Yeah," Syl says. "Ethan's ex-wife."

"Her name is Kaiwen? I think I've met her!"

"What?" Syl and Dread both say.

"She came to dinner at my house once. Maybe . . . a year or so ago? Ethan introduced her as his girlfriend."

"Why didn't you say so earlier?" Syl asks.

"I never heard any of you say her name aloud." Rock sounds genuinely shocked, and I realize how many of our conversations he's missed out on, thanks to being grounded.

"Did we know they were still in contact?" Dread asks.

"Nope," Syl says.

Thoughts spin through my mind. Ethan and Kǎiwén were dating again a year ago.

Right around when she showed up at Mom's.

"Damn. Well, Yumei was Kaiwen's sister. Yumei was the one who took Ethan's daughter hiking and fell off Rattlesnake Ledge," Syl says.

"The next prisoner is Francesca De Rossi," Dread says.

"Oh! I know why these names are familiar," Syl says. "They were all in that article I read . . . Let me pull it up."

"The last prisoner is Ethan," Rock says.

"Found the article!" Syl reads the *Seattle Times* article aloud. It mentions the names of all four prisoners in the level, along with details of Yumei and Brooke's fall. When Syl's done, we're all quiet for a moment.

I break the silence. "I guess we're supposed to decide if each of them is guilty? The trail map those mobs dropped earlier must be a clue."

"Yeah," Syl agrees. "I think this is related to the day Yumei and Brooke died. Maybe the question is guilt or innocence in the baby's death?"

Rock sounds contemplative. "Ethan Wainwright, Yumei Li,

Francesca De Rossi, and Leo Anden. The baby's dad, the baby's aunt, the officer on scene, and the witness from the article."

"Why would the two witnesses be guilty?" Dread asks.

"Something happened that day," Rock says. "And the way Cixi has this level set up, we can't just guess by submitting different combinations of guilt and innocence. We need to do some research. Find out the full story."

They don't know that Kǎiwén is my aunt or that Ethan hired a PI to investigate me last year or that Yumei looks like my mom.

Rock is right. To beat this level, we—they—need the full story. And I might be hiding more than one key piece from them.

It's past sunset by the time Slate and I go out for our evening walk. I'm still wearing my headset, connected to my phone instead of my laptop. For the third time in a row, I call the number Emma gave me and listen to Kǎiwén's voice mail message. In her short greeting, Kǎiwén sounds lighter, more playful, and more relaxed than Mom ever was. I leave her a message telling her it's her niece and I need to talk to her. I give her my phone number.

I stop myself from calling a fourth time. Instead, I connect to the team's voice channel via phone app. Slate whines, and I let him drag me to a patch of grass that looks exactly like every other patch of grass but is apparently the perfect place to pee.

Slate seems subdued. I feel horrible about how little time I've spent with him lately.

As my friends talk, I'm only half listening, thoughts pulled in too many directions. Everything I learned about Kǎiwén and Ethan this afternoon.

And Yumei the prisoner, with Mom's face.

Is it possible Mom has—had—an identical twin?

". . . consider what might really have happened that day on Rattlesnake Ledge," Rock says. "Syl, want to run scenarios for us?"

"Sure. Okay, scenario one. Everything is exactly as it seems. Yumei Li, carrying baby Brooke, accidentally fell off the ledge. Leo Anden witnessed the fall as described in his testimony, and Officer Francesca De Rossi happened to be in the area, so she was first on the scene. Ethan was not involved except that he was Brooke's dad."

"In that case, they'd all be innocent," Dread says.

"Unless someone is angry about the baby's death," Syl says. "Someone might blame Yumei for carelessness."

"I hardly think anyone would *want* to fall off a ledge," Rock says.

"Some people might," Dread says.

"Even if Yumei wanted to commit suicide, she'd never take her niece with her." Rock sounds horrified.

"We don't know anything about her," Syl says.

They don't know anything about Yumei. But maybe I do.

I let Slate lead us forward as I force myself to consider. *Is* Yumei Mom? It would mean she didn't really die on the hike. And if she faked her death, then what about baby Brooke?

I swallow hard, remembering what Mom said to Kǎiwén.

I saved Lia from becoming another one of your pawns. She doesn't need you.

Mom believes she saved me from Kǎiwén. Because . . .

No. *No.* It's not possible.

It's *not.*

"Okay, so scenario one is that it was an accident and everyone's innocent," Syl says. "In scenario two, Yumei committed suicide and took Brooke with her, in which case Yumei is the only guilty one. Scenario three: someone pushed them off the ledge."

"Someone like . . . Leo Anden? The witness?" Dread asks.

"Maybe," Syl says. "Does anyone else think he goes into a bit more detail than most people would?"

"I don't know," Dread says. "He did watch people die. Babbling could be a reaction to experiencing shock."

"Maybe," Syl says. "But inexperienced liars tend to overtell, especially if they've spent a lot of time memorizing what to say. A good lie is succinct."

"In that case, Leo would be guilty and the rest innocent," Rock says.

"Can you imagine? Pushing a woman and a baby off a cliff?" Dread says. "I kinda hope that isn't the case. I'd like to keep some faith in humanity."

What if Leo Anden did lie, like Syl thinks . . . but for an entirely different reason? Because his testimony was faked?

What if Yumei and Brooke aren't dead?

Slate whines, startling me out of my thoughts. I start to lead us back, but he gives me mournful, pleading eyes. I look at him, thinking of all the nights he let me fall asleep with my head on his fur, even though huskies overheat fast. He's always there when I need him, and I made a promise that he'd always have a home with me.

I think about how, if I tell my friends everything I know, they'll ask where I live now.

I think about how, if I told them about the restaurant and one of them let it slip, Bette and Jimmy would get in trouble, and Slate and I would be without a home.

I think about how, if I don't tell them what I know and we lose the level, there will be no restaurant to save—or Syl's brother could die.

I have to tell them. I *have* to.

"Scenario four," Syl says. "Leo and Francesca are both in on it. According to the article, she's an officer who just *happened* to be in the area. But what if that was part of the plan? She could've been the lookout, making sure no one saw Leo push Yumei. Then she got the call, arrived on the scene, filed the incident report, and ensured no one investigated too closely."

"You're terrifying," Rock tells Syl.

"Thank you."

That's it. If both Leo and Francesca were in on it, then it *is* possible that they helped Yumei fake her and Brooke's deaths . . . so they could start over under new names.

My heart sinks.

"Night, you still there?" Syl's voice makes me jump. Slate perks up, on alert. I pet him, trying to assure him that everything's fine, even though the truth is, I feel like falling to my knees and screaming at the top of my lungs.

"I'm here." My throat feels tight.

"You okay? You've been quiet."

"Just thinking." I swallow hard, forcing out the words. "Maybe we can all do a video chat in fifteen?"

"Sure, I guess," Rock says. "Why a video call?"

Because I think it would be better if I say it to your faces.

"I just think it would be helpful. We can make it quick."

"Actually . . . I have a better idea," Rock says.

"What?" Syl asks.

"Yesterday, I looked around my parents' home office for info, and I found something I didn't know they had. Can you all sneak out tonight?"

CHAPTER 40

One Year Earlier

"Ten minutes, Lia!" Mom's voice carried up to my room, where I scrambled to finish packing. We were going to LA for the weekend. We were supposed to go last weekend for my birthday, but . . .

I bit my lip, hard. It was over now. Everything was fine. I was fine.

I stuffed my sketchbook and favorite pencils into the front pocket of my backpack. It was already bulging with clothing and toiletries.

"Ready!" I swung my bag onto my shoulder and hopped downstairs. Mom was waiting at the bottom, smiling.

"Lia." She rested her hands on my shoulders, and I tried not to flinch. *She's your mom. She loves you.* "You're growing up now; nearing adulthood. You should have some say in our lives. So, I took your request into consideration. Before we visit Los Angeles, we'll stop by the Venice Beach boardwalk."

She'd actually listened to me?

"Thank you, Mom!"

"Sure. And, Lia, I'm giving you a big responsibility. I'd like you to keep our emergency cash in your backpack."

"Oh!" I unzipped my bag and let Mom tuck the roll of cash into an inner pocket. She trusted me. Maybe things really would be okay now. Maybe Basement Mom was gone forever.

I was relieved to have something other than—

Don't think about it.

—something exciting to fill my imagination. For so long, I'd dreamed of exploring the boardwalk, a quintessential California attraction that I, a Californian, had yet to visit. I wanted to see the artists and street performers. I wanted to dip my toes in the water and walk on the beach. I wondered if Mom would let me try funnel cakes.

Mom thought boardwalks were overcrowded and low class. But she was going to take me anyway. Because she loved me.

I grabbed my flip-flops and headed for the garage.

"Is that what you're wearing out?"

I looked down at the graphic tee I had put on that morning. "Yeah. You said it's hot in LA."

Mom pursed her lips. "Venice Beach is colder than LA."

"Oh. I'll get my jacket." I moved toward the coat closet.

A hand clamped around my wrist and pain shot up my arm.

For a long moment, I didn't dare breathe.

"It would be *better* to wear something with sleeves." Mom let go and eyed me. "Like what I'm wearing."

I looked at Mom. Seeing her cold expression, I stepped back. "But . . ."

"I'm disappointed, Lia. I thought you were mature enough for this trip. Maybe I was wrong. Maybe we should cancel."

Cancel?

She was the one who said to dress for hot weather when she'd told me, a few weeks ago, that we were doing a birthday trip.

A few weeks ago.

Before the basement.

I inhaled sharply as understanding dawned. My wrist throbbed. The cuts that had been healing slowly over the past week felt raw again, like someone had torn them open.

We were going to be surrounded by people. Someone might see things they weren't supposed to see.

Mom wanted me to wear long sleeves.

"I'll change now. I'm sorry, Mom."

As I walked back upstairs to change, I felt her eyes on me.

I wondered if her wrist hurt the way mine did.

CHAPTER 41

We're breaking into Ethan's house.

The four of us walk up to a mansion in a bougie neighborhood. I pass out food prep gloves I took from the restaurant, and we all put on a pair. Rock types into a keypad on the front door—the numerical code he found in his parents' office.

"That doesn't seem very secure," Dread whispers.

"My parents were always bugging Ethan to get a better home security system," Rock whispers back.

The door clicks open, and we step inside.

"Have you been here before?" Syl asks Rock.

"A few times, but he usually came to our house."

Syl locks the door behind us, and I glance around. Ethan lived alone, which means everything we see is an extension of him. No one to compromise with. We're invading his private space.

Everything about him feels different now, with the thoughts racing through my head.

If Yumei Li and Brooke Wainwright started new lives as Jade Tang and Lia Tang, then Ethan is my . . .

I draw in a shaky breath.

I should tell my friends *now*.

First step: get everyone's attention.

I clear my throat, mentally steeling myself.

But Dread's already halfway down the hall. He ducks his head into several rooms, then disappears into one.

"What are you doing?" Syl asks him.

"Bathroom!"

"Wait, won't that leave evidence?"

"I'll flush twice," Dread says, closing the door.

Syl sighs.

"All right," Rock says to me and Syl. "Let's fan out and begin searching."

"We should be methodical about it," Syl says. They start discussing like they're planning a *Darkitect* mission.

Should I wait for Dread to come back? If I wait too long, I'm afraid I'll lose my nerve. But I also don't think I can get the words out twice. Anxiety fills my throat, making it hard to breathe.

They finish discussing, and Rock disappears into another room. Then it's just me and Syl, standing in the foyer.

"Help me search the living room?" Syl says. "This place is freakin' huge!"

I'm relieved when she doesn't wait for a reply. I try to follow her lead, searching through drawers and shelves. My heart isn't in it, torn between worry over how my friends will react when I finally tell them everything and the emotions that keep threatening to pour out when I think about whose house I'm in.

My whole life, Mom told me my dad was dead.

"Hey, I found something!" Dread calls from somewhere down the hall.

Syl heads in the direction of his voice, and I trail behind. We find Dread sitting on the floor of a bedroom, holding a black cloth-bound book.

"Should we get Rock?" I try my best to sound normal.

Syl sits down next to Dread, crossing her legs. "He's working on Ethan's computer. Didn't you hear us talk about the plan?"

I shake my head as I join them on the floor. I look at the cover of the book in Dread's hands. It's printed with simple gold letters.

BROOKE MADELINE WAINWRIGHT

In Memory

This is it. This could be the thing that proves my theory wrong. I hug my knees to my chest.

Dread flips the first page. It's a photo of an impossibly tiny baby with a scrunched, red face. Brooke looks cozy, swaddled in an elephant-patterned blanket.

"She would have been sixteen now," Syl says.

I chew on my lip.

Dread flips another page. This time, a smiling woman holds the bundled baby. Kǎiwén —wearing the same face as my assassination target from *Darkitect*—looks tired but proud.

"Night, she looks kinda like you," Dread says.

I dig my nails into my leg, hard enough to hurt.

In the next photo, Ethan has an arm wrapped around Kǎiwén and Brooke. He's wearing a big, goofy grin.

I feel tears form in my eyes, and I blink them back.

In the next few, Brooke gets older. Her eyes open wider, and her newborn wrinkles smooth out. A onesie that looked huge a few pages back suddenly looks like it'll barely close.

Ten or so pages in, a new face appears, staring intently at baby Brooke.

I recognize the frown on her face, and the downturn of her lips when she's annoyed. The jade bangle on her wrist. *It's Mom.*

Syl says, "That must be Yumei."

Yumei *is* Mom.

And a little scrawl on the page says Brooke is two months old in the photo, so this must have been taken in July that year.

In July, Mom should've been eight months pregnant with me.

Her stomach is completely flat.

I let out something between a gasp and a strangled cry. I can't deny it any longer.

It's me.

I'm Brooke Madeline Wainwright.

"What is it?" Syl touches my arm.

I can't speak. Too many things are rushing through my mind. Kăiwén's words to Mom. *Well, where is she? Aren't you going to invite me in? The girl should know her own . . .*

I'd assumed that sentence ended with *aunt.*

I was wrong.

"Seriously, Night, are you okay?" Dread asks.

"Bathroom," I stammer, and stand up.

I stumble out of the room, past a floating shelf full of designer vinyl figures. I wonder if Ethan—my *dad*—picked every one of these out. Would he have explained each one to me? Told me the story of where he got them and what they meant to him?

He pulled me aside to talk to me in his office on Friday. He had someone following me. He knew I was his daughter. He had to have known.

What happened? Why didn't I grow up in this house with Ethan and Kăiwén? How did I end up with Mom?

I slip into a small bathroom. Inside, I close the door, pull off my gloves, and wash my face, staring at myself in the mirror. Looking for traces of Ethan. I look so much like the pictures of Kǎiwén in that first photo, when she's flushed and happy and bare-faced. Less so in the others, where makeup transforms her.

I feel a sharp sting. The woman I've been calling Mom is my aunt. Kǎiwén is my mom. But I can't stop calling the woman I grew up with Mom, not even in my own head. Not after so many years.

I used to wonder, seeing my hair in the mirror after showering. I'd watch my soggy, wet locks dry into a natural wave, and know my dad probably had wavy hair. Mom would never tell me anything about him.

Now I know why.

Truth is, I'm not sure I can see Ethan in my features. His hair was cut too short for me to tell if it had a wave. And our conversation—the only conversation I'll ever get to have with my dad—was so short. During the tour, I was focused on the building. And when he pulled me aside, I was thinking about my artwork, about how I'd use the money Apocalypta offered me, about how excited my friends would be that I scored us all PAX badges.

I finally found my dad only to squander the chance to talk to him, and then watch him die right before my eyes.

I pound my fists against the sink, hearing the hollow ring of ceramic. It doesn't feel like enough. I want to punch something. Destroy something. Scream at the top of my lungs. Knock over every bottle on the shelf.

Instead, I wash my face again and again, the cold water mixing with my hot tears. It's a long time before I can bear to leave the bathroom.

I can't face anyone yet, so I duck into a bedroom at the end of the hallway. The king-size bed is unmade and it's a primary suite, so it's probably Ethan's bedroom. I open the drawers on his night-stand, but there's nothing interesting inside.

The closet is full of clothing similar to what Ethan wore on Friday. It's organized except for a box of stuff shoved into one corner, piled with clothes and an old pair of shoes. Items to donate, maybe?

I look inside.

The first thing I find is a sealed letter. I tear it open.

I'm sorry. I can't live like this. I can't live without you. I'm sending you back everything you left at my house, so you'll know that I understand why you need space. But I hope you'll move in again, someday. Please talk to me. Please, let's start over. I promise to tell you everything.

—E

Beneath the letter is a red silk nightie. I pull out a heap of makeup and a few outfits, setting them on the floor. Beneath the clothing and shoes, I find a small booklet and peek inside.

A family of three smiles at the camera.

妈妈, 爸爸, 我

Māma, Bàba, Me.

The picture is faded and yellowing, and the hairstyles are definitely outdated, but the girl looks a lot like me when I was younger. I tuck it into my backpack.

Something on the side of the box catches my eye: an address for Kaiwen Li.

Beside Kǎiwén's address, there's a "returned to sender" sticker and a handwritten note, scrawled in Sharpie.

Delivery refused by recipient.

Gently, I peel off the address label and stick it in my backpack.

At least I'll have something tangible to offer my friends. Maybe they'll hate me a little less.

I can't keep avoiding them.

I take a deep breath, get to my feet, and look for them.

I wind through Ethan's house until I hear their voices coming from a room I haven't been in yet. I walk toward the sound.

"Hey, I think you'll want to look at this," Dread says.

Syl gasps. "Oh my God, is that his *will*? Gimme!"

There's the shuffle of papers as Dread says, "Of course, Ms. Future Lawyer. Only you would voluntarily read a bunch of contracts."

"You're just jealous my vocabulary is way bigger than yours."

I keep walking toward the sound of my friends chatting and shuffling through papers. I'm ten feet from the doorway when Syl shouts, "This is it!" Her face lights up. "He's leaving half of his assets to charities. But the rest goes to someone named . . ."

Dread uses his fingers to tap out a drumroll just as I step into the room. He stops, and they both look up at me. Syl sets down the stack of papers she's holding and stands. "Marina, what happened back there? Are you okay?"

I swallow, shaking my head.

Dread's eyes flick to my wrist. "Do you want to talk about it?"

"Yeah." The word comes out quiet and indecisive. I clear my throat and try again. "Yes. I need to tell you—all of you—something."

"Okay." Syl draws out the word. She looks unsure, but her eyes are filled with worry too. I savor her concern, knowing I'm about to shatter her trust in me. She takes my arm. "C'mon. Rock's down the hall."

Syl leads the way, and I follow. Dread walks behind us. Several doors down, we enter Ethan's office. Rock is seated at a desk, working on the computer.

"Hey, Rock," Syl says.

"Hey." He doesn't look up. "Remember that PI, Sloan, who was following us around? I found the files they sent Ethan! They were hired to find someone named Lia Tang."

"That's who Ethan left half his money to in his will!" Syl's voice fills with excitement.

"What?" I say, as the shock of what their words mean hits me.

Rock is still clicking through something on the computer.

"Oh, I mean . . ." Syl looks guiltily over at me. "You wanted to say something to us."

I nod, steeling myself. Taking another deep breath. "I should have told you earlier, but . . . it's complicated. It has to do with my living situation, and anyway . . . the thing is—"

"What the hell?" Rock looks at his screen in disbelief. Then he looks up. His gaze lands on me, and his eyes narrow.

The rest of my rambling words catch in my throat.

When he speaks, his words carry a mix of anger and disbelief I've never heard before. "Bloody hell. Sloan sent Ethan photos of the person they were hired to follow. It's *you*, Marina. Or should I call you *Lia Tang*?"

CHAPTER 42

One Year Earlier

The car ride to Venice Beach took us nearly seven hours.

I spent the entire time thinking about what Mom said before we'd left.

It would be better to wear something with sleeves.

We arrived, and Mom parked. We walked down the boardwalk, Mom making snide remarks about passersby. Sweat seeped into my shirt, plastering it to my arm. I longed to roll up my sleeve, to peel it away from my skin. To look at the pink, bumpy words newly carved into my wrist.

I was finally here. On the boardwalk, belatedly celebrating my fifteenth birthday.

And I wasn't enjoying a single moment of it.

We sat down for an early dinner at a noisy café overlooking the beach. People surfed and splashed in the water. Kids played in the sand. Beautiful palm trees towered above, so picturesque they looked straight out of a movie.

A bored-looking waiter in a bright T-shirt and surf shorts took our orders. After he left, Mom shouted over the music, "Did you have a good day, Lia?"

I nodded, trying to smile back.

"Good. LA will be fun too. You'll love the Huntington Botanical Gardens. We should do more outings like this. You seem mature enough to handle them."

Mature.

I thought you were mature enough for this trip. Maybe I was wrong. Maybe we should cancel.

I took a sip of water to mask my expression, but I choked on an ice cube. Mom gestured for a waiter, looking annoyed when no one appeared.

"I'm fine." I choked out the words.

"There's water all over your shirt. I'll get paper towels from the bathroom." She looked around and disappeared down a corridor.

I was alone.

Before I could think about what I was doing, I got to my feet. Instinctively, I grabbed my backpack before heading for the door.

No one stopped me.

I walked faster.

And then I was outside, breathing in the warm, salty air. There were people everywhere walking in small groups, stopping here and there. I walked fast, like I had someplace to be. Didn't look anyone in the eye.

I wove through the crowds.

What was I doing?

I was almost as giddy as I was terrified.

Mom was going to kill me.

I kept going.

I imagined what Mom would do, feeling a strange mix of contradictory emotions. Fear, delight, concern. Would she think I'd been kidnapped? Could she track me somehow? I'd never been allowed to have a phone. I didn't own any electronics. Everything I used was borrowed from Mom or Helen.

Helen will be taken care of.

Something twisted in my gut when I thought of the way Mom had said it.

She'd done something to Helen. I was sure of it.

If I stayed, maybe she'd *take care of* me.

I walked faster, rolling up my sleeves. I felt the shirt peel away from my skin; drew in a sharp breath at the pain. My wound had torn back open.

What was I doing?

I should go back now. Beg Mom's forgiveness.

I stopped and looked at my wrist. Stared at the words cut into my skin. Twenty-nine painful strokes.

Staying meant never talking about what she had done.

Staying meant agreeing to wear long sleeves to cover up *her* crime.

Staying meant Mom punishing me again, for this.

A rush of fear shot through me at the thought, and the pain in my wrist flared again.

No, no, *no*, I couldn't go back.

But I had nowhere to go, no one to take me in.

A voice drifted into my thoughts, the way it had drifted upstairs, two weeks earlier, to where I'd been hiding in the shadows.

I came all the way from Seattle to see you!

I didn't know my aunt, but I knew one thing.

I couldn't stay here.

I took a deep breath and approached someone, asking for directions to the bus station. They didn't know. Nor did the next person, or the next. Each failed attempt set me further on edge.

Nervousness crashed through me like the ocean waves I could see from the boardwalk. I imagined Mom charging through the crowds of relaxed, happy vacationers.

The thought made me sweat.

I finally thought to ask a street vendor, who pointed me in the right direction. As I turned to leave, a far-off voice called my name.

A chill ran through me. The voice had been distant enough that I couldn't tell if it was Mom. Faint enough that I might have imagined it.

Now that freedom was close enough to taste, the idea of Mom finding me felt unbearable. I wouldn't let her find me. I wouldn't go back.

I took off running.

CHAPTER 43

Sunday, 11:00 p.m.

"What do you mean she's Lia Tang?" Syl says. "Night, what's he talking about?"

"I was trying to tell you, just now." The words come out too fast. Jumbled. "I swear I didn't know how involved I was until tonight, with the album. I mean, I suspected, but I didn't want to say unless I was sure."

"But . . . how exactly are you involved? Or why? I don't even know what to ask!" Syl throws her hands up.

"Yes. Explain, please." Rock glares at me.

I draw in a breath. "So . . . Jade Tang is my mom. Only she's not really named Jade and she's not really my mom." *Wow, good start, Marina.* "I only just realized that she's actually Yumei Li. And, um . . ."

"Oh my God." Syl claps a hand over her mouth. "You're *Brooke*."

"The . . . dead baby?" Rock furrows his brow.

"Right. Only . . . I'm not dead." *Oh my God.* "I mean . . . Yumei and Brooke didn't really die. I think Yumei stole me away from my real parents, Kǎiwén and Ethan."

"Holy shit," Dread says. "Ethan is your dad."

"Cixi's whole game is about *you*, isn't it?" Rock's eyes pierce into mine. "That's the reason we've been sneaking around, breaking laws, and being threatened. Someone is after you."

I know I don't deserve it, but a tiny part of me hopes someone will jump in and say that it's not my fault. But no one says anything. My heart sinks. "I think so." Tears form in my eyes. "I honestly didn't know about any of this at the start."

"But you pieced it together along the way, didn't you?" Rock says. "And you didn't tell us."

"I was going to. I was trying to find the right time."

"We've spent practically every minute together for the past three days." Syl won't look me in the eyes.

"I know, but there are other things I was worried about, and—"

"You lied to all of us," Dread says. "You could have trusted us. We're a team. We're supposed to be in it together."

"I know that! I do trust you." I want so badly to tell them how I ran away a year ago, and why. I want to explain that I couldn't say anything, because then they'd have power over Bette and Jimmy. How the only time I've ever told a secret to someone I trusted, they betrayed me and ruined my life.

I want desperately to tell them everything, to explain all my reasons.

"You don't understand. It's . . . I'm trying to keep people safe. I . . ." I stare into my friends' eyes, looking for some glimmer of understanding that I can latch onto.

Instead, all three of them glare back at me. Everything I say is making things worse.

"I . . ." I try again, but I don't even know where to start.

All this time I've been hiding so much from them. I think of

Rock at Apocalypta HQ, trusting me with his story, his identity. I think of Dread at the library, telling me there are people who love me. I think of Syl's hands on my waist, keeping me steady on the library balcony.

They invited me into their group, made me feel welcome. They've been open with me; they've shown me they care.

And now they know I didn't reciprocate. Now that I've proven I don't trust them, they can't trust me.

My heart sinks. I can't risk them knowing I'm a runaway. I can't give them that kind of power over me.

People do rash, thoughtless things when they're upset.

Some of us run from our problems.

Others do things they can't take back. One of them might decide to tell someone that their so-called friend is a runaway who lives illegally at a restaurant.

My silence hangs thick in the air.

Syl draws in a deep breath that feels forced. "You're Ethan's daughter. That's why he's leaving half of his money to you."

I blink. I haven't even had time to process what that means, let alone what it means for this whole case.

"You really didn't know any of this before?" she asks.

"I found it all out while we investigated. Most of it today. There were some things that didn't add up. When we were in the latest *Darkitect* level, Yumei's face looked a bit like my mom's, and I suspected . . ."

"But you still didn't tell us." Syl's tone is flat.

Rock's still glaring at me. "If this is all because someone is after you, do you know who Cixi is?"

That's when we hear a chime ring through the house.

We freeze, then turn to look at each other, faces full of horror. Someone just rang Ethan's doorbell.

When the doorbell finally stops ringing, we sneak out the back door. On our way to Dread's car, we catch a glimpse of the people at Ethan's door.

It's Rock's parents.

We don't know why they're here, but it can't be a good sign.

We climb into Dread's car. Sitting in the back seat, I wait for the barrage of questions, but everyone's too mad at me to talk. Rock turns up the volume on the music and I stare out the window until Dread drops me off.

After they leave, I walk back to Bette's Battles and Bao.

My hand trembles as I reach the door in the alleyway and jam my key into the lock. Now that I'm alone with my thoughts, Rock's words replay in my mind. *This whole game is about you, isn't it? The reason we've been sneaking around, breaking laws, and being threatened. Someone is after you.*

I know what he really meant. *This is all your fault.*

My fingers fumble. I'm exhausted, and I miss Slate. I hate that I have to spend yet another night without him. I hope he's not too anxious, that he still knows I'd never abandon him. I hope he's able to get some sleep at Bette and Jimmy's.

Finally, I manage to unlock the door and step inside. I weave carefully through the dark kitchen until I reach the back office. I feel the hairs on the back of my neck prickle, and I don't know if it's nerves or if someone is watching me again.

As I get ready for bed, my friends' angry words repeat themselves like the world's worst memory reel. Between that and the way

I keep obsessing over what might have happened between Kǎiwén and Ethan and Mom, I know I won't be able to sleep right now.

I turn on my computer. There's a new file in our team's shared drive. Rock must have uploaded the PI files from Ethan's computer before taking a look.

I open them.

I read Sloan's notes from their trip to San Francisco. They started with Mom's and my old apartment address. The rental unit's owner had a daughter who sometimes babysat me. Sloan spoke with the daughter, who swore she'd seen me and Mom at Lanhua Teahouse recently.

At the mention, I feel a pang of longing. I miss their flaky buns.

Sloan describes their stakeout of the teahouse, how they tailed us home. Our brief conversation when I caught them photographing the house.

As I read, the page begins to blur. I thought I'd be out of tears by now, but I'm not. Ethan—my *dad*—went looking for me.

Sloan found me in July of last year—the month before my fifteenth birthday, when everything changed. When Mom decided she needed to teach me a lesson.

In mid-August, the messages back and forth grew frantic, Sloan trying to calm Ethan down. Because the target had disappeared.

The target.

Me.

I was already on my way to Seattle by then. I left three days before my dad was going to fly to San Francisco to find me.

I have the worst luck.

I read Sloan's interview with Helen from right after she was fired. She seems worried.

And then I read a line that stops me cold.

Helen Huang: Lia is talented at drawing comics. They are beautifully drawn, and they're always adventures undertaken by the same heroine.

Of course. Helen knew I always called my comic heroine Marina Chan.

That's how Ethan knew my new name.

The pieces click together in my mind. When Ethan was at the Mukherjees' house for dinner, Rock told him about a teammate who drew *Darkitect* fan art. Rock must also have told him my name is Marina Chan.

And Ethan connected the dots.

Sloan notes that they tried to follow up again with Helen, but she stopped responding. I swallow hard, wondering—as I often have this past year—if she's okay.

The last thing in the file is a photo—the one Rock must have seen. Me, standing in front of the house where Mom and I lived.

I close the files and turn off the computer, but my mind is stuck in what-ifs. How different would my life be now, if only I'd stayed a few days longer? If only Ethan had flown down earlier?

If only.

I'd thought reading Sloan's notes—getting more answers about my past—would calm my mind. Instead, I feel more agitated.

I want more. I want to know why Kǎiwén threatened Mom, what happened between them. I want all the missing pieces.

I want to understand more about the woman in the photo from the hospital, the tired new mother who looked at me with such love.

I reach into my bag and pull out the scrapbook I stole from the box of Kǎiwén's stuff in Ethan's closet. It's too dark to see, so I look for my phone to use as a flashlight, but I can't find it and I'm too tired to search. So, I reach up to pull the shades open, letting moonlight stream in.

The book is simple and unpolished, but it looks like it was put together with care. Its pages are full of photos, pasted-in cutouts, stickers, and handwritten notes.

At the start, the photos show a family of three—mom, dad, and little girl—in Shanghai. When the girl turns five, they move to California. A year later, a new baby girl shows up.

妈妈，爸爸，我，玉梅

Māma, Bàba, me, Yùměi

Kǎiwén seems to adore her baby sister, holding her tight. I watch them grow up. In one photo, Yùměi looks up adoringly as if her older sister was her entire world. Shortly after the family celebrates Yùměi's ninth birthday, another baby girl appears. There's a whole two-page spread featuring 画兰. Huàlán.

I do a quick calculation. Kǎiwén must be fifteen at this point. She holds baby Huàlán as Yùměi stares at them from the background, looking unhappy. Kǎiwén sprinkles in brief diary entries here and there. Most describe cute baby things Huàlán's done, but a few mention how jealous Yùměi has become. How she's grown annoying, always wanting Kǎiwén's attention when she's busy trying to help their parents with Huàlán.

And then . . . suddenly, the pages turn black.

It takes me a moment to realize it's the same white paper as the rest of the scrapbook, but covered entirely in marker. Layer after layer, like someone pressed a Sharpie into every millimeter of the page.

Frowning, I flip through pages of angry black.

Then there's a big photo of Huàlán, smiling wide with food on her face. Around it, there are little flower stickers and messages handwritten in writing so tiny I can barely read it.

I miss you so much, Huàlán.

I'm sorry. I was supposed to protect you, but I failed.

I love you, Huàlán.

I stop breathing for a moment.

When I turn the page, the tone of the book is different. No more playful, colorful stickers. No cursives, no frills. It's all black washi tape and neat letters.

There are no family photos for a while, only brief notes here and there. When the family does appear again, there are only four of them.

Is Huàlán dead?

I flip to the end. And then I see the phrase.

相依为命. *Xiāng yī wéi mìng.*

I snatch back my wrist, as if someone had pulled the words from my skin and pasted it on the page. When I check the clock on my computer, it's midnight.

It's officially my birthday.

CHAPTER 44

One Year Earlier

I realized I'd started biting my nails again when I tasted something salty and metallic. Wrinkling my nose, I leaned forward on the leather seat to inspect them. The tips were stained with streaks of reddish brown; a reminder that I needed to stop scratching my cuts, or they'd never heal.

My cuts.

The blade, sharp as a needle, piercing my skin.

Blood rushed through my veins, hot and fast, and a full-body shudder racked me. My heart pounded so loudly it was hard to believe all the passengers around me couldn't hear it. The air on the bus had been stale to begin with; now it was stifling, strangling.

I clutched the armrest, desperate to find something for my mind to grab ahold of. Anything to keep thoughts of the basement away.

"Honey, are you okay?" The woman across the aisle took in my features. "Is there an adult with you?"

"I'm eighteen," I muttered. "Excuse me." I grabbed my shark backpack and practically ran to the bathroom.

Inside, I closed the toilet lid and sat, hugging my backpack.

As tears streamed down my face, the bus jostling me each time it hit a bump in the road, I wondered if I should give up.

I hadn't thought this through. How could I possibly navigate the world alone? There were so many little things I hadn't considered. Like the age thing. If anyone found out I'd just turned fifteen, it would all be over. And then . . .

The thought of being sent back sent shivers through me.

No. I couldn't give up. I still had money left, and no one had caught me yet. All I needed to do was find Kǎiwén. I had to keep going.

I wiped my tears. I still felt shaky, but the wave of panic seemed to be subsiding.

While I was alone, I might as well check on my wounds. I couldn't seem to stop picking and scratching at them.

I peeled off the old bandage, hissing in pain as some of the scabs went with it. Using paper towels and the bathroom sink, I cleaned and dried the area as well as I could. As I was applying a new bandage from the emergency first aid kit in my backpack, someone knocked. I finished up quickly and grabbed my backpack.

I opened the door and brushed past whoever had knocked without looking. Don't look at anyone. Don't draw attention. I could do this. I just had to learn the rules, to stay unnoticed until I found Aunt Kǎiwén. It was my only chance forward.

Walking back up the aisle, I glanced at someone's open laptop screen, noting the time. Six hours left; the final stretch. Six more hours until the bus stopped in Seattle, where everything would be different. Six more hours until my new life.

No more looking back.

CHAPTER 45

My sixteenth birthday starts with a rough, wet tongue licking my face. I open one eye. "Slate?"

He breathes directly into my nose, which is gross, but my heart flutters that he's nearby. Then I scramble upright. Slate wasn't here when I finally fell asleep last night.

I look up. "Jimmy?"

The gruff older man eyes me with a frown. "Bette says you slept at friend's house."

"Yeah. I got back early this morning."

Jimmy grunts. "Terrence will be here soon." He leaves.

I put on shoes and stash away my bedding. Why didn't my alarms wake me?

Slate follows me around as I search frantically for my phone. Did I leave it at Ethan's house? Did it fall out of my bag in Dread's car? I might have missed messages from my teammates.

Or maybe they started a new group text without me. After last night, I wouldn't blame them.

I'm not ready to face them, but that doesn't matter. We have another level to beat. Without my phone, there's only one place to check. I log into *Darkitect* and open the team roster. Everyone is offline.

Now what?

I grab a veggie bāozi from the kitchen and take Slate for a walk. It feels weird going out without a phone. Slate's subdued again this morning, walking closer to me than usual. I think of him sleeping on the floor of Bette and Jimmy's for the second night in a row, not knowing it's only temporary. I stop to whisper reassurances that I love him, that he didn't do anything wrong. He cocks his head like he understands, and I wrap him up in a hug.

When we get back to the restaurant twenty minutes later, I check the game again, but everyone's still offline. We need to beat tonight's level before eight. And unlike Cíxǐ's other levels, I don't see a path forward with this one, which makes me nervous as hell.

I'm tempted to stay here and guard against anyone setting the building ablaze, but based on the previous videos, Cíxǐ probably rigged something in advance. Plus, the restaurant is connected to the whole row of small businesses. If one goes up in flames, they all do. I can't singlehandedly search or guard every shop. And no one will take it seriously if I call in a threat unless I reveal how I know, which could endanger Syl's brother. If we tell someone, Cíxǐ might just carry out all the remaining threats.

I really need to talk to my friends—if I can still call them that.

I'm a nervous snacker, so I head to the kitchen to dig around for something, even though my stomach's still full of bāozi. Maybe Syl's right and I am starting to act more like Dread.

Dread.

Today's Monday, which means Dread's at work. I *do* know how to find one person.

I let Slate and Jimmy know I'm leaving, grab my backpack, and head out.

I take the bus and walk the last few blocks to Apocalypta HQ. Inside, I ask the front desk guard to call Andrew Hunt for me. After a few minutes, Dread shows up.

"Let's talk outside," he says, and I follow him out the front door.

As soon as we've left the building, I turn to face him. "Hey, I'm really sorry. About yesterday. About not saying anything earlier. I should have told you all what I found out."

Dread's expression darkens. "Yeah, you should have. Marina, we *barely* beat those first two levels! And you still didn't say anything." He clenches his jaw and kicks the sidewalk. "Be honest. When did you find out you were involved?"

I swallow hard. "That first night. After you dropped me off at home, I signed on." I lower my voice. "Cíxǐ took over my computer with a message for Lia."

"*The first night?*" Dread makes a frustrated sound, and his hands ball into fists by his side.

"I really am sorry."

"Friends are supposed to trust each other. I'm not saying you have to tell us everything." His eyes dart toward my wrist. "But when your silence puts us and our families in danger, you'd better have a really damn good reason for it."

I draw in a breath. "I do. I, um . . . don't live with my mom anymore."

"You mean Yumei?"

"Yeah. But . . . if I tell you about my living situation now, some people who have been very kind to me could get in serious trouble."

"Night, what are you talking about? Are you safe?" Dread's voice is suddenly tense and alert, the anger temporarily gone.

"Yeah, I'm fine. I just don't want to get anyone in trouble."

"Then why didn't you just tell us *that*?"

"Because! I know you'd all be dying of curiosity. You'd want to know more. And you'd want to try to help. But even when people have good intentions, sometimes their *help* is the worst thing possible." I think of the last time I saw Helen, and I have to bite my lip to still the tremble. Despite everything, I miss her. I never got to say goodbye.

Dread chews on this. "Maybe we would try to figure out what's going on with you. But only because we care. And we wouldn't do anything behind your back."

I didn't think Helen would either but look what happened.

I shrug.

Dread shakes his head. "We should talk about all of this later. But I don't want to be late for our meeting with Nina."

"Who?"

"Nina Cohen. Ethan's assistant? The one HR was forming a case against." Dread sees the blank look on my face. "Didn't you read any of the messages this morning? I thought you were here to question her with me."

"I lost my phone."

Dread badges us back into Apocalypta HQ, and we take the elevator to the third floor. I follow Dread down a hallway, past a big open area full of people working. We stop at a door that says "<Error 174>." He peers in through the window.

"Error 174?"

"Development team inside joke. There was this one error that kept popping up." Dread pulls open the door. "Sweet! We're first."

He plops down on a black couch on one side of the small room, across from two beanbag chairs. In the corner, there's a small bookshelf full of graphic novels and video game art books.

"This is a conference room?" I ask, incredulous.

"Yep."

"Beanbag chairs? Really?"

"That's why I picked this room. She'll be stuck in the shorter seat. We'll have the high ground."

I stare at him.

"You know, like Jedi? *Star Wars*?"

I sit next to him. "Never seen it."

"You've . . . what?"

The door opens to reveal a harried-looking woman. I recognize Nina from the photo in her personnel file. Nina looks at Dread, then me, confused. But she relaxes her face into a smile.

"Hi, Andrew." She sits. The beanbag beans crunch as she sinks in. "And . . . I'm sorry, I thought I knew all the interns. You are?"

"Hello, Cíxǐ," I say.

"I'm sorry, your name is . . . Sishee?" Nina turns red, probably because she knows she pronounced it wrong. She turns to Dread. "Andrew, I thought you wanted to talk about a surprise the interns are planning for Ethan."

"Funny you should mention him," Dread says, "when you're working against him."

Nina's lips part in surprise. "What? Why would you . . ."

"We know about your little side hustle. If you don't tell us who you're working for and everything you know about them, we'll go to the police." Dread hands Nina a sheet of paper. He must have taken it from her personnel file.

As she reads it, her face falls, and she slumps. "I know how this looks. But there are things about Ethan that you don't know."

"Then tell us," Dread says.

"Look, I was in a bind. My ex-husband is . . . he . . . was abusive." She swallows.

It feels wrong, pushing her to dredge up bad memories and reveal details of her personal life. But we have no choice.

"No one believed me. He was a charmer . . . at least when other people were around. Anyway. This woman approached me. Said she had a history with Ethan. She didn't even know about my ex, I swear, but I recognized the type when she told me her story. I knew what she was going through. I *had* to help her." She sounds like she's trying to convince herself as much as us.

"Did she tell you her name?"

Nina bites her lip. After a pause, she nods. "Her name is Kaiwen. She used to be married to Ethan, over a decade ago. He hurt her in secret, in places that wouldn't show. One time, in a rage, he . . . he hurt their baby. She couldn't let it happen again." Nina stops to wipe away tears. "Her sister was the baby's nanny. Kaiwen wanted to get out of her marriage, but she knew he wouldn't let her go. Not when they had a child together. So, she and her sister hatched a plan."

"What kind of plan?" I ask.

"Kaiwen's sister took the baby and ran. They found a sympathetic police officer and acquaintance to help them fake their deaths, so that Ethan wouldn't look for them. Kaiwen divorced him a year later."

"So, why would Kaiwen want you to steal information for her now?" Dread asks.

"Because," Nina says, defiance seeping into her voice, "her

sister left in a hurry and she couldn't take anything with her. Not without looking suspicious. She'd been working on a project before it all happened. Ethan found that project and, thinking the sister was dead, claimed it as his own. Kaiwen only found out much later that it was her sister's work he'd stolen. Seamless Server Technology."

With that, she looks up at us, challenging.

My stomach knots.

Professor Park told us Ethan was average. He'd credited Ethan with working hard and learning fast. But wasn't that what everyone always thought about people like Ethan?

Nina claims Ethan stole Yùměi's—Mom's—work and used it to build his entire empire. And that he hurt both of us.

It doesn't fit with the man I met three days ago, but monsters often hide in plain sight. What do I really know about him? How much can people change in sixteen years?

"What does this have to do with you stealing information from Apocalypta?" Dread asks.

Nina sits up straight, which looks ridiculous in the beanbag chair. "I'm helping Kaiwen because it's the right thing to do. She asked me to help her compile information that would expose him. Ruin his reputation."

"And the expensive house you moved to had nothing to do with it?" I say.

Nina turns red. "I told you what you wanted to know. Don't you dare judge me. You think an executive secretary's salary is enough to support me and my child? Seattle has one of the highest costs of living in the nation. Childcare alone eats up almost my entire paycheck. My son shouldn't have to live in squalor. I'll do what I need to for his sake."

"Ethan didn't come into work this morning," Dread says. I try not to show my surprise at his words. "Are you sure Kaiwen only wanted to ruin his reputation?"

A look of fear flashes across Nina's face. "I have nothing to do with that, I swear. All I did was . . ." She looks away. "I scheduled the offsite and your tour for a date she specified." She bites her lip. "And I gave her some private info from his computer. Passwords and stuff. But that's *all*. I have no idea where he is."

"It might be good for you and your kid to have a backup plan. Somewhere else to stay for a while," Dread says, more softly now. That's when I realize why he's dropping a pointed hint. Cíxǐ has killed before. Dread's afraid she might do so again.

"I'll . . . look into it." Nina looks shaken.

"One more thing," Dread says, as Nina turns to leave. He pulls out a photo of Kǎiwén—he must have taken it from the album in Ethan's house—and holds it up to Nina. "Is this Kaiwen?"

Nina studies the photo, then nods. "She looks older now, but I think it's her."

After Nina leaves, Dread and I stay in the conference room. I take the photo of Kǎiwén, studying it. I look into her eyes.

I came so far to find you.

"I don't think Nina was lying." Dread's words are curt; it's clear he's still upset at me.

"Me neither." I can't tear my eyes away from Kǎiwén's beautiful smile. My mother.

"Do you know anything about Kaiwen?"

"No. I didn't even know she existed until a year ago."

"So, you don't know if she would do something like this."

I think back to Kǎiwén's visit. The thump as she'd slammed Mom against the wall. Mom's strangled reply.

"I didn't see her, but I overheard one conversation between her and Mom—Yùměi. And Kǎiwén was . . . violent. I don't know how much of what she told Nina is true, but Nina admitted to setting up our tour for her and giving her access to Ethan's computer."

"Could Kaiwen and your mom be working together?"

"Probably not. They were really pissed at each other." I chew my lip. I don't *want* Cíxǐ to be Kǎiwén, and I don't want to believe Ethan abused us. If it turns out both my biological parents are horrible, what does that say about me?

But all the evidence is lining up, and it's growing hard to deny.

I might have come all this way, risked so much this past year, all to end up in this tidy little trap, set by someone who's willing to toy with all our lives for reasons I still don't understand.

I take a deep breath and hand Dread the photo. "I think Kǎiwén is Cíxǐ."

CHAPTER 46

Ten Months Earlier

It was pouring out. Again. I had never minded the rain before. Back then, I didn't have to sleep in it.

Nearly two months had passed since I'd arrived in Seattle. I'd thought my wad of cash would get me a hotel room. Then I'd go to the library, borrow a computer, and start looking for my aunt. As it turns out, hotels require ID. And I was too scared to go to the police or a shelter—they might send me back to Mom.

The longer it takes to find a place, the longer you go without a shower. And the more your body odor begins to build up, the less sympathetic the looks become. One day's grime loses you a sliver of compassion. The slivers add up and soon, they forget you're human. And you end up huddled by a dumpster in an alleyway, waiting for the last light to wink off while your stomach growls traitorously.

Every night, I wondered if it would have been better to keep living Lia's life after all. But I was too afraid to go back.

The last light went out.

I waited in the rain for as long as I could stand. Then I dashed across the alleyway toward my favorite spot to spend the night. The overhang behind this restaurant stuck out the furthest, and there was a step between the door and the alley, so the rain didn't collect.

I reached the landing and stopped short.

There was a folded blanket tucked away in the shadow of the landing. A little brown to-go bag sat on top, stamped with the logo for Bette's Battles and Bao, with a tag that said, *For You.*

I almost turned and ran. Did they know I slept here? I always left early in the morning.

Curiosity won, and I looked in the bag.

I pulled out each item, marveling. Water, Calpico, rice crackers, three guàbāo, a pineapple bun, a fantasy novel, and a portable reading lamp.

My eyes grew watery. I dug in, filling up my starving body, trying to go slowly so it wouldn't all come back up.

I stayed up and read with the blanket wrapped around me like a cape. Finally, I fell into the least restless sleep I'd had in a while.

When I left in the morning, I took the book with me.

When I returned that night, there was another bag.

After one week of bags mysteriously appearing, I summoned my courage. I waited until evening when customers would be gone, but before the light winked off.

I knocked on the magical door in the alleyway.

The door opened.

A middle-aged man with a wispy beard and solid build appeared.

I gulped and tried to talk, but my voice caught in my throat, heavy from disuse. I cleared my throat. "I don't want to bother you. But . . . thank you. For everything."

"It's nothing," he grumbled. "You need a place to sleep."

"Well, I . . . have been sleeping here." I looked down. He knew that, obviously. Still.

He shook his head, pointing inside. "Here."

Before I could protest, he had opened the door all the way, revealing a short corridor leading to an industrial kitchen.

"Wait here." He disappeared through a door leading to the front of the restaurant, leaving me alone in the back. I looked around, afraid to move. The kitchen wasn't huge, but there was enough space for five or six people to work comfortably. There was another door to my left. I craned my neck, looking in to see a simple office with a computer desk, chair, and rolled-up sleeping bag.

Should I run? I imagined the headlines. "Unhoused Girl Lured into Kitchen, Murdered, and Cut into Pieces." It would have to be something gruesome like that, because otherwise no one would care about one runaway. The food, the novel, and the blanket seemed too good to be true. If this was the start of a horror film, then I was the extra about to die.

A part of me wasn't sure that would be a bad thing.

I shivered, hugging the blanket closer. The door to the alleyway was still open. It wasn't too late to run.

But he had left me alone in his kitchen. He was trusting me like I was trusting him. Trust for trust.

I stayed.

A few minutes later, the door burst open, revealing a stout middle-aged woman with kind eyes and black hair tied up in a bun.

"Hello!" Her booming voice filled the room. "I'm Bette."

She stuck out her hand. Startled, I shook it. Bette didn't flinch or wipe her hands afterward, though I knew I must smell awful. I was accustomed to it now, but the wrinkled noses and people crossing to the other side of the street told me enough.

"That was Jimmy." Bette pointed to the doorway where the man had disappeared. "Grumpy man, but good husband." She turned to look me in the eyes. "You can stay here now."

I opened my mouth to protest, but Bette shushed me. "I wish our apartment was bigger, but Jimmy takes up too much room." She waved her hand at him as if annoyed, but there was fondness behind the gesture. "You can come to our apartment in the day. Shower, wash clothes, have meals with us if you like. Sleep here."

Bette beckoned me toward the office, gesturing at the sleeping bag. She opened a tiny closet and pulled out a pillow and another blanket. As she began setting up the bedding, my eyes filled with tears.

"I'm Marina," I said. "Marina Chan."

I thought I'd feel silly using my character's name. Instead, speaking it aloud felt right. Marina was brave enough to start anew. I could be brave too.

Bette smiled. "Welcome home."

TECH MOGUL GOES MISSING

By Ian Alwin

Posted on Patch Notes, a video game blog

Ethan Wainwright, the CEO of Apocalypta Games, has been reported missing. Wainwright was last seen at work on Friday afternoon. According to sources at the game studio, Wainwright never badged out for the weekend. He did not show up to work Monday morning. Friends who have tried to reach him since Saturday have been unable to do so.

Wainwright is best known as the creator of Seamless Server Technology. More recently, he founded Apocalypta Games, the studio behind MMORPG *Darkitect*, a niche game with a cult following.

If you have any information on Ethan Wainwright's whereabouts, please call the police tip line.

CHAPTER 47

Monday, 11:45 a.m.

If I can get Kăiwén to talk to me alone, maybe I can figure out what she wants and work something out with her. Convince her not to hurt anyone. Obviously, she's dangerous, but it's the middle of the day, and I'll be careful.

Deep down, I know it's still a risk, but it's worth it. If there's a chance I can end the game here, I have to try.

The floor outside the conference room feels tense. A pair of workers walks by, and I hear Ethan's name whispered. News of his disappearance must be spreading. We agree that it's too risky for me to stay at Apocalypta HQ any longer.

As Dread walks me out, I show him the shipping label with Kaiwen's address on it. He looks it up on his phone, whistling when the map loads. "That's in Queen Anne. Bet there are a *lot* of zeros in that house price."

"Let me see." I change the map to bus directions, memorizing them. Then I give Dread his phone back and wave goodbye.

After leaving Apocalypta, I hop on a bus from downtown to Queen Anne. It's a cloudy day, and I shiver as I step onto the sidewalk. I wind through several blocks until I spot the three-story-tall, boxy house. I pull out the torn shipping label to double-check the address. And triple-check.

I know I'm stalling.

Thoughts and emotions rush through me in a swirl, and I don't know how to feel. Why is Kǎiwén doing all of this?

Maybe, in some twisted way I don't yet understand, she invented the whole game *for* me because she loves me. Would that be so impossible?

Or she's getting back at Mom, somehow, and the game has nothing to do with me at all.

I shake my head, shoving the thoughts aside as I walk up to the front door.

Light thumps sound from inside the house, like footsteps muffled by socks or carpet. I ring the doorbell. Eerie notes chime, echoing throughout the home's interior.

No one answers, so I knock.

Still nothing.

"Kǎiwén! Hello?" I shout.

No reply.

Something inside me breaks. Why is she doing all this? Why toy with so many people? Why not just come *find me* at the restaurant, or at least answer one of my many phone calls?

I start pounding on the door, nerves and frustration pouring out. I heard something earlier. Someone *must* be home.

When it's clear that all my knocking is fruitless, I peer in through a front window. The interior is beautiful, with patterned hardwood floors, a small entryway table full of fresh flowers, and a mirror. The edge of the staircase is just visible, and I can see a frame on the wall.

There's a noise from somewhere above. I step back and look up, feeling the hairs on the back of my neck stand up. The blinds in one of the third story windows are shaking, settling.

I ring the doorbell once more, listening as the eerie tune sounds again, my heart pounding. I'm too shabby for this picture-perfect neighborhood. How *did* Kǎiwén afford this place on a makeup artist's income? I remember the box in Ethan's house. He sent it to her address. Did he buy her this house?

I notice the next-door neighbor glaring at me through his window and jump. The older man narrows his eyes at me before moving out of sight.

I look back up at the blinds that moved. They're still now. I walk around to the side of the house, out of the nosy neighbor's line of sight. Through the window, I see a furry black tail dart away.

Oh. Just a cat.

Kǎiwén has a *cat*. She really isn't like Mom, who hates pets.

I head back to the front. The neighbor's still glaring. He holds a phone to his ear, probably about to call the cops. I glare back at the old man and leave.

Half an hour later, I'm back in the restaurant office with Slate. I sign on again, but still, none of my teammates are online. I get up and pace nervously. We have to beat Cíxǐ's dungeon level soon.

"Marina! Nǐ de péngyǒu láile!" Bette practically twirls into the office.

"Which friend is here?" Have they figured out I live here?

"I put Tamyra in wolf booth. Go wash up and look nice." She gives me such an obvious wink that I turn bright red. "Wǒ lái bāng nǐ huàzhuāng!"

"Uh, that's okay."

Bette looks disappointed when I don't take her up on her offer to help me do makeup, but I do stop by the bathroom to wash my face and smooth out my shirt. Slate's already sitting by Syl in wolf booth. Syl coos and pets him.

"Hey, Syl." I clear my throat. "What are you doing here?"

"You said you were coming in to work today, and Dread said you lost your phone."

I nod and sit. Slate lies down beneath the table. I reach down to stroke his fur, and he nuzzles my hand. "Work can wait. Listen, I'm really sorry . . ."

"I don't want to hear it right now."

"But . . ."

"Night, *stop*. You don't get to just apologize everything away. I talked to you about Jamal. You knew Cixi threatened to kill him, and you *still* kept all these secrets from us!" She wipes a tear away, careful not to smear her makeup. "If he gets hurt, I'll never forgive you. If we make it through . . . I don't know. Let's just focus on finishing these levels."

My own tears threaten to spill, but I swallow them back. "Okay," I whisper.

"Great." Syl's tone turns curt and businesslike. "Did you see the article?"

"What article?"

Syl hands me her phone.

Tech Mogul Goes Missing

"Dread says the office rumor mill is flying," Syl says. "He's staying the full workday to gather intel and avoid suspicion, but he'll try to book a conference room and log into *Darkitect* this afternoon if he can. Oh, and Rock's parents are stressed as hell. Apparently, the reason they were at Ethan's house last night was that he hadn't responded to their texts all weekend. They were checking on him."

"Did Dread tell you what Nina said?"

"He hasn't had time."

I spend the next ten minutes updating her on the lunch confrontation with Nina Cohen.

"Do you think Nina is telling the truth?" Syl asks when I'm done.

"I think so. Kǎiwén must have used the passwords to access Apocalypta's internal systems. Maybe to set up the whole screen with the rules of the game. But the rest? I don't know if Kǎiwén told *her* the truth. Seems convenient that Kǎiwén and Nina happened to have the exact same marital situation."

"Yeah. But I still don't get the whole elaborate charade involving *you*." Syl's emphasis on *you* is a sharp reminder that she's still angry. She's only being civil because she needs us to beat this level. "If Kaiwen is Cixi, why the game? If she wanted revenge on Ethan, she could've just gotten all the info from Nina and exposed Ethan. Or killed him and been done with it."

"That's the part I don't get either."

"Maybe it's not about revenge," Syl says.

"What else could it be?"

"Power. Control. Money. Those are almost always the things that drive villains."

"I guess Cíxǐ's game gives her temporary power over us? Though it seems like tons of work for a few days of controlling our lives. As for money? She obviously paid Nina well. What could she possibly get out of this that's worth the effort of setting this up, plus however much Nina's bribes cost?"

Syl gasps.

"What? What is it?"

"Money," she says.

"Yeah, I just said it would cost a lot to do all this."

271

"No, I mean . . . how rich do you think Ethan Wainwright is? *Was?*"

"Why would that matter?"

Syl looks intently at me, wide eyes framed by her long, curled eyelashes. "You're still a minor. And Kaiwen is your biological mother. If she finds a way to get custody of you, then she'll have control over *all of your assets.*"

My mouth drops open as the pieces fall into place.

Ethan Wainright was incredibly wealthy.

And he left half of his fortune to *me*.

Syl and I are video chatting with Rock. His parents are at Apocalypta trying to find clues about Ethan's disappearance. We're all nervous about that, but at least it means Rock is free for a bit. Like the others, he isn't super happy with me right now, but we have more important things to worry about. We have to figure out which of the four witnesses to Yùměi and Brooke's supposed deaths are innocent or guilty and write our guesses on the scrolls for the dungeon level.

"Reasons to lie and help someone fake their death. Go," Syl says.

"Helping a friend out," Rock says. "Following your conscience to do a good deed for a stranger. Accepting payment because you're in a bad spot."

"Because someone coerced you into it," I say. "Being a pathological liar. Using it to take revenge on someone."

"Incurable addiction," Syl says. "Accepting payment to fuel a bad habit or because you're a greedy bastard."

Through the screen, Rock shakes his head. "Remind me never to cross you two."

"Which do we think is most likely?" I ask.

"The thing is," Syl says, "Leo and Francesca didn't just lie to help someone fake their death. They lied to help someone kidnap a baby from her parents. You only participate in something like that if you're a heartless bastard . . . or if you believe the parents are heartless bastards."

"Why does everyone have to be a heartless bastard?" Rock asks.

"They don't have to be. Sometimes they just are." Syl's phone buzzes, and she picks up. "Hey, cuz. We're all here . . ." She stops talking and I hear Dread's voice through the phone, sounding panicked. After a few minutes, Syl says, "Okay. Good luck." She hangs up. "Shit."

"What happened?" I ask.

"Dread's being questioned by the police."

CHAPTER 48

Nine Months Earlier

It was evening, and everyone else had left for the night. I sat in front of my new laptop. Well, new to me; it was definitely used. Bette had gotten a deal from a restaurant regular who worked at a computer repair shop. I couldn't afford it, but Bette had lent me the money.

I'd promised to pay it back through restaurant shifts and whatever I could do to help out. Bette hadn't wanted repayment, but I insisted. She and Jimmy were already risking so much. Besides, working at the restaurant was interesting. I liked observing everyone. I hadn't been surrounded by this many people since elementary school.

I signed onto *Darkitect*, a game I'd picked up in a Steam sale. As it loaded, I admired the art. It was gorgeous in a vaguely creepy way. The visuals had inspired me to draw characters and game scenes on my lunch breaks.

I queued up, waiting for a random group to join. I was learning how to be helpful to teams as their fourth player.

Group found. Click to join mission.

The upper left portion of my screen populated with three characters' names: *RockSplice (team leader), Dreadnaughty, Syldara.*

Syldara: hi!!! we're on voice chat, wanna join?

My heart raced. Most groups I'd run missions with used the game's built-in text chat or didn't talk at all. I'd never had anyone invite me to voice chat. Would it be dangerous? I was trying to stay under the radar.

A wave of longing hit me. It was lonely, being here by myself every night.

I joined.

Three voices greeted me at once, startling me.

"I thought we agreed that I'd be the welcoming committee!"

"But I'm our leader. Clearly, this is a privilege befitting the most important member of the team."

"Ignore the two of them. Hi, I'm Syl."

"She's the one who uses too many exclamation marks and probably scared you off."

"No, you saying stuff like *that* is what scares people off, cuz."

They were so in sync with each other, talking so fast that it was hard to keep up. I was relieved to hear they all sounded like teens.

"Um, hello?" I looked at the screen, unsure which voice belonged to who. Then I noticed each character name lit up when that person talked. Phew.

Dreadnaughty: "Behold, our mysterious stranger speaks!"

Syldara: "Shhhh, don't say that!"

RockSplice: "Children, shall we discuss strategy?"

Syldara: "Have you played this mission before, Night? Is it okay if I call you Night?"

NightMar3: "Um, sure. And, nope, haven't played this one yet."

Syldara: "Oooh, it's a fun one!"

RockSplice: "It's timed. Once we begin, we won't be able to take breaks until the end, so we like to do a rundown of strategy beforehand. That all right with you?"

NightMar3: "Sure!"

I listened to RockSplice lay out the plan. I loved the excitement in everyone's voices and how seriously they all took the game.

We all confirmed readiness, and then our mission began.

On the first run-through, we wiped on the second boss. While we rested up and prepared to try again, a chat message popped up on my screen.

Syldara: hey! just wanna say your icon is really cool!

My heart fluttered in my chest. *Darkitect* allowed players to use their own icons for characters. I'd used Bette's phone to take a picture of my drawing to upload.

NightMar3: thank you!

Syldara: the art is like a cross between darkitect's art and something softer in style

Syldara: like . . . amulet. Or ghibli!

I burst into a grin.

NightMar3: you really think so? amulet and studio ghibli characters were what i used for practice when i was first learning to draw!

Syldara: wait

Syldara: WAIT

Syldara: YOU DREW IT?

NightMar3: yeah!! do you draw?

Syldara: no lol I letter but don't draw. ALSO omg do you take commissions?

NightMar3: i've never done that

Syldara: you should consider it! people would totally pay good money for it

Syldara: i'll be your first customer if you do

NightMar3: i'll think about it!

By the time RockSplice called it a night, after we'd played

through the mission six times, I was thoroughly in love with the team. I wished, with a fierce ache, that I could be part of a group like this. To have *friends*.

I'd resigned myself to our parting ways when Syldara spoke. "Hey, we're planning another run tomorrow night. Want to join?"

I nearly burst into happy tears. "Yeah, I'd . . . yeah."

"Cool. We can add each other as friends and meet at the same time tomorrow."

"Sounds good. 'Night, everyone."

As I signed off, my face hurt from smiling. I hadn't felt this happy in a long, long time.

CHAPTER 49

It's the dinner rush, and Bette kicked me and Syl out of the wolf booth in favor of paying customers, so we're back at the library, sitting across from each other with our laptops open. Syl's phone buzzes with another call. This time, instead of declining or sending it to voice mail, she turns it off completely.

"What if Rock or Dread needs to reach us?"

"They can find us through the game. It's not like we can do anything until they sign on anyway." Syl shakes her head. "I can't deal with dodging more calls from my parents. They might remember to turn on Find My Friends and show up here."

Through the family grapevine, Syl's parents heard about the police questioning Dread. They have questions, but we have less than two hours before we need to complete the level. And to do so, we need Rock and Dread.

The wait is excruciating.

I glance over at Syl's notebook, where she's written down the answers we plan to give Cíxǐ.

Francesca De Rossi—INNOCENT. She helped Yumei save a baby from abuse.

Leo Anden—INNOCENT. He helped Yumei save a baby from abuse.

Ethan Wainwright—GUILTY. He was abusing his child.

Yumei Li—GUILTY. She was supposed to help her sister save Brooke from an abusive parent, but instead she took the baby for herself. She lied to Leo and Francesca to convince them to help.

We're most uncertain about the last one. Our best guess is that Mom was supposed to fake our deaths and then meet up with Kǎiwén a year or two later, after Ethan and Kǎiwén divorced. But Mom went rogue, stealing me away. I remember Kǎiwén accusing Mom of being jealous, of coveting her life, and I wonder if she was right. Maybe that's why Mom never brought me back to Kǎiwén.

"What if we're wrong?" I ask.

"I don't know. I've left messages for Jamal asking him to be careful. Telling him I had a premonition he'd get hurt. It all sounds pretty flimsy, though, and he told me not to worry, he's always careful. What about you?"

I shake my head. "Let's just not be wrong."

An in-game alert pops up on both of our computer screens.

Dreadnaughty is now online.

"Finally!" Syl says. We both put on our headsets.

"Traffic was shit today," Dread says. "I got home as fast as I could."

"How did it go with the police?" I ask.

"I'm not sure. They asked a lot of questions about Ethan and Carlos, since I was the last one to see both of them. If anyone mentioned plans for after work or whatever. I told them about the tour. Said it ended, and we all went home. They told me not to leave town."

"That doesn't sound good," Syl says. "What if they have footage of Night going back up in the elevator with Ethan after the tour?"

"I'm assuming Cíxǐ did something to the security footage," I say.

"Have you heard from Rock?" Syl asks Dread. "We're running out of time to finish the level."

RockSplice has come online.

"There you are!" I say.

"Actually . . . that's also me," Dread says. "He gave me his login info."

Damn. That's true trust.

"He's not signing on at all?" Syl sounds worried. "Dread, do you even know how to heal?"

"Eh, give me a few minutes to try out his character."

"This is a terrible idea," Syl says.

"Yeah," Dread agrees, "but Rock's parents are back home again, and they know both Ethan and Carlos are missing. He's under too close a watch. There's no way he can sign on right now without them seeing."

"All right." Syl sounds dissatisfied, but what choice do we have?

It takes us a long time to get through the early parts of the level without Rock's help. We die several times to trash mobs that would've been easy with all four of us. Thankfully, Dread learns fast. By the fourth round, he manages to heal us just enough. He's switching back and forth between one character on his home computer and another on his work laptop. I try to help pick up the slack, being extra careful to keep mobs off our squishiest team members, Syldara and RockSplice.

Finally, we make it back to the huge chamber with the four

captives. Each of us heads to a different corner. I end up standing in front of Leo Anden.

For each character, we "write up" our answers on the scrolls. Together, we enter the next room, where Cíxǐ is waiting. We hand in our scrolls. Syl and I look nervously at one another.

"I guess we wait now?" Dread says.

"I guess," Syl says.

We watch the timer tick down. It took us so long to get through the level that we only have eight minutes left. We learned everything we could. We *have* to be right.

The timer runs down to zero and flashes once as Cíxǐ looks up from the scrolls.

She wears a frown.

"You have failed. Now you face the consequences." Red flames flash from her eyes before we're kicked out of the level.

Syl and I look up from our laptops, our eyes meeting. Icy terror shoots through me, and a strangled cry escapes my lips as the realization hits.

"Oh my God, oh my God . . ." Syl grabs her phone, fingers fumbling. Her hand shakes.

"What do we do?" Dread sounds panicked.

"Damn it!" she yells, and someone at a nearby table looks up. She ignores them, waiting for her phone to turn on and thumping her foot on the ground.

I tear off my headset and run downstairs to the line of public phones. I grab one and dial the restaurant, heart in my throat.

No one answers.

I call twice more before trying the print shop down the street from Bette's Battles and Bao. I've passed by so many times that I have the phone number from their huge banner memorized. The phone rings once. Twice.

"Phoenix Printers, Libby speaking. How may I help you?"

Then I hear it.

It's faint at first. I press the phone to my ear, as if I need to hear better. As if I didn't know what the sound growing louder and louder in the background of the phone call means.

Sirens.

I drop the phone, and it hits the wall behind me, clanking. Someone shouts at me as I whiz by, nearly tripping over them, but I don't stop. My mind is full of flames, burning, smoke.

Bette, Jimmy, Slate. The staff. The patrons.

I run outside and, like fate has spoken, there's a bus headed in the right direction. It's pulling away from the stop, so I do what I've always vowed never to do. I scream and shout and wave my arms, and the bus driver takes pity on me. When the door opens, I grab the rail and practically leap up the steps, fumbling around for my Orca card.

The bus starts moving. One person pointedly places their bag next to them; another scoots into the aisle seat. I get it. No one wants to sit next to the sweaty maniac. I can't sit anyway. I'm jittery as hell, ready to burst with panic. *Slate Slate Slate Slate someone please remember Slate, please make sure he gets out safely.* I'm worried for everyone else too, but no one's going to forget to save them. What if Slate's sleeping in the office? Tears form in my eyes.

I promised him I wouldn't abandon him. I promised him I would keep him safe. I should have been there.

Angrily, I wipe them away, and wait the excruciating twentyish minutes it takes to get from downtown to Fremont. I can't panic yet. Maybe the fire trucks were headed elsewhere. Maybe it's not related.

Maybe Syl is the one who's about to get bad news.

I hate myself for the thought, and for not waiting to learn if her brother's okay, but there's no time to dwell on it. We're here.

I hop off the bus and start running. It's only a few blocks from here to the restaurant.

From several streets away, I can already see the smoke.

It feels like all the air has been sucked out of me.

This time, I don't bother to wipe away the tears. My restaurant is on fire. My home is on fire. And three members of my family—my real family, the one I'd choose for myself—might be inside.

I run, faster than I'd ever have thought possible, into the chaos. The firefighters. People watching, pointing, whispering. Standing huddled together in groups, like they can't tear their eyes away.

There are so many people outside the restaurant. Some look shocked and disheveled, smelling of smoke. Oh God, the dinner rush. Others have their phones up, filming or photographing Bette's Battles and Bao as it burns. When I get there, I shove two surprised gawkers aside, knocking a phone out of one of their hands. I run past the surprised crowd before anyone can catch me and straight into the building, calling Slate's name.

I shout Slate's name again, and then the coughing starts. Smoke fills my lungs, leaving no space for air, and I'm choking. It happens so quickly.

Strong hands grab me, pulling me backward roughly. I cry out as my leg touches the metal of the doorframe. It's scorching hot. Then two massive arms hand me to someone. There's shouting.

"Don't do this!" someone says. I look up to see a big-framed guy who looks absolutely furious. "You've just wasted precious time the firefighters could've used to rescue someone else."

My eyes fill with tears again. It's strange how my eyes can still produce tears when my throat is so dry. My leg hurts where it touched the doorframe.

Someone hands me a water bottle, and I take a swig. When the coughing finally subsides, I look at them.

"My dog. Has anyone seen my dog?"

The people around me shake their heads, giving me pitying looks.

"Come on," a woman says. "Let's move out of the way so the firefighters can do their work."

"No. Slate's in there. I have to find him. And the owners of the restaurant. Has anyone seen them?"

There are collective gasps, and I turn to see two firefighters rush out of the building. They're holding a limp body between them.

It's Jimmy.

I cry out. He's always been gruff and stoic. Now he's being loaded onto a stretcher, unmoving. I pull myself out of the lady's grasp and run over to him.

"Is he going to be okay?" I ask a medic.

"We're rushing him to the hospital. They'll do their best for him."

"He insisted on helping everyone out of the restaurant first," a voice says woodenly, and I recognize Christina, the hostess. Her eyes are red-rimmed, and she looks like she's in shock.

I want to go with Jimmy, but I need to make sure Slate and Bette are okay. It's what he'd want me to do.

"Slate? Bette?"

Christina shakes her head, and I let out a horrible cry, thinking she means the worst. That snaps her out of her mood. "No, sorry, I mean . . . they're not here. Bette took Slate on a walk maybe fifteen minutes before the fire started."

A huge weight lifts.

Bette's kindness saved her and Slate from the fire.

Still, I won't trust that they're well until I see with my own eyes that they're both safe and sound. And I need to tell Bette about Jimmy.

I thank Christina and take off again. Bette and I occasionally walk Slate together, so I know the path they would've taken. My long-sleeve shirt is soaked with sweat, and people give me a wide berth, the way they used to when I lived on the streets, but I keep running. I don't care about anything but finding Bette and Slate.

I round a corner into a quiet street and gasp.

"Bette?" My words come out strangled.

She lies on the ground, not moving, her black hair stained with blood.

CHAPTER 50

Eight Months Earlier

Everywhere I turned, their eyes greeted me. The younger ones were hopeful, the older ones wary. I wished I could take them all home. Jimmy would be picking me up in fifteen minutes. He never said it aloud, but I knew he worried about me being alone at the restaurant every night.

I looked into the tiny, hopeful eyes of Buttercream, a cheerful golden retriever mix puppy. It would be so easy to fall in love with her. An adorable little companion who would be around for years. Who had never been hurt or felt broken.

But my eyes kept drifting to an older husky lying down in the back corner of his cage, head lowered. He seemed exhausted by the barking puppies and excited kids. Each time I glanced over, he looked at me, but he didn't move otherwise.

Our eyes met. I knew that look. I wondered if Jimmy had seen it on my face when he opened the alley door for me that first time.

"Do you have questions about any of the animals?" Lara, the lady who had been helping me earlier, asked.

"Yes." I read the name on the husky's cage. "Do you know Slate's story?"

"Slate's had a rough past." Lara pursed her lips. "He's happy and cheerful by nature, but he's eight years old and he's already had three previous families. Because of this, he has separation anxiety and a fear of abandonment. Slate really needs someone who can commit to keeping him for life. To be honest, I'm not sure he'd survive being abandoned again."

Tears welled up in my eyes as Lara described Slate's history up to his last owner, an older gentleman who'd recently died.

I stepped into the enclosure and sat near Slate.

"Hey, Slate," I whispered. It wasn't hard to see where his name had originated. My eyes traveled across the beautiful swath of slate-gray fur that adorned his back. "I'm Marina, and I have a rough past too."

I swallowed hard, thinking about all the things those two words encompassed.

"I know what it's like to leave behind the place you called home for so long. I know how hard it is to start over. But this is it for us, okay? I'll take you to where my new life began and where yours does, starting today. I promise I'll never abandon you. I promise I'll never leave you behind."

Slate's ears perked up, and he looked straight at me, listening to promises I didn't know I could make.

"Slate." I let the name roll over my tongue. "It's perfect. A new start for both of us. A clean slate." I looked into his wary eyes. There was a glimmer of hope in them if I searched hard enough.

Tentatively, he moved his paw forward until it was just touching my leg, the tiniest patch of fur against my skin.

"We'll start over," I whispered. "I promise you from now on, the only thing that matters is our future together." I stood. "Come on, Slate. Let's go home."

CHAPTER 51

Monday, 8:50 p.m.

Tears stream down my cheeks as paramedics load Bette onto a stretcher.

She looks so helpless.

Bette blinks awake, looking confused as her gaze moves from the paramedic to me. Her eyes settle on my face and there's a hint of relief. She tries to sit up.

"Please don't move, ma'am," a paramedic says. "We don't know what injuries you've sustained yet."

Bette mutters a curse in Mandarin, but she lies back down. I squeeze Bette's hand. She turns toward me, her face scrunched in frustration, like she's trying to remember something.

"Bette? What happened?"

"Slate," she says finally, and my heart constricts. "She took him."

"She?" I can hear the dread in my voice.

"Duì, wǒ liúgǒu le. Tā xíjīle wǒ, qiǎngzǒu Slate."

Rage fills me at the thought of someone attacking Bette and taking Slate. "Who?"

Bette shakes her head.

"You've never met her before?"

"Bù."

"Does she look like me?"

Bette frowns. "Yes, a little. Tā hěn shòu. Yītóu hēisè de cháng fā. Huàle hěnduō zhuāng." She waves to indicate her face.

Very thin, long black hair, wears lots of makeup.

Sounds like Kǎiwén.

Someone steers me out of the way as paramedics load Bette into the ambulance.

"Is she going to be okay?" I ask.

"I can't tell you more unless you can prove you're related to her."

"I'm Bette's adoptive daughter."

"Sorry, kid." The paramedic shuts the ambulance doors. At my look, he adds, "We'll run some diagnostics. Make sure she's okay. She's in good hands. I promise."

He leaves me with a card listing the hospital's info, and then they're off.

I'm torn between finding a way to the hospital or going after Slate. But there are people making sure Bette and Jimmy are cared for, and I'd just be in the way.

Slate has no one but me.

I take off running for the bus stop.

———

There are no lights on in Kǎiwén's house. It's dark out, and I can barely see what I'm doing, but I have a few tricks up my sleeve from when I was unhoused—on really cold or rainy nights, I sometimes crept into abandoned houses.

I sneak around the side of the house, looking for a window. After several tries, I find one that opens. I leave my shoes under a nearby bush and climb in, landing softly on hardwood floor.

I close the window carefully, relieved it wasn't too hard to break in. Was it *too* easy? Is this a trap?

It doesn't matter. I'll do whatever I have to do to get Slate back.

I listen for sounds. All I hear is the light whisper of air moving through the house.

Then I hear a faint noise that pushes everything else from my mind. A bark I've heard many times before, so muffled I can't tell where it's coming from. Slate.

I creep through the house, not daring to call his name. My eyes slowly adjust, but it's still hard to see more than blurry outlines. I tiptoe past the living room, then stop in the kitchen and look for a knife, just in case. In the darkness, I can't find anything sharp, so I grab a small cast-iron pan with both hands—the perfect size for hitting someone on the head.

From the end of the hallway, I hear another faint bark, followed by a whine. I wield the pan like a baseball bat and turn to look through each open door as I pass, imagining someone leaping out to grab me.

Someone stares back at me.

Startled, I scream and swing the pan. It smashes against the person, and then there are glass shards everywhere.

It's just a mirror.

I freeze, heart racing, and listen to see if anyone shows up.

No one does. The house must be empty.

My heart pounds as I carefully dust off pieces of shattered mirror and continue walking.

Finally, I'm at the end of the hallway, where there are stairs down to a basement. I step back instinctively. It's hard to breathe and my hand clutches at my wrist, almost frantic in the tracing motions now.

One, two, three, four, five . . .

When I reach twenty-nine, I can still feel the panic choking my lungs, crowding out rational thoughts. I start over.

One, two, three, four, five . . .

This time, when I finish tracing the twenty-ninth stroke, I can hear myself think again. I don't want to enter the basement, but Slate's down there.

Maybe I heard wrong. Maybe the sound came from elsewhere. Maybe I don't have to go down there.

This time, there's no bark. Just a low whine. It's definitely coming from the basement.

I steel myself and reach around for a light switch. Everything will be okay. I just have to find the light, run down there, get Slate, and run back up. I made a promise to him and promises weigh more than fear.

My hand finds the light switch. I flip it, but nothing happens. I try again, then feel around for a second switch, but nothing works.

Gulping down my nerves, I take the first step down into the abyss.

I thought my eyes had adjusted to the darkness, but this is different from the ground floor, where moonlight still streamed in through uncovered windows and cracks in the blinds. Here, there's no light at all. With each step down, I walk straight into pitch-black darkness.

I shiver and draw in my whole body tight while keeping one hand on the railing. When I'm far enough down that my head is below the floor of the ground level, I call out softly. "Slate?"

He lets out a panicked whine when he hears my voice, and my voice catches in my throat. I squint, trying to see. Where is he? Is he okay? I take the next few steps more quickly, and next thing I know, there aren't any steps left. I've hit the bottom. I turn in the darkness, wishing my eyes would adjust faster. "Slate?"

Slate starts barking just as a bright light flashes directly in my face.

Instinctively, my arms move to cover my eyes. Something cold presses against my neck. I hear a hum, then there's a burst of sharp pain and I scream, falling backward like someone shoved me. The pan falls from my grasp, clattering to the ground. Slate barks and scratches somewhere in the distance.

I have just enough time to realize I've been Tasered before a crackle fills the air, and I'm hit with another blast of pain. I whimper, trying to recover muscle control. My attacker flashes the light in my eyes again and my lids close reflexively. This time, I feel a needle slide into my neck and try to swat it away, but my arm won't cooperate.

I try to call out for Slate, but it's impossible to get any words out. Darkness descends.

CHAPTER 52

I can't see anything. I open my eyelids, but it's still pitch dark. Where am I?

I have a killer headache. I try to reach for my temple, but my arms are bound, one to each chair arm. As sensation returns, I realize my waist and legs are tied to the chair too, ropes tight enough to leave indents.

"Slate?" Speaking makes me cough.

There's no response.

I try to move, but all it does is make the ropes burn against my skin. I clear my throat and shout louder. "Hello?"

No response.

"Kǎiwén? What do you want?"

Still nothing.

I start screaming at the top of my lungs.

My throat feels raw and ragged, but I keep screaming anyway.

A light clicks on, startling me silent. My eyes water from the sudden change, and I take in my surroundings. Slowly, my vision adjusts to reveal that I'm sealed inside a glass wine cellar within the larger basement. Surrounding me are floor-to-ceiling wooden wine racks.

I'm not alone.

Kǎiwén is seated with her back to me, wearing a formfitting dress and stilettos. Beside her, there's a glass-topped side table with several sharp-looking devices laid out next to a vase of fresh flowers. Her toned legs are crossed, and she leans back casually with a glass of wine in one hand, like she's relaxing after a long day. I hear the clicking of her nails as she taps the side table absently.

"Where's Slate?" I demand, looking around.

"Soundproof glass is expensive." Her voice is sweet and icy, but poison lurks beneath. "Especially if you pay a generous tip so no one asks any questions."

Tap, tap, tap. Her nails hit the glass in a repetitive motion. The sound draws my gaze, and I see that her ring and pinky fingers wear long, clawlike golden nail protectors, sharpened at the ends. Just like the ones Empress Dowager Cíxǐ always wore.

"It's worth the price, though, if you want to talk to someone." She stops tapping and stands, turning on her heels to face me. "In private."

She sets her wineglass on the table and inspects me. My throat goes dry, but I try not to show her my fear. I barely know anything about her, and every expression on my face is a tool she can use against me.

Kǎiwén is thinner than Mom, cheeks hollow where Mom's were always full. The contours of her makeup only enhance the sharpness of her face. Her lips are red and lined, and cat-eyed wingtips shape her thick, smoky eyes. She wears her hair loose and long, and her brows are perfectly plucked into thin, arched lines.

I wonder what it was like for Mom, growing up with this impossibly glamorous sister. Cathy at Emerald Salon said Kǎiwén was naturally charming. *People just loved her.*

I doubt anyone has ever said the same about Mom.

Kǎiwén's heels clack against the marble floor as she walks toward me. She's beautiful, with flawless skin and long, curled lashes. As she leans in to inspect me, I can see past the veneer of cover-up and foundation. There's a crack here, a telltale sheen there where she's covered up a pimple or blemish of some sort. Her lashes are so long they must be fake. She leans in so close that I can see her eyelash extensions are individually glued in.

"Is this because of the inheritance? You can have all the money. I just want my dog back."

She doesn't reply, but a soft, disappointed sound escapes her throat.

"Why do all of this?"

I don't ask the question burning in my mind.

Why don't you love me?

She stands up straight. "Because I had to."

My nose wrinkles. "That's not a real answer."

She shrugs.

"I thought you were coming to get me." The words come out sadder than I planned. "To save me from Mom. But you're just as bad as she is."

At this, her eyes flash, a tempest of rage behind them that startles me for a moment before they calm. I draw in a sharp breath and look. *Really* look.

I've seen that expression. Exactly one year ago, in another basement in another city.

And then it all begins to make sense.

"She couldn't afford this house," I say, the realization dawning. "You could."

Kǎiwén never called her old workplace to quit.

Kǎiwén would only speak on the phone with Emma, never in person.

Kǎiwén refused the box of personal items Ethan sent her.

Kǎiwén ignored my calls and messages.

Kǎiwén hasn't tried to look for me in the past year.

"You're pretending to be her," I whisper.

Mom lifts an eyebrow. She doesn't look like the mom I grew up with. She's thinner than I've ever seen her. She has a cat. And she's made up. She's wearing *lipstick*. Mom despises lipstick. But Kǎiwén doesn't.

Where is Kǎiwén?

And then I'm pushing back rising bile. Because I know. I *know*. I don't know how it happened, but I *know* what Mom did.

"She's dead. You killed your own sister."

Mom flinches and her eyes betray her startlement for a second, though I'm not sure why. Surely, she knew I would guess. Surely, she wanted me to guess.

"Your own *sister*," I say again, horrified.

"Oh, you mean Kǎiwén." Mom drops the vocal affectation, and a chill passes through me, hearing the sound of her real voice for the first time in nearly a year. She makes a flicking motion with her fingers, as if to say Kǎiwén mattered no more than a passing fly.

Her response gives me pause. Who else would I mean?

Oh my God.

The blacked-out pages in Kǎiwén's scrapbook.

I miss you so much, Huàlán.

I'm sorry. I was supposed to protect you, but I failed.

I love you, Huàlán.

"You killed Huàlán too, didn't you? Your baby sister. You killed both of your sisters." I struggle against my bonds.

"They deserved it." Mom's quiet, vicious words sit in the air.

Will you say the same about me?

My mind races through everything I know. Kǎiwén's words from the conversation I'd overheard come back to me now.

I know you better than anyone ever has or ever will. How could you forget the most important thing I taught you? Xiāng yī wéi mìng. You and I are bound together after what you did.

I picture Kǎiwén's little scrapbook. The photo of baby Huàlán, surrounded by words, like snippets from a eulogy. Then the black, warped pages. I imagine Kǎiwén writing a confession, then covering it over and over in Sharpie.

Mom killed their baby sister, and Kǎiwén knew.

"Huàlán was a baby." I can't keep the disgust from my voice.

Mom narrows her eyes. "Kǎiwén was *my* sister. She was supposed to love me."

I swallow hard, thinking about our phrase. She's always told me that I'm the only person she loves.

Can she only love one person at a time?

Was Kǎiwén that person, once upon a time?

I imagine teenage Kǎiwén, teaching Mom the phrase that was supposed to bind them together forever. Xiāng yī wéi mìng. It's supposed to describe a bond so strong it transcends the normal bounds. A love that's more than love, more than any kind of love out there.

"Kǎiwén taught you the phrase. She loved you."

"She was a terrible older sister. She only pretended to love me. She taught me the phrase, but from her lips, it was a lie."

Why didn't Kǎiwén tell anyone what Yùměi did? Was she afraid she'd be blamed? Maybe she was afraid to lose her only remaining sister. Or maybe Kǎiwén couldn't trust her parents. Maybe Mom's violent streak came from one of them.

I look up into Mom's face, searching for the monster lurking beneath. This entire time, she's been waiting patiently. Watching me put the pieces together.

"How did you kill them?" It's not important, but I have to know.

"Oh, Huàlán died peacefully in her sleep. For the most part." Mom smiles lightly.

I gulp, imagining nine-year-old Yùměi smothering her baby sister in the crib. "And Kǎiwén?"

"Ah, she was trickier." Mom tilts her head to one side. "She demanded I meet her in secret, bringing cash in return for her silence. She figured out about the computer work I did to cover the trails in, ah, making people *disappear*. She thought to extort me, but I surprised her when she was leaving to meet me."

Mom's wicked grin sends shivers crawling across my skin.

"I was right. You kill people for a living, don't you."

Mom purses her lips. "No. I didn't have to until Kǎiwén came to ruin everything. And the rest is your fault. If you hadn't betrayed me, Helen and Ethan would still be alive. I've only ever done what was necessary to keep us safe."

I feel sick to my stomach. "I thought there was some big secret. That Ethan might have secretly hurt you or done something horrible to you. That Kǎiwén was a cruel older sister. That you rescued me because you're a good person."

There had been no evidence of abuse on Ethan's or Kǎiwén's part. Yet, part of me had wanted to believe that there was a reason Mom was the way she was.

I try to move, to test the ropes. They're too tight.

"But you didn't have a reason for kidnapping me as a baby. You took me from my parents because you're selfish and insecure! And when they finally found me, you *killed both of them*! You took away my chance to know them forever."

Tears arrive in full force. I hadn't known how much I hated her for taking away Ethan—and now Kǎiwén—until I said it aloud.

Mom's face twists into an ugly smirk. No regret, no apology, not even an ounce of sympathy.

A smirk.

She laughs. "Are you done with your little outburst?" The smirk turns into a smile. Something about it is slightly wrong, a little off. It's the same expression I've seen all my life, but I didn't realize how strange it was until I spent ten months with Bette's genuine, warm smile.

"You have it all worked out, don't you? Evil witch Yùmĕi stole her niece and ran away in the night. Kǎiwén and Ethan would have been the perfect, loving, fairy-tale parents. Instead, they spent fifteen years thinking their precious daughter was dead. When they finally found out, they came to rescue her."

The bonds feel like they've tightened, even though Mom hasn't laid a hand on me.

"They turn every stone. Look in every corner of the world for their baby girl. Finally, the girl and her *mother* are almost reunited. Then the girl and her father are reunited. Sadly, the girl's evil aunt steals them away again. Isn't that right?" Her eyes flash, the rage beneath barely contained.

My mouth goes dry. She's too gleeful. My entire body fills with dread.

"You want to believe your father was so heroic." Mom spits the words. "You want to know something about your perfect father?"

No. My lips form the word, but no sound emerges. Mom is messing with me. She's shown me just how twisted she is. And there's an eager anticipation in her eyes. If the past few days have proven anything, it's this. She loves her mind games. I can't let myself believe whatever she's about to say. It isn't true.

Whatever she says, it's a lie.

Mom looks straight into my eyes.

"He. SOLD. You."

CHAPTER 53

One heartbeat. Two heartbeats.

Lies lies LIES lies.

Lies.

My lips part to spit the accusation out, but words escape me.

Mom smiles.

"We met in class. Two aspiring programmers. He was failing the course. I was not. But he was a charmer, and I was a fool." Distaste coats her words. "I loved the attention he lavished upon me. I thought attention meant love. But all he loved was having someone he could rely on to help him fake being a more talented programmer than he was.

"In the end, he was a bigger fool than I. He fell for Kǎiwén." She lifts her chin in disdain. "They had you. And then they had the audacity to ask me to be your live-in nanny. He knew how I felt, and he asked me to *set aside my little crush* for your sake, so that we could all be a happy family together. He said he knew I needed a job, and they preferred to *keep things in the family*."

"He was doing what he thought was best for me!"

Mom continues as if she hadn't heard. "I accepted. I would

earn money watching you while I worked on my own project. My way to make a name in the world." She looks at me then, but I get the feeling she's seeing a different version of me. Maybe me as baby Brooke.

"And then something unexpected happened." Tenderness softens Mom's gaze for a moment. "I fell in love with you. And already, I could see what you would become, with the two most selfish people in the world for parents. A little carbon copy of them."

"That's how you justified stealing a baby from her rightful parents?"

Mom grips my wrist, digging her claws in painfully. "Don't you *dare*."

I keep quiet this time.

Mom takes a long breath, relaxing her grip. "I wanted you. And I was willing to give up anything for you. *Everything* for you. Ethan wanted to prove himself, to show his family he didn't need their hand-me-down business. We cut a deal."

No. *No.*

"He sold you—for a piece of technology. My project."

No no no no NO.

"I gave him Seamless Server Tech and he gave me you."

"You're lying." There's no conviction in my voice. Tears form and I blink, willing them away. I don't believe her. I *won't* believe her.

Mom sighs, as if explaining something to a very foolish child. "He helped me fake our deaths with the help of an officer who knew his father and a childhood friend of his. In exchange for his help starting over, I solved any problems that came up with the software until he sold it to reach the wealth and acclaim he dreamed of."

Mom is lying. She's just saying it to get a rise out of me.

"We stopped speaking. It was a forever bargain, no take backs. But he broke his promise. He promised never to seek us out, never to contact you. I kept my bargain. I never told a soul the dirty little secret behind Seamless Server Tech. He broke his promise."

"No, he didn't! Not until you drove me away from home. He never contacted me when I lived with you!"

I hate what I'm saying. I'm admitting there might be truth to her words. But it doesn't matter. She's claiming she killed him because he contacted me, but he *didn't*.

"Oh?" Mom cocks her head. "He had *regrets*. He hired a PI and confessed his sins to my sister. He is the reason Kǎiwén came after us."

"And you murdered her because she wanted her child back?"

Mom's tone is wry. "You think she came for you? She just wanted recompense for not being cut into the deal to begin with. She didn't want you. She wanted money."

"Stop lying," I whisper. Then something occurs to me. A thread of hope I cling to. "I know you're lying because if the truth was that bad, you would've just told me all of this instead of inventing an elaborate game."

She raises an eyebrow. "And you would've believed me?"

I bite the inside of my cheek. Without all the evidence my friends and I uncovered—things that couldn't have been faked by Mom—would I have believed her, if she'd told me?

The answer isn't comforting.

Mom looks at me, face full of pity.

I blink back tears. I can't let myself fall apart. I need to focus on finding out what I can while she's willing to talk. "I still don't understand. How did you know where I was? And why not bring me back earlier?"

Mom lets out a long-suffering sigh. "I've always known where you were."

I suck in my surprise, unsure if I should believe her.

"You'd made it clear you couldn't be trusted, speaking to outsiders of assassins and other sordid things. You promised never to betray me again, but I had to test your loyalty."

"The boardwalk." I thought I'd been so lucky that day, finding a moment where Mom left me alone with a backpack full of cash. I was so naive.

"You caused a mess of problems. The people I worked for don't like complications. If they'd caught wind of the rumors you were spreading . . . well. Suffice to say, I needed to cut ties. Luckily, I had a fresh identity on hand. A real one, without any connection to their business. Someone who, conveniently, looked quite a bit like me."

Bile rises in my throat as I look Mom over again. This is why she's been playing the part of Kǎiwén for the past year.

"It's better this way. No more *business trips*, no more time apart," Mom says. "It really is just us now."

My brain hurts, trying to process everything. Mom has been living here, probably keeping tabs on me. Maybe she thought I'd eventually give up and return to her. I might have—if it weren't for Bette and Jimmy.

When I didn't, she must have grown angrier each day. She could've dragged me back by force, but she risked me running, again and again. And each time I defied her, I hurt her pride. She likes pretenses. She wants to control me, but a part of her wants to believe I'd choose her of my own accord.

"It's clear you've learned nothing in the past year. It's time for another reminder."

For your birthday this year, a reminder.

No, this can't happen. Not again.

I renew my effort, struggling against my bonds.

Mom turns away for a second, picking something up from the table. I hear the sound of fabric rustling against skin. When she turns back, she's wearing gloves and holding a knife. I try to kick or throw an elbow, but I'm tied too tightly to the chair. Mom's grip is firm. She waits patiently as I sap my strength. My reserves still feel low. All the running, the restaurant fire, working on an adrenaline high for days, and whatever Mom injected me with has taken its toll.

"I had hoped the truth would make you understand. That if you learned for yourself what kind of person he really was, you'd know why I had to keep you safe from him. But it seems I've been overly optimistic. Now, hold still. It would be a shame if you moved too much. Things might . . . go wrong."

I struggle. Mom can't convince me to play the willing victim again.

"Did you know? Severing even one muscle in the forearm can cause a person to lose their ability to draw. Forever," Mom says conversationally as she flips open the pocketknife and moves it toward my right wrist.

I'd been about to kick again. At Mom's words, I freeze. I'm not Lia anymore. I won't let Mom do this to me. Not again.

But if I can't draw anymore . . .

Please let it be over soon.

My whispered prayer opens a crack in my heart, letting in the self-hatred.

Just like that, I'm Lia Tang again. The obedient daughter who will let her mom do anything, who lets herself play the victim. I squeeze my eyes shut and stop fighting.

The cold blade pierces my skin.

"Once upon a time, there was a mother and a daughter. They were everything to each other and for the mother, that was enough. But the girl wanted to know why her father had abandoned her, and no answer would satisfy. She grew belligerent in her ravings. When the girl began seeing things that weren't there, cutting her own wrists, and talking of killing her father, the mother grew desperate."

Sweat beads on my forehead as I put all my effort into holding my right wrist still. The blade slides across my skin. I can feel the panic rising and bite my lip to keep it at bay. Panic means moving. Moving might mean one wrong cut.

"The mother didn't want to believe there could be madness in her precious daughter's veins, but the girl's tutor brought a wild story to her attention. A hallucination the girl had shared with her. Talk of assassins, secret relatives, and murdered strangers. At last, the mother could hide from the truth no longer."

I force myself to pay attention to Mom's words instead of the blade.

"The mother tried to get help for her daughter. But her daughter refused aid and fled, finding someone to take her in."

Each stroke is so careful, so deliberate. I close my eyes, trying not to shake. *Please be over soon. Please.*

Mom smiles at me. "What happens to our mad little girl? Well, the story isn't finished yet. Endings are hard to write, aren't they?

You can help me decide how this story ends. Maybe the mad girl befriends three local teens. They spend nearly every night talking online, but none of her friends' parents have met her. If they had, they might have noticed something is very, very wrong with her."

A cry escapes my lips, and I bite my lip so hard that it begins to bleed.

"She concocts a plan and convinces them to join her. Together, the four teens plan to get Ethan alone and kill him, then invent an elaborate game to blame it all on some unseen murderer. The girl lures Ethan in with the promise of reconciliation with his daughter. Tamyra fires the deadly shot. Rajesh tampers with the security footage and invents the game. Andrew has access to the building, allowing them to return under cover of darkness to move the body and clean up."

My arm shakes, and Mom lets out a hiss. I don't want to move, but I can't help it. With her free hand, she presses my wrist down hard, stilling my movement. I whimper.

"The girl promises them a cut of her inheritance money. Tamyra needs the cash for her brother. He won't have to work a dangerous summer job anymore. Andrew will use it to pay for his expensive private school tuition, and perhaps to start his own game company someday. Rajesh doesn't need the money, but he wants revenge. He's never admitted it to his parents, but Ethan did things to him that were . . . unpleasant."

Blood drips off my wrist, staining the arm of the chair.

"The girl tells her friends they'll frame her aunt for the murder, and they believe her. Sadly, she betrays them in the end. She disappears right when they're caught red-handed at the place where they've buried Ethan's body."

What?

"In the weeks and months after the girl's disappearance, more evidence appears, supporting everything the four teenagers did. Rajesh's parents hire an incredible legal team, who fight every charge tooth and nail. They convince him to accept a plea bargain in exchange for selling out his friends. Rumors and speculation begin appearing on internet forums. The shadow of suspicion follows him for the rest of his life and ends up ruining his parents' business—the one he tried so hard to save."

Her words slide in, and I try to process them before they fall out, slipping away with my blood.

"The justice system isn't kind to people like Tamyra. A judge can choose to try her as an adult in the case of murder. She's likely to spend time in some *very* unpleasant places. As for Andrew? He just turned eighteen. He'll be imprisoned, possibly for life, while his parents are further indebted by his legal fees."

Mom sets the blade down, pulls out a first aid kit, and begins pouring rubbing alcohol on a gauze pad. "Fortunately for poor Rajesh, Tamyra, and Andrew, the story can also end another way."

She smiles and begins dabbing at my freshly cut wounds. I scream, unable to hold back any longer. The alcohol stings so badly.

"When the mother finds her daughter again, the insanity has already taken hold. The mad girl convinces her mother to help her take revenge upon the father who abandoned her as a baby. Her mother refuses at first, but it soon becomes clear that her daughter is determined to follow through with the plan no matter what. If the mother tries to stop her, she'll lose her daughter forever."

I feel so weak, so tired. Mom gently wipes away my blood. The gauze pad turns red and dark.

"The girl tells her little friends that someone came in and killed Ethan. That she had nothing to do with the murder. Only, no one saw it happen, did they? She lied to her friends about her life, her past, and what she was doing to them at that very moment."

I clench my teeth through the pain, forcing myself to focus. To pay attention to what Mom is saying. "I . . . couldn't have done . . . those things. I was with them . . . when the rules appeared. I was . . . at the library when you set the restaurant on fire." I stumble on the words, remembering how paramedics took Bette and Jimmy away on stretchers.

"You misunderstand." Mom's still smiling. "She's not alone. She was never alone. She and her mother do everything together. *Everything.*"

I inhale sharply.

This is what the game was about. She wants it to seem like I'm the mastermind. Either my friends and I did it, or Mom and I did. If I fight her, she'll frame all four of us. If I agree to whatever she wants, she'll make sure my friends think she and I were in on it together.

Why? Why would she do this?

The dull, throbbing phantom pain I've carried on my arm for the past year flares up. It's enough of an answer.

Mom is jealous. Possessive. And if she's not lying, if she really did trade her greatest invention for me? Then she won't be able to stand me loving anyone else. She'll do anything to break the only bonds I've ever formed without her—and she wants them to stay broken forever. If I somehow manage to break free and explain this all to Bette and Jimmy, to Rock, Dread, and Syl, why should anyone believe me?

I played right into her hands. Keeping secrets. Lying over and over.

I look up. Meet her gaze. She's paused her story to let me take everything in. Watched me piece it together. Her lips turn up at the corners. "Mother and daughter flee the country, leaving behind the evidence of what they've done. Knowing neither can ever return. Together, they board a flight and start over. A clean slate."

Clean slate.

Slate.

Slate needs me. He's been abandoned three times already. He might not survive a fourth time. *I promised him.* I vowed to be there for him, always. I picture his eyes looking up, tail wagging when he sees me.

I may not have anything—or anyone—else to fight for, but I still have Slate.

I need to agree to whatever Mom wants. Play along and escape later. If I cooperate in her twisted games, there's a chance I'll live to find my way back to him.

I summon all the lies I've ever told, each one practice for this moment. I bite my lip and soften my eyes, careful not to overdo it. Mom's too smart. I need exactly the right balance of contrition, defeat, and longing for my old life.

"I don't know if it will work, Mom. The police . . . they'll figure it out. They'll come after me. They'll come after us."

Mom studies me.

Please buy it.

Please please please please please.

She narrows her eyes.

"Not good enough."

"Mom?" My heart sinks and fear seeps into my voice. I've failed.

"I see you're not quite convinced yet. We'll have to do this the hard way, then."

CHAPTER 54

Mom is gone now, and my mind's racing. Before leaving, she showed me one more thing. My phone, which she must have stolen last night. She texted my friends, pretending to be me. Told them I'd found my phone again and made up reasons why I couldn't go with them. She'd given them my *Darkitect* password, the way Rock had given Dread his. One of them must have logged on as me, so they could get started on the last level.

My friends set off to complete the final mission without me. They've been texting updates. Syl and Dread are at an address they got from the game. They're breaking in, looking for evidence.

What they'll find, instead, is Ethan's body.

When they cross a certain threshold, they'll trigger the silent alarm that will call the police. If all goes as Mom plans, they'll be standing over the body when the cops arrive.

I can stop it from happening.

I can keep them safe.

All I have to do is leave everyone I've come to love behind. Including Slate. If I go with her, Mom will make sure it looks like she and I murdered Ethan together. That I fooled my friends. She has travel plans in place; we'll go somewhere the law can't find us. And I'll never be able to return.

But if I stay, she won't just brand me the murderer. She'll frame all four of us. I have no doubt she'll go as far as needed.

Leave, spend the rest of my life with Mom, and be branded a murderer forever.

Stay, ruin all my friends' lives, and end up in prison.

Either way, I abandon Slate.

My thoughts are interrupted by a blurry shape in the distance, moving closer.

No. NO!

And then the tears come. Because I know. I *know*. It's all hopeless because I'd do anything to protect my bundle of fur. Even if it means living with Mom forever.

I crane my neck and look through the glass, so relieved and horrified at the sight that I feel like I'm going to lose consciousness. My favorite being in the whole world is panicked and confused.

Mom looks pissed. She's always hated animals.

Mom leads him in through the glass door.

"Slate!" I let the tears run down my face now. I try to be brave for him. He barks and growls, but not as loudly as I'd have expected. In fact, he looks a little sleepy. "You drugged him!"

"You really should train him better. He's troublesome."

"He's trained well if he fought you!"

What am I doing? I need to convince Mom I'll go with her, not antagonize her. But the thought of Mom feeding him drugged food or injecting him with something infuriates me beyond reason.

Mom pulls Slate forward and I make a low, horrible sound when I see that she's put a choke chain on him. He follows, nearly stumbling as he walks forward.

"Relax, Lia. He's just a little subdued. Some dogs—and people—need it."

I grit my teeth, trying to reign in the simmering rage. Slate's safety depends on me. Mom wants me to be emotional. People make mistakes when they're emotional.

"What do you want?" My tone is as civil as I can manage.

Mom and Slate are just out of reach. Slate tries to move toward me, but Mom yanks on his leash firmly, and he whimpers.

"You would never lie to me, would you?" Mom winds the leash around her hand.

No, of course not, I want to say. That would be an obvious lie, but I'd have to be a fool to admit I'd lie to her. What's the right answer?

I hate her mind games.

"I try not to lie."

"How does the story end?" Mom asks.

The story?

Oh, the choice she gave me earlier. I take a deep breath and close my eyes for a moment, letting Mom see my resignation.

"The girl starts a new life with her mother. Together, they work to cure her madness. They start over. Clean slate."

A new start for both of us. A clean slate.

Only I'll be starting anew with the wrong person.

Mom nods. "I believe you, Lia."

I breathe a small sigh of relief.

"All you need to do is write that you're sorry."

That's it?

Mom reaches for the table and pulls out a knife. I shrink back, but all she does is cut loose the rope tying my right arm to the chair. I try moving my arm, and the pain makes me lightheaded. I can feel every fresh cut in my wrist and every indent where the ropes burned my skin.

On my leg, Mom sets down the knife and steps back, out of reach.

I stare at it. It's clean now, wiped free of my blood, but I shudder, the memory of the cold blade on my skin surfacing . . .

All you need to do is write that you're sorry.

Mom didn't give me a pen.

Mom prefers words cut from flesh.

I swallow. I can do this. I have to do this, to get us out of here. But what will happen to Slate? "If I do this, you'll let him go? Bring him back to the restaurant before you and I catch the plane?"

I don't know if I can count on Mom for anything, but I have no choice. Besides, if she really does want us to be together again, she'll fulfill her promises, so we start on the right foot. Flimsy logic, right? But it's all I have.

"I will." Mom's voice and gaze hold steady. How do monsters manage to look so earnest?

I long to turn the knife on Mom. If I were my character, Night-Mar3, I'd throw it, bound hands or not. It would fly straight into Mom's heart, and she'd fall backward, shock and betrayal splayed across her face. Then the level would be over.

But I'm here in a real basement with a real monster.

And I'm still tied up. I know if I try to saw away at the ropes, Mom will stop me. And I have Slate to consider. Whatever actions I take, the consequences will doubtless fall upon him.

It's my turn to nod.

I reach out with my fingers, just managing to grasp the end of the handle. My arm is stiff and awkward. Even holding the knife feels painful, but I grit my teeth and position the blade over my other palm.

对不起. *Duì bu qǐ.*

I'm sorry. I picture the three Chinese characters and count the strokes. Nineteen. I can do this.

I'm about to cut the first stroke when Mom clears her throat and shakes her head.

She pushes Slate forward. Sits him down next to me, putting his paw in my lap. Then she looks at me and cocks her head.

All you need to do is write that you're sorry.

That's when I realize where she wants me to write it.

CHAPTER 55

The blood drains from my face.

I can't—*won't*—hurt Slate. No matter what Mom does to me, I'll refuse. I'd die first.

But then Mom will kill him. She barely values human life. She won't care about one dog.

Is it better to hurt him? A few cuts to save him from something worse?

If I do, a part of me will die. Is saving a life worth betrayal and brokenness? I think about taking the knife, picking up his paw. Imagine him waking up at my touch, his trusting eyes watching me . . .

NO.

I can't can't won't can't . . .

STOP PANICKING AND THINK.

I tamp down the urge to beg Mom for mercy. The words long to escape, but it would be the wrong thing to say.

When it comes to Mom, there's no right thing to say.

There's no way out of the ropes, no miraculous escape.

Mom is too smart, too careful, and too much in control.

"Don't disappoint me again, Lia." Mom locks eyes with me.

Lia.

Mom's name for me.

Mom was able to set the perfect trap because she knows me. Lia, the girl she raised. The girl she spent fifteen years obsessively shaping to be just the daughter she wanted. I'll never be able to escape Mom's trap for Lia.

But Mom doesn't know Marina.

I think of Syl and the team.

I think of Dread saying the only way to beat someone this prepared is to do something unexpected.

I think of Bette and Jimmy and the chance they gave me, the life they've helped me build.

I think of Slate, who is always there for me.

I think of the girl I used to be. Scared, obedient, always listening to my mom.

I think of the girl I am now.

And I brace myself.

I scream, plunging the knife into my own leg.

There's a horrible sound as the sharp blade cuts through denim and meat and hits bone. My piercing shriek splits the air as the pain arrives. The shock of what I've done nearly makes me pass out, but I force myself to focus through the pain.

Mom lunges forward, just as I'd hoped. Just as I'd feared.

Tears leak out of my eyes from the sharp pain. I summon all the strength I can muster and yank the blade back out. There's a horrible ripping sound as it pulls free of my leg. Blood bursts out, terrifyingly red and liquid. It's coming out fast. Too fast. What if I hit an artery? What if I never walk again?

The knife is drenched in my blood, but I tighten my fingers

around the handle so it won't slip out of my grasp. Mom reaches out to snatch the knife from my hand.

Mom can't believe that her precious daughter isn't in her control.

Mom has no idea how much I've learned in the past year.

Mom will never understand what lengths I'd go to for Slate, for my friends, for Jimmy and Bette. To protect the people I love.

I use every last ounce of strength and willpower and rage in me to fuel the motion of my arm as I plunge the knife into Mom's chest.

The violent swing of my arm tips me off balance and the chair I'm tied to begins to fall, pulling me toward Mom. I have just enough time to elbow Slate's limp paw out of the way before Mom and I both crash to the ground.

The knife, still tight in my death grip, sinks deeper into Mom's chest with the full weight of me and the heavy wooden chair behind it. Several wine bottles fall, shattering when they hit the floor.

I scream again as blood soaks my hands and shirt. My voice cuts off as something wraps around my neck. Fingers, hands, feeling for my windpipe and finding it and squeezing, squeezing, *squeezing*. Desperate, I try to turn to one side or the other. Anything to escape that grasp. But I can barely think past the overwhelming pain in my head and when I gasp for air, the scent of spilled wine fills my nostrils, making me gag. No matter how hard I try, I can't move.

I'm wedged in tight, my head stuck in the crook between Mom's neck and shoulder. She has her legs wrapped around my ankles, arms around my neck, and she's not going to let go for anything. I feel her fumble around for something in her pocket—some backup plan, no doubt—but I can't move, can't do anything to stop her.

Mom's mouth is close to my ear and her voice sounds wrong now. It's breathy and wild and sharper and more venomous than she's ever sounded before. She pours words into my ear.

"I gave . . . Kǎiwén . . . *everything*. But nothing . . . was ever . . . good enough . . . for . . . your . . . *mother*." She spits the last word, as if it were a fly on the tip of her tongue. "And you"—something needle-sharp presses into my neck—"are the same."

Maybe Kǎiwén could tell that you're a monster inside.

The words won't come out. There's pressure; the hiss of a needle. Mom's grip on my neck relaxes, but there's no relief for me, only a wave of intense dizziness and the feeling of falling. Out of the corner of my vision, I see something blurry, moving into sight. The glass door bursts open, and a panicked voice calls out.

A sweet, beautiful, lovely voice that I thought I'd never hear again. "Night?"

Before my eyes close, I have one last thought.

Take care of Slate for me, Syl.

The world drifts away.

CHAPTER 56

Two Days Later

Everything is soft. So soft. Soft and fluffy and light and . . .

And everything hurts.

Also, my eyes don't work. My lids are so heavy, and I can't open them and . . .

"Night?"

I know that voice. A finger touches my cheek, strokes it gently.

"Night, are you awake?"

I finally win the struggle. My eyelids open. I'm looking up at . . .

Syl?

Wait, did I say that out loud? No, I don't think so. I open my mouth to say . . . something. Then the coughing begins. My head throbs and there's something wrong with my throat. Instead of words, a strangled croak escapes and I draw in a sharp, mortified breath.

The breath sets my throat on fire. I can feel something wrap around my windpipe. My hands shoot up protectively, wanting to pry the fingers off my neck, but there's nothing there.

Syl reaches out for my hand, and I feel a familiar little jolt when our fingers touch. She wraps my hands in hers and gives them a squeeze, drawing my attention away from the memory of the basement and the horrible tightness in my throat. Then her hand is gone, and I feel briefly forlorn again, until she reaches out to put her hands on my back, helping me sit up.

Even sitting up slowly and cautiously hurts.

Syl hands me a glass of water from the bedside table and I lift my arm to take a sip. I almost drop the glass as pain shoots up my wrist.

This isn't the wrist that's supposed to hurt.

"You're safe, Marina." Syl wears a soft, concerned expression. She has black streaks under her eyes. I squint, realizing that it's smeared mascara. She's been crying.

Crying seems like the right thing to do.

My vision blurs as tears drip down my face. My breath is still ragged and even the thought of speaking is painful, but I need to ask. "Where's . . ."

"Slate is safe," Syl promises, touching a finger gently to my lip to shush me. "He's sleeping, but he's here. Promise." She points downward and I summon my strength, needing to see for myself. I turn my head and look down.

Slate is curled up on the floor, snoring.

There's no blood on him. He looks okay. If I hadn't already been crying, the sight of him would have made me start. I found us a way out of Mom's lair. I saved Slate. I found a way to win after all.

Why does winning hurt so much?

Slate's really okay.

Now that I'm more awake, more aware, twinges of pain begin to flare. My leg feels like . . . well, like someone stabbed it. Hard. And I find myself fighting the constant urge to keep my hands protectively near my neck. Or to stare at the new scars on my right arm.

Tears leak from my eyes, faster now, and Syl hops up onto the bed next to me. Cautiously, she put her arms around me and leans into a hug, careful to avoid my wounds.

It still hurts like hell, but I don't protest or pull away.

She doesn't say a word as I alternately cough and sob, leaking snot all over her sunny yellow dress. Every breath *hurts*. She doesn't offer any words of comfort or reassurances, just moves closer to me, and stays there until we're both soaked with my tears. Until my eyes run out of sadness. Until finally, dry-eyed, I lean on her shoulder.

She doesn't pull back until I do. Then she takes something out of her dress pocket.

I accept the handkerchief, and a snort bubbles out of my nose.

"Old-school." My words come out in a dry croak that makes me cough again. I wipe away my snot.

Syl's burbling laughter tumbles out and I wish I could bottle it up. Save it in a jar for a dark day.

"Shut up," she says, smiling. "It's made of bamboo. I'm trying to be eco-friendly!"

At that, I can't help but smile back. There are so many things I want to talk to Syl about. I wish we could talk here, endlessly. I wish I hadn't lied to her about a million things. I wish we could pretend that we're just two carefree teenagers getting to know each other better. Just for a little while longer.

But the worry won't stay away.

Syl must see it reflected on my face. Her expression grows somber. "There's a lot to sort out."

Understatement of the year.

"But we *are* going to sort it out, okay? There are a lot of people rooting for you. Dread was here earlier. He had to go to work, but he brought you some cupcakes from his favorite bakery. They're in the kitchen."

My heart lifts. Eating doesn't sound appealing in the least, but I've worked at Bette's Battles and Bao long enough to know what some people are really saying when they bring food.

Bette's Battles and Bao. The restaurant fire.

"Do you know if Bette and Jimmy are okay?" Tears spring to my eyes again.

"They're recovering. They'll be okay."

And then something occurs to me. Syl said the cupcakes are in the kitchen. And I haven't heard the bustle of doctors, nurses, or anyone else you'd expect to find in a hospital. There are only a few machines in the room. The television screen is too big, the chairs too new. And Slate is lying on the carpeted floor.

"Where are we?"

Syl grins. "I was wondering when you'd notice! It's Wednesday afternoon and we're at Rock's house."

I blink. Rock, whose parents are friends with . . .

"Do his parents know?" I can't say it aloud. Now that I'm not caught up in a messed-up game or lying to everyone in sight, I have plenty of time to think about how I lost my dad right after I finally found him.

It turns out I have more tears left after all.

Syl nods, her grin gone as quickly as it came. "Yeah, they know about Ethan. They're grieving, but they're good people. They want you to have the best care while everything gets sorted out. We all do. Rock says his parents insisted that you stay with them. They rented some hospital equipment and have a nurse coming in to check on you."

"But . . . why?"

"I think they feel partly responsible for what happened. It turns out that your mom . . . um, Yumei . . . was working for them, disguised and under a pseudonym. That's how she was able to access a lot of Apocalypta's security systems."

I stare at her in shock. "That explains a lot."

"They also know you're Ethan's daughter," she adds quietly.

Oh.

A memory flashes to the front of my mind. Syl's voice, right before everything faded.

"How did you know where to find me?"

"When you ran off, leaving your computer behind, we knew Cixi must have carried out your threat. Dread and Rock said they didn't care if they were grounded for life. Rock snuck out, Dread picked him up, and we all met at the restaurant. Or . . . what was left of it." Syl winces. "We followed your trail and found a very loud and angry Bette. She'd been trying to get someone to listen to her. She said you disappeared, and she was worried you were in danger. She described the woman who had taken Slate."

"But how did you know I'd be *there*?"

"Dread saved Kaiwen's address from when you borrowed his phone. We figured we'd give it a try, but to be honest, we weren't sure what we'd find." Syl shifts in her seat. "The three of us had discussed how you might be, uh . . . a little too close to Cixi for us to trust you completely."

Ouch. It hurts, even if I deserve it. I hate to think how close Mom's contingency plan was to working. She might really have convinced everyone I was in on it.

"We found your shoes outside the window. We weren't sure what to think, but we had to go in, in case you were in trouble." She takes a deep breath. "I was scared that if you were, we might be too late."

I imagine my friends sneaking in through the window. Knowing they were willingly entering a murderer's home with who-knows-what traps, to find a friend who had lied to them for as long as they'd known her. I feel a rush of guilt along with a warm, fuzzy feeling that they care this much about me.

"We found Carlos first," Syl says. "She . . . uh . . . Cixi was impersonating the AC repair person the day of the tour. She lured Carlos to her van somehow."

"What?" My eyes must be bulging out, picturing the friendly security guard dead somewhere upstairs in the house. Oh God.

Syl's hand goes to her mouth. "I didn't mean . . . oops. No, he's fine. He's alive. He was starved for three days and kept drugged for most of that time, but he'll be fine. I think the only reason he's not dead is that killing him would've caused problems for her. She needed him to log into the security company's secure messaging app and send the right things so no one would grow suspicious too soon and ruin her game. She threatened to hurt his family if he did anything to sabotage her."

"But he's okay."

"Yeah. He's recovering."

I'm hit with a wave of relief. At least his kids won't lose their father.

The thought brushes too close to something painful, so I push myself to focus on the rest of Syl's words. The three of them were at the house. But . . . something still doesn't fit quite right. I furrow my brows, trying to remember. "Wait, no. You couldn't have been at her house. She showed me the group texts. Said you were following the clues from her fourth mission."

Syl laughs. "We didn't know if that would work! We were all together and we knew your phone had gone missing. Rock

326

suggested it would be the perfect way for her to infiltrate our group, stealing your phone. So, we played along, just in case."

"But she showed me the texts she sent, saying I'd found my phone. How did you know it wasn't me?"

"We weren't sure, but something about them felt off to me. The texts didn't mention anything about Bette and Jimmy getting hurt. I couldn't imagine you leaving that out." Syl sobers. "When I saw you covered in blood . . ." This time, she's the one who starts sobbing. I lean forward and wrap her up in a hug, not caring how much it hurts.

As I sit there with my arms wrapped around Syl, another question forms. I need the answer, but I'm not sure I can ask. I gulp, willing the words out.

"Where's Mo . . . where's Yùměi?"

It comes out so quietly that I'm afraid I'll have to repeat it. I try not to think about the knife going into Mom's chest. Mom's ugly, hateful expression at the end. I don't look at my wrists or reach for my throat. I have a lot more than scars on one wrist now. So much of me bears evidence of the mother that either loved me too much or not at all.

"She's at a hospital, under guard," Syl says gently. "There's a police investigation underway, trying to figure out everything she did. There's a lot to sort through. But it's going to work out."

"Maybe."

"It will. We'll figure it out together." She leans back to look me in the eyes, and I'm suddenly aware of how close we are. Of how we're sitting together on a soft bed. Of how my arms are still wrapped around her waist.

Of how, for the first time since we met, I'm not hiding a single thing from her.

I move my hand ever so slightly, and my fingers dip below the hem of her shirt, brushing bare skin. Her breath hitches, the sound filling me with daring. I trace a circle on her back, and she brushes a stray hair out of my face.

Syl leans forward, our lips so close I can feel the tickle of her warm breath.

"Is it okay . . ."

"Tamyra." I gasp, a breathless little sound. And then I pull her close. Her mouth presses against mine, soft and warm and lovelier than every fantasy I've had.

CHAPTER 57

Two Weeks Later

"Are you sure you don't want us to walk in with you?" Syl asks.

"I'm sure." I try to project confidence I don't feel.

"Good luck," Rock says.

"We'll be right out here," Dread adds.

I nod, thanking them wordlessly, and step out of the car. The hospital looms large. A huge, rectangular building with tons of windows.

I stand with my back straight, channeling Syl's self-assured, confident walk. At first, it's a put-on for my friends, so they don't spend the entire time worrying. It takes me a few minutes to realize they're not the only ones who need me to be all right.

It's okay to do something for me.

It's colder inside, but I ignore the goose bumps prickling the flesh on my bare arms. I'm not covering up today. I'm never covering up again just to hide her crimes. I didn't do anything wrong.

For too long, I've felt guilty and ashamed. For not being my mother's perfect daughter. For whatever I must have done to make her hurt me. For all the crimes she's committed.

I remind myself it's not my fault, pushing away thoughts of Jimmy's new burn scars, of Bette's bloodied hair when I found her.

Of Slate, drugged on the basement floor. Those things happened to them because I was in their lives, but I didn't hurt any of them.

I'm here to face the woman who did.

I stay polite and follow all the procedures, not wanting anyone to take particular notice of me or find a reason to throw me out. Rock's parents managed to secure me a private visit with Mom, something a minor like me shouldn't be allowed to do with a defendant. Rock says his parents worked it out using a loophole their lawyer found. I hope whatever they did was legal, and some other time I'll think about how unfair it is that wealth buys you privileges no one else gets, but for now I'll borrow their influence and money for this one thing.

"Ten minutes," the guard at the door says. "Yell if you need anything."

I step inside. She's lying on the bed. I expect her to sit up when I enter, but she stays still. I'm not sure she's even awake.

"Mom?" My voice comes out soft, tentative, not at all like what I intended. I wanted to be brave in this moment, to stand strong. But the sight of her here, like this, wipes all of that away for a moment. I've never seen her vulnerable before.

My eyes travel to the spot where I stabbed her, expecting to see a dramatically large, bloodied bandage, or something. But there are blankets layered atop her chest, and I can't tell if there's a bandage underneath or not. Besides, it's been two weeks. From what I hear, she had an emergency operation. I missed her heart, but still, she almost died from blood loss.

I did this to her.

I can't tell if I'm horrified by my own handiwork or disappointed that I didn't finish the job.

Without noticing, I've closed the distance between the door

and her bed. I'm so close now that I could lean forward and brush the corner of the bedframe with my fingertips. I imagine reaching my arms out, gripping her narrow, pale throat, and squeezing. Ending her life, the way she tried to end mine. There would be some sort of poetic justice in it, wouldn't there?

And then I close my eyes against the rage. I stand straighter. I think of my friends, waiting anxiously outside in the car.

If I take my final vengeance against Mom, she wins. She'll have nurtured the monster in me. I owe so much more to everyone who believes in me. Everyone who's risked so much and lost so much to get me here.

I step closer to Mom, but I don't reach for her throat.

Her eyes snap open, and I expect them to be smoldering, furious. I wait for her face to twist up into the monstrous, hateful look it took on in those final moments before I passed out.

But her expression is empty.

"Lia." Her tone is so even and robotic that I don't recognize it.

I wait for her to scramble up to her elbows. Most people don't like the idea of looking up to talk to someone. She's already vulnerable. I don't think she'd want me to see her this way.

But she doesn't move. Just keeps her eyes open, devoid of emotion, looking up at the ceiling.

"You were wrong," I say.

I see her nostrils flare. The only indication that my words anger her.

"Xiāng yī wéi mìng is a lie. Kǎiwén didn't teach it to you because you meant the world to her. She did it because she was afraid of you. *My mom* knew you'd turn your murderous sights on her someday. She was right. Did you also hit James Steinberg with a car, making it look like Ethan did it?"

The quirk turns into a faint smile, like she can't help it. There's a strange sort of pride in her silence. I don't know if it's pride in orchestrating everything she did, or if it's pride in me for figuring it out. I don't want to know.

"Well, you failed. I'm not like you. And you couldn't keep the truth hidden from me. I found the journal in Kǎiwén's belongings."

Police found Kǎiwén's stuff stashed in an upstairs room of the Queen Anne house. She didn't scrapbook anymore, but she kept an occasional journal. If her entries were to be believed, Ethan rekindled their relationship early last year. Kǎiwén had no idea Mom was alive until she found the PI files on Ethan's computer. When she confronted him, he admitted what he'd done, saying he was planning on fixing it.

He begged her forgiveness, saying he was young and foolish in his ambition, but he'd get me—their daughter—back. Enraged, Kǎiwén told him she'd never speak to him again, and immediately left to find me. She'd been planning to lure Mom out of the house so she could snatch me back that night.

That's where the entries end.

"You said you knew where I was the entire time. How?" It's been bothering me.

Mom smiles. "Your backpack."

I open my mouth to speak, then close it again, as the truth dawns.

"You put in a tracking device before our trip."

"Smart girl," she says.

I hate myself for the warmth that fills me up. One sarcastic little comment, and I rise to the bait like a child drowning from lack of praise.

"I still have family," I say, feeling petulant. I'm losing the thread of this conversation. But what does it matter if I win or lose this confrontation? Mom is the one who loves mind games, not me.

"The Wainwrights?" Her derisive snort tells me what she thinks of them.

Yes, I suppose I have the Wainwrights. Mom killed my parents, but I still have two aunts, at least one set of grandparents, and two cousins.

Cousins. I have *cousins*.

It's a shock to everyone. They thought I died long ago. They're processing Ethan's death. I don't know if they'll want to meet me anytime soon. What if I end up hating them? What if they end up hating me?

Even if that happens, it'll be okay.

They're not who I meant.

I already have a family. The family I've been lucky enough to find. The family I've chosen for myself. The family I'd choose every time.

Rock's parents assure me that I'm welcome there for as long as I need. I'll stay with them while everything is sorted out. They'll see what they can do about adopting me themselves if that's what I choose.

They don't know me. And I was the one who dragged their son into all this trouble. But I know it's not really about me. It's about the friend they lost. They're making sure Ethan's kid is taken care of.

When I recover, I'll help Bette and Jimmy rebuild the restaurant, using the money Ethan left me in his will. The little office room Slate and I called home is gone, but Bette and Jimmy are safe. I'll still see them.

I'm a girl with no family and the best family.

I don't have to be afraid anymore. I can stay here and keep the new life I love.

For that alone, tears rise to my eyes.

Mom wears a light smile. She must mistake my tears for sadness over her. She thinks I'm still hers. She thinks I'll continue to visit her, once she's behind bars. She thinks she's still in control.

I almost tell her that she could've had everything if she'd only let me keep Slate. That, if she hadn't been too petty and selfish and jealous to let me have *one* companion that wasn't her, she might have won. I'm tempted to leave her with the perfect parting words. To hurt her, the way she hurt me.

Then I realize that I don't need to hurt her. I don't need anything from her anymore.

I pull my gaze away from the woman who raised me and walk out, closing the door behind me.

EPILOGUE

One Month Later

"Everyone ready?" Rock asks.

"Yeah!" Dread, Syl, and I shout.

All four of us are set up with our laptops in a room in Rock's house. Even though we've gamed together countless times, this moment feels monumental. None of us have signed on since Mom's last, twisted level. She put us through so much, and we're still working through it all.

Mom tried to ruin us through the game we loved.

But *Darkitect* is what brought us all together. Today, we're reclaiming it.

My heart swells as I look at each of my teammates. Dread, who convinced me that dealing with my trauma would help the healing process and referred me to his sister's therapist. Rock, who talked his parents into letting me stay at their house indefinitely. And Syl, who's taking me out for a very belated birthday dinner.

Just the two of us.

I asked her for advice on what I should do, now that I know the birthday I've celebrated my whole life wasn't my real one. It's just an arbitrary date Mom picked. Syl told me to observe both. Life is too short to pass up any opportunity to celebrate.

She said when my real birthday comes around in May, we'll go out to celebrate eight months together.

Syl looks at me, and we share a secret smile. We haven't talked to the others yet. We want to see if we fit together before saying anything. But I think Dread suspects. He glances at us with raised eyebrows, and I look down again. There will be time to sort everything out.

And there's still so much to sort out. Even though my friends say they understand, I know my lies hurt them. I know I have a lot of trust to earn back, and I'm ready to put the time in. I have a lot of relationships to rebuild, along with new ones to build. It seems Ethan never said a word to any of his family about finding me.

I don't like to think about that. About what Kǎiwén wrote in her journal. About what Mom said.

But at night, my mind wanders, wonders. I had three parents. Two who did terrible, twisted things. One gave up everything to keep me and the other gave me up by choice, to make a name in the world. Another parent who was kept in the dark. I'll never know what she would've been like now.

I'm still staying at Rock's. Slate and I have a real bedroom now, with walls and a bed and a closet. Tomorrow will be my first day of school. Rock's parents managed to get me enrolled. An actual building with other students my age and different teachers for every subject, not a private tutor at home.

Every time the nervous knot threatens to tie up my stomach at the thought of high school, I look at my wrist.

Not the scar from my fifteenth birthday, but the new one, on my other wrist. The one Mom carved while telling me a story without an ending.

切记. Qièjì.

Remember.

I don't know why she picked the word. Did she want me to remember our phrase, the words that were supposed to bind us together forever? Or was it meant for once we left the country? Did she want me to remember what she was capable of? Did she want me to remember that I could never return?

I didn't ask her in the hospital, and now I'll never have the chance. But it doesn't matter what she thinks anymore. It's my phrase now.

I *will* remember.

I will remember that I could have stayed, and let my friends take the fall for something they didn't do.

I will remember that I could have carved the words into Slate and left to start over with Mom.

I will remember that instead, I found my own way to save him.

I will remember that my love is stronger than whatever twisted blood I might have inherited, or the lessons I've learned from the woman who raised me.

Tomorrow, I'll worry about making friends at my new high school.

Right now, I'm going to stow away my worries, clear my mind, and become someone else.

I type in my password, hit enter, and sign onto *Darkitect*.

ACKNOWLEDGMENTS

In 2017, an idea popped into my mind—what if a gamer girl found someone dead in a video game before that person was murdered in real life? In the seven years since that initial spark of a concept, Marina and her friends have seen me through many milestones—having two kids, moving cities, and changing careers—and all the quieter moments between. In that time, I received support, encouragement, and assistance from numerous people. Words on a page can never be sufficient for your collective generosity, but know my thanks are heartfelt.

To my agent, Jennifer Azantian—I could not have asked for a better partner in navigating this industry. Your enthusiasm, compassion, integrity, and expertise shine bright in everything you do. Thank you for believing in me and my stories.

To my editor, Camille Kellogg—your sharp editorial eye, your strong vision, and the immense time and care you put in made all the difference to Marina's story. Thank you for acquiring my manuscript, and then for helping me improve it by leaps and bounds.

To the entire team at Bloomsbury, including Jeanette Levy, Oona Patrick, Briana Williams, Erica Barmash, Faye Bi, Mary Kate Castellani, Erica Chan, Jennifer Choi, Nicholas Church, Phoebe

Dyer, Beth Eller, Alona Fryman, Lex Higbee, Donna Mark, Kathleen Morandini, Andrew Văn Nguyễn, Daniel O'Connor, Laura Phillips, Valentina Rice, and Sarah Shumway—thank you for the hard work you've put into this book at every step along the way. I know my debut novel is in good hands with you all.

I was fortunate enough to have quite a few early readers for this book, many of whom read multiple versions. For your notes and support, thank you to C.G. Drews, Jena Brown, Eleanor Thomas, Maraia Bonsignore, Sophie Normil, Pearl Yu, Nora Foutty, Collin Yu, Corbin Yu, Bilan Todd, Christine Lee, Erin Hartel, Elise Dubois, Carl Laviolette, Clare Edge, Jill Tew, M.K. Pagano, Nikki Brown, Samantha Hunt, Maranda Medina, Gwen Mitchell, Tara Michelle, Ben Baxter, and S.R. Appavu.

Though writing is often a solo endeavor, I've rarely felt lonely in this industry. In addition to those named above, thank you to the following for your friendship, advice, encouragement, and commiseration: Ai Jiang, Dana Vickerson, Leah Ning, Marissa van Uden, Marie Croke, Anna Madden, Amy Henry Robinson, Rebecca E. Treasure, Marie Baca Villa, Carina Saal, Mackenzie Moody, Stephanie Cheng, Cara Klein, Shari Beltran, Sana Shams, Joséphine Kühn, Gagan Kaur, Soren Dominguez, Mercy Gonzáles, Krizelle DeGuzman, Brittney Arena, Rachel Griffin, Emily Lawhorn, Virginia See, Aun-Juli Riddle, Julia Wang, Thamires Vitello, Carolyn Brooks, Hazelmae Overturf, Cameron Overturf, Teresa Weitz, Zoe Zhou, Catherine Yu, Ashley Deng, Michelle Tang, A.D. Sui, Sarah Chen, Patrick Kreuch, Alex Kreuch, Chatham Greenfield, Meredith Adamo, Leah Stecher, and Erin Luken. Thank you also to all the friends I made through Bookstagram, Twitter, Discord, and Slack—your support of my writing journey has meant the world to me.

Without my family, publishing my books and stories would not have been possible. Mom and Dad—thank you for filling my childhood with books and for fostering my love of reading. To both of you and to my in-laws, Bob and Carol—thank you for your encouragement in my writing career and for all the times you watched the kids while I wrote.

To my husband, Tal—none of this could have happened without your continual support. Thank you for being my first reader for every piece, for making sure I have consistent writing time, and for listening to me talk endlessly about my stories. You are patient and kind and wonderful, and I am forever grateful we found each other.

And to everyone who blurbed, reviewed, read, bought, shared, or recommended my books and stories—you've helped make my dream career possible. Thank you, thank you, thank you.